# Fiction

## From Sadie's Sketchbook
*Shades of Truth (Book One)*
*Flickering Hope (Book Two)*
*Waves of Light (Book Three)*
*Brilliant Hues (Book Four)*

## The Girls of Harbor View
*Girl Power (Book One)*
*Take Charge (Book Two)*
*Raising Faith (Book Three)*
*Secret Admirer (Book Four)*

## Boarding School Mysteries
*Vanished (Book One)*
*Betrayed (Book Two)*
*Burned (Book Three)*
*Poisoned (Book Four)*

# Nonfiction

*Faithgirlz! Handbook*
*Faithgirlz Journal*
*Food, Faith, and Fun! Faithgirlz Cookbook*
*No Boys Allowed*
*What's a Girl to Do?*
*Girlz Rock*
*Chick Chat*
*Real Girls of the Bible*
*My Beautiful Daughter*
*Whatever!*

## Check out www.faithgirlz.com

D0956882

# Sophie
## and Friends

## Also by Nancy Rue

*You! A Christian Girl's Guide to Growing Up*
*Girl Politics*
*Everyone Tells Me to Be Myself ... but I Don't Know Who I Am*

### Sophie's World Series
*Meet Sophie (Book One)*
*Sophie Steps Up (Book Two)*
*Sophie and Friends (Book Three)*
*Sophie's Friendship Fiasco (Book Four)*
*Sophie Flakes Out (Book Five)*
*Sophie's Drama (Book Six)*

### The Lucy Series
*Lucy Doesn't Wear Pink (Book One)*
*Lucy Out of Bounds (Book Two)*
*Lucy's Perfect Summer (Book Three)*
*Lucy Finds Her Way (Book Four)*

## Other books in the growing Faithgirlz!™ library

### Bibles
*The Faithgirlz! Bible*
*NIV Faithgirlz! Backpack Bible*

### Faithgirlz! Bible Studies
*Secret Power of Love*
*Secret Power of Joy*
*Secret Power of Goodness*
*Secret Power of Grace*

the beauty of believing

# Sophie
## and Friends

**2 BOOKS IN 1**

Includes *Sophie's First Dance*
and *Sophie's Stormy Summer*

Nancy Rue

ZONDERVAN.com/
AUTHOR**TRACKER**
*follow your favorite authors*

ZONDERKIDZ

www.zonderkidz.com

*Sophie and Friends*
ISBN 978-0310-73852-7
Copyright © 2013 by Nancy Rue

*Sophie's First Dance* Copyright © 2005 by Nancy Rue

*Sophie's Stormy Summer* Copyright © 2005 by Nancy Rue

This title is also available as a Zondervan ebook.
Visit www.zondervan.com/ebooks

Requests for information should be addressed to:
Zonderkidz, 5300 Patterson Ave. SE, Grand Rapids, Michigan 49530

Published in association with the literary agency of Alive Communications, Inc., 7680 Goddard Street, Suite 200, Colorado Springs, CO 80920. www.alivecommunucations.com

Zonderkidz is a trademark of Zondervan.

*Printed in the United States*

13 14 15 16 17 18 19 /DCI/ 24 23 22 21 20 19 18 17 16 15 14 13 12 11 10 9 8 7 6 5 4 3 2 1

*So we fix our eyes not on what is seen,*
*but on what is unseen.*
*For what is seen is temporary,*
*but what is unseen is eternal.*

—2 CORINTHIANS 4:18

# Sophie's First Dance

# One

"Are you going to feed us something weird for your report?" Sophie LaCroix looked up from the library table into the disdainful face of B.J. Schneider. *Disdainful* was a word Sophie's best friend, Fiona, had taught her, and this word definitely worked when B.J. or one of the other Corn Pops narrowed her eyes into slits, curled her lip, and acted as if Sophie were barely worth the breath it was taking to say something heinous to her.

"As a matter of fact, yes," that same Fiona said as she tucked a strand of dark hair behind her ear. It popped back out and draped over one gray eye. "We thought we'd dish up some sautéed roaches on a bed of seaweed with a nice snake venom sauce."

Sophie dragged a piece of her own hair under her nose like a mustache.

"It is so disgusting when you do that," said another Corn Pop, Anne-Stuart — with the usual juicy sniff up her nostrils.

*Not as disgusting as you and your sinus problems*, Sophie thought. But she didn't say it. All of the Corn Flakes had taken a vow not to be hateful to the Corn Pops ever, no matter how heinous THEY were to the Flakes.

B.J. put her hands on her slightly pudgy hips. "I KNOW you aren't really going to serve something that nasty for your culture project," she said.

Fiona pulled her bow of a mouth into a sly smile. "Then why did you ask?"

B.J. and Anne-Stuart rolled their eyes with the precision of synchronized swimmers.

"What are y'all doing for your presentation?" Sophie said, adjusting her glasses on her nose.

"We AND Julia and Willoughby—we're doing a folk dance," Anne-Stuart said. "And we're going to make the whole class participate."

"You're going to 'make' us?" Fiona said.

Sophie cleared her throat. Sometimes Fiona had a little trouble keeping the vow. It *was* hard with the Corn Pops acting like they ran Great Marsh Elementary, especially when school stretched into Saturdays at the town library.

"Then everybody can get used to dancing with each other," Anne-Stuart said. She sniffled. "That way, SOME people won't feel so lame at the graduation dance."

"What graduation dance?" Sophie and Fiona said together. Sophie's voice squeaked higher than Fiona's, which brought a heavy-eyebrowed look from the librarian.

"What dance?" Fiona said again.

B.J. and Anne-Stuart both sat down at the table with Sophie and Fiona—as if they'd been invited—and B.J. shoved aside the *Food from Around the World* book they'd been looking at while Anne-Stuart leaned in her long, lean frame. Sophie was sure she could see moisture glistening on Anne-Stuart's nose hairs.

"The dance the school is having at the end of the year for our sixth-grade graduation," she said.

"Duh," B.J. put in.

"Who decided that?" Fiona said.

"Just the entire class. Back in September." B.J. gave her buttery-blonde bob a toss. "You were probably off in one of those weird things y'all do — making up stories — "

"No," Fiona said. "I wasn't even HERE yet in September. I moved here in October."

"I know YOU were here," Anne-Stuart said, pointing at Sophie.

Sophie shrugged. She knew she had probably daydreamed her way through the entire voting process. That was back before she'd gotten her video camera, and before she and the Corn Flakes had started making films out of their daydreams instead of getting in trouble for having them in school and missing important things like voting for a stupid dance.

"What were the other choices?" Fiona said.

"Who cares?" B.J. said. "We're having a dance, and everybody's going to wear, like, dress-up clothes, and — "

"So if you didn't even know about the dance," Anne-Stuart said, "then you obviously don't have your dates yet."

"Dates?" Sophie said.

"You mean, as in boys?" Fiona said.

Anne-Stuart snorted and covered her mouth. B.J. waved at the librarian, whose eyebrows were now up in her hairline.

"You know," Anne-Stuart whispered. "Boys. The ones with the cute legs."

"Cute LEGS?" Sophie's voice squeaked out of her own nostrils, and she was sure Anne-Stuart was going to drip right out of her chair. B.J. kept smiling at the librarian.

"People are actually coming to the dance with DATES?" Fiona said.

"You meet your date at the dance, and he doesn't dance with anybody else but you the whole night." Anne-Stuart put her hand on Fiona's and wrinkled her forehead. "You don't HAVE to. I mean, if you can't get a boy to be with you, then you can't."

"I don't WANT a boy to be with me, thank you very much," Fiona said. She snatched back her hand.

Sophie was doing the mustache thing with her hair again. What boy in their class would she even want to get within three feet of? One of the Fruit Loops — Tod or Eddie or Colton? The thought made her feel like she had the stomach flu coming on. She shrank her already tiny form down into the chair.

Tod Ravelli had a pointy face like a Dr. Seuss character and acted like he was all big, even though he was one of the shrimpiest boys in the class. Acting big included trying to make Sophie feel like a worm.

Colton Messik wasn't any better. He seemed to think he was cute the way he could make the Corn Pops squeal when he told a joke. Sophie and the rest of the Flakes thought the only thing funny about him was the way his ears stuck out.

And Eddie Wornom was the worst. He acted like Mr. Football, but mostly he was what Sophie's mom called "fluffy" around the tummy, and he was louder than the other two put together, especially when he was calling their friend Maggie "Maggot" or some other lovely thing.

"I doubt any boy would ask you anyway," B.J was saying to Fiona. "Not unless it was one of the computer geeks. Vincent or one of the boy-twins or — I know! Jimmy Wythe — he's like the KING of the computer geeks. You could go with him."

Fiona let her head fall to the side, closed her eyes, and pretended to snore. Sophie watched the librarian march toward them. B.J. lowered her voice. "But you'd better hurry up because there are more girls than boys in our class. You COULD get left out."

"We have to go," Anne-Stuart said. She grabbed B.J.'s hand, pulling her from the chair, and cocked her head at Mrs. Eyebrows. Silky-blonde tresses spilled along the side of Anne-Stuart's face.

"We tried to get them to be quiet, ma'am," she said. She and B.J. trailed off.

"Come on," Fiona said. "Let's wait for Kitty and those guys outside."

Sophie left *Food from Around the World* on the table and followed Fiona past the glowering Mrs. Eyebrows and on outside—where a corridor of trees sheltered the library and Poquoson, Virginia's City Hall from the road. Big, fluffy hydrangea bushes provided a getaway spot for the two of them. Sophie sat down on the curb and wriggled herself under a snowball cluster of blue flowers with Fiona perched next to her.

"Just when I think they couldn't GET any more scornful, they reveal yet another layer of contempt—" Fiona's eyes narrowed, Corn Pop style. "They're evil."

Sophie nodded. "And Julia wasn't even with them. Or Willoughby."

"Julia always lets them do the dirty work, being the queen and all. And Willoughby—you can hardly tell if she's even a Corn Pop anymore. Have you noticed that sometimes she's with them and sometimes she's not?"

"I invited her to hang out with us that one time—"

"And the Pops snatched her right back. Even if THEY don't want to be her friends, they don't want US to be her friends. I told you—they're evil."

Sophie squirmed. "What about this dance thing?"

"It's lame. I vote the Corn Flakes just don't even go. We have better things to do. Hey—I have an idea." Fiona nodded toward Sophie's backpack. "Get your camera out. Let's hide in this bush and film Kitty and Darbie and Maggie when they get here."

Sophie felt a grin spreading across her face. "Let's pretend we're secret agents——"

"Hired to do surveillance on——"

"A new group of agents being gathered for a special mission——"

"Quick—here comes Maggie's mom's car!"

As Senora LaQuita's big old Pontiac pulled into the parking lot, Sophie climbed into the hydrangea bush with Fiona, fished the camera out of her backpack, and became—

*Agent Shadow. With a practiced hand—and eye—Agent Shadow framed her fellow agent in the lens. Wide-set brown eyes, dark chin-length hair, and a classic jaw line revealed her Latino heritage. An experienced agent knew these things. The dark-haired agent didn't say goodbye as she drew her boxy-square frame from the car, but, then, according to classified information, this was not a smiley spy. Agent-from-Cuba was known as the most serious of this collection of agents from all over the world.*

Yeah—an international group. That was good, Sophie decided.

As Maggie plodded up the library walk with her leather backpack, Sophie panned the camera, but Fiona gave her a poke and pointed back to the parking lot. A van was pulling up.

"There's Kitty," Sophie whispered to Fiona.

*Agent Shadow focused the camera and watched the girl hop down from the van, her black ponytail bouncing. Agent Shadow continued to film Agent Ponytail as she stood on tiptoe to talk through the window to the driver. Agent Shadow was sure Ponytail was getting ALL the instructions about when to be back at headquarters—for the fourth time at least. This agent's documents had revealed that* she could be scatterbrained at times. Just as Ponytail turned, Agent Shadow got a good shot of her profile—an upturned nose that looked like it had been chiseled out of china. Agent Ponytail was very un-agent-like. That must be part of her cover.

"Hey, Mags!" Kitty called up the walk.

Agent Shadow jumped and collided with Agent Big Words, nearly tumbling the two of them from their hiding place—

"Better let me," Fiona said. She picked up the camera from where it teetered on a hydrangea branch.

Agent Shadow grew more intent as she crept deeper under cover. She had been in the field for forty-eight straight hours without sleep. Perhaps it was time to let Agent Big Words take over the filming.

She watched, her mind razor-sharp, as Agent Ponytail hugged the neck of Agent-from-Cuba. Agent Ponytail appeared to be the slobbery type. Agent-from-Cuba obviously was not.

"Psst—here comes Darbie!" Fiona hissed.

Agent Shadow swiveled her gaze to the figure getting out of a BMW. She was the newest agent to be recruited into this gathering. Recently arriving from Northern Ireland, she would have much to add to the mission internationally speaking, especially when Agent Shadow determined just what the mission was—which would come later. It always came later.

Refreshed from her short break from the camera, Agent Shadow snatched it back from Agent Big Words and zoomed in on the subject striding up the walk. She was swinging her arms and her reddish hair and taking in everything with flashing black eyes.

"Agent Irish will be helpful in giving each of our agents new names and identities," Agent Shadow told herself. "Once we figure out what dangerous, risky, and utterly vital mission we'll be on. But first I must see just how observant she is. Can we remain hidden—or is she just as sharp as her file says she is?"

17

*Even though Agent Shadow burrowed herself deeper into the treacherous tangle of brush, she could see Agent Irish growing bigger in her lens—and bigger—and bigger—*

"Don't be thinking you're sly, you two," Darbie said, her nose pressed against the camera lens. "You're just a bit obvious."

"But we got you on film!" Fiona said. She crawled from behind the bush, shaking tiny blue blossoms from her hair. Sophie wriggled out after her.

"Our next Corn Flakes production should be a spy film, I think," Sophie said.

"My mom could make us trench coats," Maggie said.

Fiona bunched up her lips. "That's better than dance dresses."

"DANCE dresses?" Kitty's clear blue eyes were lighting up like tiny flames. "That's right—the sixth-grade dance!"

"You knew about it?" Fiona said.

"Of course she did. So did I." Maggie shrugged. "They do it every year."

Darbie gave a grunt. "You won't be seeing me at a dance. Those Corn Pops already made me feel like an eejit about my dancing when I first came here." *Eejit* was *idiot* in Darbie's Northern Irish accent. It was one of her favorite words. "I'd rather be making a spy flick," she said.

"Exactly," Fiona said.

Sophie looked at Kitty, who was poking at a weed growing up through a walkway crack with the toe of her pink flip-flop.

"You WANT to go to the dance, Kitty?" Sophie said.

"Kind of," Kitty said. "It would be fun to be all, like, dressed up. We don't HAVE to dance." Kitty's voice was starting to spiral up into a whine. Whining was one of the things she did best.

"You just want to get dressed up and go stand around?" Fiona said.

"Maybe we could just dance with each another — "

"And pretend we're agents in disguise, keeping the Corn Pop organization in our sights," Sophie said.

"That definitely has possibilities," Fiona said, rubbing her chin. "What if we could foil their plans with their 'dates'?"

"Define 'foil'" Darbie said.

"I think that means mess them up," Sophie said.

Darbie giggled. "You mean, like mix them up so they end up dancing with each other's boyfriends?" she said.

"The only thing is," Sophie said, "we can't be hateful to the Pops just because they're hateful to us. Corn Flake code."

"I know — bummer," Fiona said. She sighed. "But you're right. We'll have to think of some other mission."

"Whatever it is, we can't let them see us filming them," Darbie put in.

"WE don't have to dance with any boys though, do we?" Maggie's voice was thudding even harder than usual.

"Absolutely not," Darbie said. "We'll have nothing to do with those blaggards."

*Blaggards*, Sophie thought, repeating the word *blackguards* in her mind the way Darbie had pronounced it. With her Irish accent, Darbie could make anything sound exciting and exotic and worth doing.

"We might look a little suspicious not dancing with ANY boys," Kitty said. "It's not like ALL of them are blackguards."

"The Fruit Loops definitely are," Fiona said with a sniff. She dropped down on the grass and the rest of the Corn Flakes joined her.

Darbie nodded slowly. "But those boys that are always raving on about computers — they aren't THAT bad."

"You mean like Nathan and Vincent and Jimmy and the twins?" Sophie said.

"Ross and Ian," Kitty said.

Sophie peered at Kitty through her glasses. Kitty was looking suspiciously dreamy, and Sophie had a feeling it wasn't about being a secret agent.

"I can't keep any of them straight," Darbie said.

"Nathan's way skinny and he got first place in the science fair, remember?" Kitty said.

"No," Fiona said. "Why do you remember?"

Kitty's cheeks got pink. "His dad's in my dad's squadron. I see him at picnics and stuff."

"Carry on," Darbie said, pointing at Kitty with a piece of grass.

"Like I said, Ross and Ian are the twins—"

"Round faces," Maggie said.

"Not Eddie Wornom-round, though," Sophie said.

"No—eew," Kitty said. "What else, Darbie?" Her eyes were shining, and Sophie could tell she was enjoying this role.

*This might come in handy when we make our secret agent movie*, Sophie thought. She was already thinking of plot twists that could make use of Agent Ponytail's powers of observation.

"Vincent—which one is he?"

"Curly hair, braces," Fiona said.

"And he has kind of a deep voice," Kitty cut in—before Fiona could take her job away from her, Sophie thought. "Only it goes high sometimes."

"I know exactly who he is," Darbie said. "He isn't as much of an eejit as a lot of them."

"You left out Jimmy Wythe," Maggie said matter-of-factly.

Kitty shrugged. "I don't know that much about him. He's quiet." She gave a soft giggle. "That kind of makes him mysterious."

"Or a geek," Fiona said.

"Okay," Sophie said. "So when we come up with a mission, if we have to dance with any boys it'll be just those not-mean ones. Is everybody in?"

Fiona stuck out her pinky finger, and Kitty latched onto it. Maggie hooked onto Kitty's, and Sophie crooked her pinky around Maggie's. Only Darbie was left.

"Are we promising there will be no dates for us though?" she said.

"Not a chance," Fiona said.

Darbie gave a serious nod, and then she curved one pinky around Sophie's and the other around Fiona's.

"It's a Corn Flakes pact then," Fiona said. "No one breaks it."

"We better get to work on our culture project now," Maggie said.

Kitty giggled and hiked herself up onto Maggie's back, right on top of her backpack. "Can't we talk about our dresses first?" she said.

"Costumes," Sophie said. "For the film."

As the Corn Flakes meandered toward the library door, Sophie held back. She had a feeling this was going to be the Corn Flakes' most important movie yet—and maybe even Agent Shadow's most important mission. It was going to take some serious dreaming to get it just right.

*And as she watched her fellow agents disappear into the agency building, Agent Shadow glanced back over both shoulders to be sure there was no one from the Corn Pop Organization spying on them even now. An agent could never be too careful.*

# Two

"All right, highs and lows," Daddy said that night at the dinner table.

Sophie stuck her hand in the air before her older sister, Lacie, could start. At thirteen, Lacie could talk longer with her "lows" than their five-year-old brother, Zeke, could when he said the blessing.

"You don't have to raise your hand, Soph," Lacie said. "You're not in school."

"It's even Saturday," Zeke said. "You don't gotta do school stuff on Saturday."

Mama touched Zeke lightly on his just-like-Daddy's ski slope of a nose. "You don't HAVE to."

"That's what I said," Zeke said. Zeke's dark brown eyes—also like Daddy's—blinked. Except for his cut-with-a-weed-eater dark hair, he looked like Daddy in every way. So did Lacie for that matter. Only Sophie looked like Mama—all but Mama's highlighted hair.

"So what's your high, Soph?" Daddy said. He had invented the high/low thing at the dinner table so everybody could tell the best thing and the worst thing that happened to them that day.

"I want to tell my low first," Sophie said. "They're having a sixth-grade graduation dance for our end-of-the-year treat."

"Why is that a low, Sophie?" Mama said.

"Because it doesn't sound like that much fun—only it's also my high."

"You're going to have to explain that one," Daddy said.

"We could be here for days," Lacie muttered into her sloppy joe.

"We all decided—you know, Fiona and Maggie and Kitty and Darbie."

"The usual suspects." The laugh lines around Daddy's eyes crunched together.

"We all decided to get really dressed up."

"I love that!" Mama said. "Just do the girl thing—THAT sounds like fun."

Mama was chattering faster than Kitty, and Sophie had a feeling it was to keep Daddy from making some Dad-comment, like, "Your high is a dress?" He had come a long way since he and Mama and Sophie had been working with Dr. Peter, the Christian therapist, but sometimes he still didn't have a clue as far as Sophie was concerned.

Lacie dragged her napkin across her mouth, smearing a frown onto it. "I don't mean to take away from Sophie's high, but I'm going to need a new dress for my party too."

Daddy looked at Mama. "How much is this going to cost?"

"Not as much as you think. I'm going to make both of them, girls."

"Mo-om!" Lacie said.

But Sophie leaned forward, dipping the front of her tank top into the pool of ketchup next to her fries. "Do we get to pick out our own fabric?"

"And the pattern," Mama said. "Don't worry, Lacie, I won't make it look like I made it."

"No offense, Mom, but—"

"Wait," Daddy said. He looked at Lacie, eyes twinkling. "Is this your low?"

"It is now!"

While Lacie wailed about how the dress she really wanted was at Rave, and that since they had made the whole family change churches and took her away from all her friends at the old one, the least they could do was get her the *dress* she wanted—

*Agent Shadow stood before the piles of fabric, rich with colors and textures—purple velvets, red silks, blue rhinestones that sparkled in the light. She had to remind herself, as she draped a filmy length of pink chiffon around her shoulders, that this was all in the line of duty.*

"I personally washed that, so it isn't dirty," Lacie said. She snatched away the spoon Sophie was gazing into. "What are you looking at?"

The next day at Sunday school, while Fiona and Sophie were waiting for Darbie to come, Fiona said, "I'm supposed to go shopping with Miss Odetta Clide today." She rolled her eyes. "She is SO the worst nanny we've had yet."

"You're getting your dress for the dance already?" Sophie said. "That's cool!"

"I don't think so," Fiona said. "She'll make me get a dress from the Dark Ages—or worse."

"Is she still being super strict?" Sophie said.

"Strict? She's a prison guard! She actually made me go back and brush my teeth again this morning because she could still smell sausage on my breath." Fiona edged closer to Sophie and huffed out some air. "Can you smell it?"

"No."

"Boppa says she's giving us more structure and that we need that." Fiona sighed, the wayward piece of hair flopping across her eye. "Who would have thought my own grandfather would succumb to her?"

Sophie wanted to ask her what "succumb" meant, but Darbie had just walked in, and Sophie waved her over.

"Did you talk to your aunt about your dress?" Fiona said, instead of hello.

Darbie sniffed. "Did you have sausage for breakfast?" Then she grinned, showing the crooked teeth Sophie thought were kind of charming. "Aunt Emily nearly went off her nut, she was so excited. You'd think I was going to be married."

"NO," Fiona said. "Remember—no boys."

"No need to be reminding me." Darbie linked pinkies with both of them.

Between Sunday school and church, as the three of them dodged the crowd in the hallway to meet Sophie's family in the sanctuary, a familiar figure was suddenly beside them, barely taller than most of the sixth graders, except for Sophie, of course. Dr. Peter's eyes sparkled down at her through his glasses. His hair was Sunday-morning gelled, but the curls were popping out anyway. To Sophie, he was the best part about going to the new church.

"How are the Corn Flakes this morning?" he said.

"We're astonishingly good, Dr. P," Fiona said. Ever since she'd started going to church with Sophie back in March, Sophie had noticed that Fiona had tried every Sunday to use a new word for him. He usually seemed impressed.

"Good one, Fiona," he said. "And how's this wee lass?"

Darbie grinned again. Sophie knew she had taken to him right away, which was good, since she was going to see him every week to help her deal with things like her mom and dad's deaths. Sophie used to see Dr. Peter every week too. Now she only went once a month for a "check-in," and she missed their weekly chats on his window seat.

"Still only three Flakes?" Dr. Peter said.

"Yes," Fiona said cheerfully. "Maggie and her mom go to a different church. And Kitty's parents don't even believe in church."

"And what are you going to do about it?" Dr. Peter said.

"Keep praying for Kitty," they all said together.

Sophie felt a little twinge somewhere. *I haven't exactly been praying that much lately,* she thought. She shut her eyes and tried to get Jesus into view.

*Hello,* she thought to him. *Um, I'm sorry—it's not that I don't love you. I just haven't had anything to ask you in a while.*

Yikes. What if God made something bad happen so she would pay more attention? Did it work that way? Was she going to be snatched from—from what?

*From her post at the Secret Agency? Agent Shadow straightened her slim shoulders. NO, that couldn't happen. She would have to double her efforts to stay in contact with Headquarters. The Big Headquarters. In the sky. Especially with some unknown mission looming on the horizon.*

"Sophie-Lophie-Loodle?"

Sophie shuddered back to Dr. Peter, who was peering at her as if he knew exactly where she'd been. He always used his nickname for her when he was calling her back.

"Did I miss something?" she said.

"Dr. Peter's Bible study starts Tuesday after school," Fiona said. "I can come if Miss Odetta Clide thinks I've gotten my room organized enough. Isn't there some kind of child labor law about that?"

"Maybe you can ask your parents about that," Dr. Peter said.

"Like I ever see them," Fiona said.

Sophie always felt bad for Fiona about how too busy her mom and dad always were—but right now she was smiling inside. She had been waiting for what seemed like a whole millennium for Dr. Peter to start the Bible study group. He was the one who had taught her how to read Bible stories, and doing that had helped her solve some *formidable* problems. That was another Fiona word.

"It's going to be just class!" That was a Darbie word—and it meant "very cool," only it sounded much more mature than plain cool.

That night when Sophie wiggled herself under her fluffy purple bedspread, she immediately closed her eyes and imagined Jesus, just the way Dr. Peter had taught her. She could almost see Jesus' kind eyes and his strong hands and she could ask him any question. The answers usually came later.

*I'm really going to try to talk to you more*, Sophie prayed when she got him in her mind. *Even if I don't actually have a question, which isn't so often because every time I think I have everything figured out—I SO don't! But I'm here, and if there's anything you want me to learn right now, please show me.*

She sighed as her thoughts grew fuzzy around the edges. *I don't guess you would want to hear about the perfect dress, would you? Gold satin with diamonds around the neck. Not real diamonds, of course.*

When Sophie met the Corn Flakes at their usual spot on the corner of the playground the next morning, Kitty started whining before Sophie could even get her backpack off.

"She's at it again," Darbie said. She and Fiona exchanged Kitty's-getting-on-my-nerves looks.

"What's wrong?" Sophie said.

"Her mom is making her wear one of her sisters' hand-me-down dresses to the dance," Maggie said.

"All those dresses are lame!" Kitty said. Her voice was getting up into only-dogs-can-hear territory. "All stupid ruffles and big old bows."

"That could be your cover though," Sophie said. "Who would think you were a secret agent dressed in some fluffy yellow thing?"

"I'll look like a canary!"

"Of course," Sophie said. "That's your new mission name. Canary."

"What's mine?" Maggie said. She was never the best at thinking up names.

"All three of you could have bird code names," Fiona said.

"I'm Heron," Darbie said. "Long legs and all that."

"I like Flamingo better," Sophie said.

"I'm not gonna be a buzzard," Maggie said with a voice-thud.

"No way," Fiona said. "You're more like an owl."

Maggie blinked.

"See what I mean?" Fiona said.

"Can I be Canary Louisa or something pretty like that?" Kitty said.

"That's too much for us to be saying to each other." Fiona said.

"But you can call yourself that," Sophie said quickly. She'd already heard enough whining and the bell hadn't even rung yet.

"What are you up to, Maggie?" Darbie said.

Sophie looked at Maggie, who was cocking her head with one eye closed, her lips bunched up into a pointy knot.

"I'm seeing what it feels like to be an owl," Maggie said.

Sophie giggled. Maggie hardly ever did the pretending thing unless somebody else did it first. *She's a Corn Flake to the core now*, she thought.

"You'll never get off the ground, Owl," Darbie said.

"WHOOO!" Maggie hooted.

She stretched her arms out and pulled her head down into her shoulders and made three leaps. Kitty squealed and clapped her hands.

"Again, again!" Darbie called out to Maggie.

Maggie looked back at them over her shoulder, still flapping her wings, and gave a wise wink. Fiona collapsed against Sophie, and they pounded on each other between guffaws.

"Go on then!" Darbie cried. "Fly!"

Maggie let out one more resounding "WHOOOO!" and thundered toward the middle of the playground, arms going so hard Sophie thought for a second she might take flight.

"It's a bird!" a male voice shouted.

"It's a plane!" another one yelled.

"It's SUPER BLIMP!" was the final cry.

On the other side of Maggie, the three Fruit Loops—Tod, Eddie, and Colton—fell into a heap, all puffing out their cheeks and poking out their stomachs.

Sophie watched as Maggie deflated like a leftover party balloon.

# Three

The Corn Flakes had Maggie surrounded before the Fruit Loops could even pick their ridiculous selves up off the ground.

Darbie hollered at Eddie, "Are you talking about yourself, Whale Boy?"

"You know you're not a blimp, Mags," Fiona said as they practically carried Maggie back to their corner. "Not even close."

"You're NOT fat, Mags," Kitty sobbed. "You're not!"

"I know."

They all stopped in mid-hug to stare at Maggie. She just blinked, owl-like.

"They're only stupid boys," she said. "I don't pay any attention to what they say."

Darbie gave her an admiring nod. "You're a class person, Maggie LaQuita, and don't you be forgetting that." She ran a steely gaze over Fiona, Sophie, and Kitty. "We'd all do good to listen to her. Boys are a sorry lot."

"Blackguards," Fiona said. "They just proved it. Pinky promise—one more time."

There was pinky-linking all around before the bell rang.

"Maggie took that well, don't you think?" Sophie whispered to Fiona as they hurried off to language arts.

"She's resilient," Fiona said. "Fruit Loop slime slides right off her. That's why she's a great agent. Now, what we have to figure out, like, IMMEDIATELY, is how I'm going to get out of shopping with that evil Odetta Clide person. Did you know that she showed me pictures of herself going to her first dance—like a hundred years ago or something?" Fiona's gray eyes grew. "The Corn Pops are going to have a BLAST if I come in looking like that."

"We'll try to think of something," Sophie said.

They pinkied up.

"I want to say my high," Mama said at supper that night. She pushed Zeke's plate with the broccoli left on it toward him. "Here's your low, Z-Boy. Work on that while I'm talking."

Zeke pretended to throw up over the side of the chair. Mama's brown eyes got all bubbly as she ignored him and said, "I was on the phone all afternoon."

"That's your high?" Daddy said. "I thought you did that every day."

Mama spread out her fingers and counted on them. "I talked to Darbie's aunt, Maggie's mom, and Fiona's new nanny. What a lovely name: Odetta Clide."

Lacie choked over her iced tea glass. "Is this person actually living in the twenty-first century?"

"She is, and she's quite—something."

*I bet*, Sophie thought. *Something from the Dark Ages.*

"Where does the high come in?" Lacie said.

"The four of us are taking you two, Maggie, Fiona, and Darbie to Smithfield to have lunch and shop for party dresses."

Lacie dropped her fork into her pork chop. "You're going to BUY our dresses! Mama, you ROCK! Only—I think we should go to the mall in Virginia Beach. No offense, but what do they have in Smithfield?"

"Loveliness," Mama said. "It's old, and Darbie's aunt says there's a museum and all kinds of little shops and cafés. And no, I'm not going to buy your dresses. We're going there to get ideas."

"Oh." Lacie folded her arms. "You know, I bet I could just take the money you were going to use for fabric and buy something. They're having a sale at Rave."

Daddy shook his head. "Rave sells nothing but Band-Aids and dental floss. Off-limits, Lacie."

Mama got up to clear the table and Lacie followed, going off about how they treated her like a total baby. Sophie picked up her own plate, walked over to get Zeke's, and imagined herself shopping for her new disguise.

*The lovely Smithfield boutique, where rack upon rack of elegant gowns awaited her choice. "It can't be anything showy," Agent Shadow told herself. She had to blend in. It was Canary and Flamingo and Owl who needed to stand out so they wouldn't LOOK like undercover agents. Canary in fluffy yellow acquired from her older sisters. Flamingo in hot pink. Owl in brown velvet that swayed as she danced with Edward Wornum, a.k.a. Whale Boy, who would whisper, eyes downcast, that he was sorry he had ever humiliated her by comparing her to a large, lighter-than-air craft—*

"Quit blowing in my ear, Soph! That tickles!"

Zeke peeled his sticky palm from Sophie's, leaving her the last mouthful of broccoli he had spit into it.

"Already at the dance, Soph?" Daddy said. He grinned at her as he twirled her around, nearly knocking Lacie inside the dishwasher. "Just keep the daydreams here, huh? You don't want to lose your camera at this late date."

He was talking about the deal they had: if she made at least a B in everything, she got to keep her video camera, which meant limiting her dreaming to filming and keeping it out of the classroom, where she was supposed to pay attention.

"So can I call Fiona?" Sophie said to Mama as she washed the green off her hand. "Does she know about Saturday yet?"

Daddy leaned against the counter, elbows propped. "You're really into this dance thing, huh? I don't know why you want to complicate your life with boys."

"Eew!" Sophie said.

"Well, I assume there are going to be boys at this dance."

"I'm not going for the boys! Sick!"

"Good attitude, Soph," Daddy said. He put out his arm just as Lacie tried to make an exit from the kitchen and he hooked her in by the neck. "Now, you, on the other hand—"

Lacie started screeching again. Sophie loaded the silverware into the dishwasher, thoughts—and stomach—turning. *I don't even want to get anywhere CLOSE to a boy! Gross me out, why don't you?*

She tried to imagine sharp-faced Tod Ravelli, Mr. I'm So Cool I Can Hardly Stand It, holding out his hand to her, asking her to dance—but even Agent Shadow wouldn't go there. *"I won't even do it to capture spies from the Corn Pop Organization,"* the agent told herself. *"I have made a promise to my people that I will never break."*

It was obvious the next day that the Corn Pops had made no such promise to each another. During first period, Sophie saw Anne-Stuart go to the sharpener with a point already on her pencil, just because Tod was there. Second period, Ms. Quelling had to call on B.J. twice because she was so busy staring at Eddie.

*How TOTALLY gross is that?* Sophie thought.

The only thing grosser was Julia walking her fingers up Colton Messik's neck while they were standing in the lunch line. He reached back to grab her hand to make her stop, and then he twisted her arm around until she was almost on the floor.

She laughed up into his face like he was James Bond.

*More like Pond*, Sophie thought. *Pond SCUM.*

"I'd break his arm if he did that to me," said the girl behind Sophie.

It was Gill, one of the four athletic girls in their class who were friendly to the Corn Flakes. Sophie and Fiona had named Gill and her friends the Wheaties. Gill was lanky, with reddish hair and very green eyes.

"I think Julia likes it," Sophie said, nodding toward Julia, who was now weaving among the tables with Colton on her heels threatening her with his juice box.

"You know it," Gill said. She nudged Sophie lightly on the arm with her fist. "But what's to like about somebody trying to squirt you with grape juice?"

"And they say YOU guys are weird," said another Wheatie, a husky girl named Harley whose cheeks came up and made her eyes almost disappear when she smiled. "They're the weird ones."

The Corn Pops got weirder after lunch, when all the fourth, fifth, and sixth graders were seated around the edges of the cafeteria on floor mats for an assembly. Julia led her group to sit against the wall, right behind the Corn Flakes.

"What's this about anyway?" Sophie heard B.J. say.

34

"We get to see somebody do gymnastics," someone answered her.

Sophie took a peek. It was Willoughby. She was finger-twirling a piece of her wavy milk-chocolate-colored hair—worn in a short cut that was shorter in back than in front. One sandal-clad foot was wiggling too. Sophie had heard Julia tell her to "quit fidgeting—you're so annoying" more than once.

"All of us can do gymnastics," Julia said, flipping her burnt-auburn ponytail. "What's the big deal?"

"It's a boy," Willoughby said.

"A boy?" Anne-Stuart said.

"Oh, brother," Fiona whispered to Sophie. "I bet you ten dollars Julia's already putting on lip gloss."

"A boy from our class," Willoughby said.

"Nuh-uh," B.J. said.

Out of the corner of her eye, Sophie could see B.J. get up on her knees to scan the sixth grade.

"It's not somebody from our class, *Willoughby*," B.J. said. She sounded like she had something in her mouth she wanted to spit out. "The only boys who could do gymnastics in our class are Tod and Eddie and Colton, and they're all sitting out here."

"Eddie doing gymnastics?" Kitty whispered across Maggie, who was beside Sophie. "He'd break the floor."

"They're not the only boys in our class," Willoughby said.

But just then Mrs. Olinghouse, their tall principal with the silvery hair and the blue eyes that could slice through somebody, stepped up to a microphone in the corner. The whole cafeteria went silent.

"We have a special treat today, boys and girls," she said. "Many of you know this young man, but you don't know that he competes all over the country as a gymnast. And today, he's going to do a demonstration for you."

35

"Life's desire," Sophie heard Julia say behind her. "Wake me up when it's over."

"I can do a cartwheel," Colton Messik yelled to Mrs. Olinghouse.

"If you can do one like this boy, Colton, I will give you a day off."

"Sweet!"

"And now, boys and girls, I give you — Jimmy Wythe!"

"Jimmy WYTHE?" the Corn Pops said in unison.

"That kid who hangs out with the computer guys?" Maggie said to Sophie.

It was the same kid, suddenly doing double backflips across the padded floor and landing on his feet. For the next twenty minutes he didn't stop — skinny Jimmy Wythe, who didn't look so scrawny in his shiny one-piece suit. He had muscles where Eddie Wornom had baby fat, total control where Colton Messik stumbled over his own feet, and speed that would have left little Tod Ravelli in the dirt.

*Colton is definitely not going to get his day off*, Sophie thought.

Sophie had never really noticed blond-haired Jimmy Wythe much before — except for the fact that he, like his friends, kept pretty much to their computers and didn't make disgusting noises with their armpits and burp "Jingle Bells" the way the Fruit Loops did. Even Kitty had said she thought he was "mysterious."

But there was no missing Jimmy now. *He moves like a deer*, Sophie thought. *A deer that does somersaults and walks on his hands.*

Whenever he finished a part of his routine, shy Jimmy Wythe faced the audience, throwing his arms up and rewarding them with a smile that flashed white against his very tan skin. The kids cheered and whistled loud and high.

As he made his final bow, Kitty leaned across Maggie again and said, "He's a babe!" Her cheeks were watermelon red.

But Kitty's excitement couldn't compare to B.J.'s and Anne-Stuart's. They were screaming so loud, Sophie turned around to make sure they weren't dying. Anne-Stuart's pale blue eyes were about to wash right out of her head, as far as Sophie could tell, and B.J. was climbing up onto wiry little Willoughby's shoulders, craning for a last glimpse of Jimmy as he left the cafeteria with a wave.

"I thought they said he was a geek," Fiona said to Sophie.

"Well, they're going mental over him now," Darbie said.

Sophie felt herself grinning. *This is ALMOST as good as if one of us did it*, she thought. *He showed those Pops they're not the only ones who can do awesome things.*

When Mrs. Olinghouse dismissed them to go to fifth period, Anne-Stuart and B.J. climbed over Darbie and Fiona and raced for the door. By the time the Corn Flakes reached it, one of them was on each side of Jimmy, tugging at his sweaty arms and saying things like, "You were so GOOD!" And "I never knew you could do that!"

"They never knew he existed," Fiona muttered.

"He WAS good though," Maggie said.

"Sorry, Maggot," said Colton, grinning at Maggie from one stick-out ear to the other.

"It's about TIME you were apologizing," Darbie said.

"Nah," Colton said. "I'm sorry she doesn't have a chance with Jungle Gym Jimmy. I heard he doesn't like fat—"

"Close your cake trap, Colton," Darbie said.

Colton froze for a mini-second, and then grinned at Darbie. "Cake trap. That's pretty good. Hey, Eddie—close your cake trap, dude! Close your cake trap!"

"We're so out of here," Sophie said. She hauled Darbie and Fiona toward the math room before they had a chance to close Colton's cake trap for him. Kitty and Maggie had already disappeared.

"Why are those boys bugging us again?" Kitty whined while Mrs. Utley was handing out worksheets. "I thought they learned their lesson during the science project."

"I don't know," Darbie said, "but I'm dying to make them pay."

"But that isn't the Corn Flakes way," Sophie said. She handed Darbie a sheet from the stack Mrs. Utley put on their table.

"Besides," Maggie said, "it doesn't bother me. They're just stupid boys."

Mrs. Utley paused before she moved on to the Wheaties. "And my advice to you ladies," she said, her many soft chins jiggling happily, "is that you wait until they get a whole lot smarter before you have much to do with them."

"We hear you," Fiona said.

Mrs. Utley smiled and took her chins to the next table. By then the Corn Pops were all standing at the pencil sharpener next to the door. When it opened and Jimmy Wythe appeared, back in his jeans and T-shirt, Anne-Stuart twirled to face him, but not before B.J. got to him, grabbed him by the wrist, and dragged him toward the Corn Pops' table.

"I think B.J. won that round," Fiona said.

"That's because she mugged him!" Sophie said.

"Anne-Stuart won't be giving up," Darbie said.

Kitty giggled. "You can't blame her. He IS cute."

The four of them turned on her. "No BOYS!" they all hissed.

"Ladies," Mrs. Utley said. She was looking at the Corn Pops, but the Flakes zipped their mouths and hunkered down over their papers.

Before five minutes had passed, Mrs. Utley moved Jimmy back to his usual "computer geek" table with curly-haired Nathan and skinny Vincent and the round-faced twins, leaving B.J. to pout her lower lip out and Anne-Stuart to go to work writing in her fake-curlicue form what Sophie knew had to be a note.

When the bell rang and everyone burst from the room for the break before science, Sophie saw Anne-Stuart tuck the folded paper into the pocket of Jimmy's T-shirt, giggle into his face, and run off to catch up with her fellow Pops.

*"But we have more important things to do," Agent Shadow told herself as she moved with the crowd out into the hallway. "If I had time—if I didn't have spies to watch—I would like to say to Secret Weapon Wythe, 'You're better than all of them.'"*

"Thanks," someone said. Sophie felt her eyes widen. Beside her stood Jimmy Wythe. He smiled a shy smile at her and backed away into the hallway crowd.

"Did I say something to him?" Sophie said.

Kitty sighed, eyes in two dreamy puddles. "I don't know what it was—but I think he liked it."

"But somebody ELSE didn't like it." Maggie jerked her head toward the water fountain.

Anne-Stuart and B.J. stood there, holding Julia's hair back while she drank, looking dead-on at Sophie.

"I think they're wishing it was YOUR head in that sink so they could drown you," Darbie said.

Sophie didn't answer. She knew Darbie was right.

# Four

Sophie didn't wait for bedtime that night. She went straight to her room after school and started praying *then*.

Sitting in the middle of her purple comforter, Sophie tried to imagine Jesus. As soon as his kind eyes came into view in her mind, the prayer-thoughts began. *Things aren't going so good. The Fruit Loops are trying to humiliate Maggie. B.J. and Anne-Stuart hate me more than ever now because they think I'm trying to steal the boy they like. And I don't even LIKE boys! Well, except for you. You were a boy. But I bet you never told any girl that she was a blimp or that she'd never get a boyfriend.*

Sophie fell back against her pile of pillows and grabbed one to hug against her. *What I want to ask you is—what do I do? I don't want them making fun of Maggie anymore. Right now, I really wish I WAS a secret agent so I could just turn them in to the government ...*

*Agent Shadow clicked the last pair of handcuffs on the third prisoner. Colton Messik was pale to the tips of his stick-out ears. He SHOULD be ashamed, the agent thought to herself. He tried to make the Owl feel bad about herself when she was in the line of duty, doing important work to do away with the likes of him and his Fruit Loop Mob. Agent Shadow breathed a deep sigh of relief as she shoved Colton Messik and his two accomplices toward the armored car, which would take them straight to solitary confinement in a maximum security prison. There wouldn't even be a trial. Everyone knew they were guilty ...*

Sophie opened her eyes and felt a smile cross her face. Putting the Fruit Loops in their place—now THAT was a mission worth going to a dance for.

By Saturday, the Loops and the Pops were miles from Sophie's mind as everyone climbed into Fiona's family's big Ford Expedition to head for Smithfield.

For the first twenty minutes of the trip, Sophie's attention was on Miss Odetta Clide, who was gripping the steering wheel with the veins on her hands bulging like blue twine. Her wiry gray hair was short and pushed back from her face with the brush marks still in it. *That hair wouldn't DARE fall in her eyes,* Sophie thought.

Miss Odetta kept glancing into the rearview mirror as if she didn't want those eyes to miss a thing somebody might be doing wrong. Before they had even gotten into the car while in Fiona's driveway, she had made Fiona go back in and put a barrette in her hair.

"She's just as strict as you said," Sophie whispered to Fiona in the far backseat.

"You haven't seen anything yet," Fiona whispered back. "But we can't talk about it now or she'll give me demerits for whispering. She says it's rude."

"Fiona—that's five demerits," said Miss Odetta Clide. "A lady does not whisper in the presence of others." Her eyes, a washed-out blue, were watching them in the rearview mirror.

"What are demerits?" Maggie said.

"Marks for being rude, inconsiderate, or irresponsible," Miss Odetta Clide said.

Fiona slid down in the seat.

"Do you get in trouble for them?" Maggie said.

"If Fiona accumulates too many she will."

Fiona slid farther.

"How many is too many?" Maggie said.

"Margarita!" her mom said.

"Not as many as you might think," said Miss Odetta Clide. And once again she gave Fiona a look in the mirror—although by now Sophie was sure she could no longer see her. Fiona was almost on the floor.

But even that was forgotten the minute they arrived in Smithfield.

"This is a beautiful little town!" Mama said.

"Isn't it precious?" Darbie's aunt Emily said.

Sophie didn't think *precious* was exactly the right word for the old courthouse that stood on the street like a wise judge—and the country store with two bent men playing checkers out front—and the ice cream parlor where she was sure they still made ice cream the old-fashioned way, whatever that was.

"It's nostalgic," said Fiona. She emerged from hiding and pressed her face to the car window between Sophie's and Darbie's.

"Look at these gorgeous Victorian homes," Mama said. "It makes you want to wear a bustle, doesn't it?"

"You'll see houses from the Federal and Georgian periods as well," Miss Odetta Clide said as if she were reading from a textbook. "A few Colonial. This town is over 250 years old. It was the peanut capital of the world at one time." Miss Odetta parked the Expedition and turned stiffly to the backseat. "A lady listens, Fiona," she said. "She learns."

Fiona moaned—although not loud enough for Miss Odetta Clide to catch her. Sophie couldn't even imagine how many demerits that would be worth.

But after they parked and started down Main Street, past the bakery and the antique stores and the houses with their wide porches, Sophie found herself sidling closer to Miss Odetta to hear what she was saying.

"British merchants started settling here in about 1752," she said in her brisk-for-an-older-lady voice. "Brought in by the sea captains up the Pagan River."

"Look at those roses," Mama said.

They stopped to look up at a house with thick white columns on its porch.

"Now this one is Civil War era," Miss Odetta said. "Might have been owned by a steamboat captain. They brought their boats up the river too, after the war, trying to build things up again."

"Would their wives have waited for them on that porch?" Sophie said.

Miss Odetta Clide squinted down at her as if she'd just noticed Sophie was there. "It would be safe to say they might have. The reason they built the porches so deep was to accommodate the women's dresses. A hoopskirt could reach from the front door to the railing. And the women were even more extravagant in the Victorian period. You need only look at their homes."

She clipped around the corner with everyone right behind her. Miss Odetta stopped in front of a pale blue house that had towers and turrets like a castle, stained-glass windows, and trim that reminded Sophie of a fancy gingerbread house.

"This is Victorian," Miss Odetta said. "The ladies who first lived in this place wore the bustles Mrs. LaCroix spoke of, and corsets pulled so tight they could barely draw breath."

"Why would they want to do that?" Maggie said. "Sounds brutal."

"That is precisely what THEIR daughters said. In the 1920s they threw away the corsets and replaced them with short dresses that had everyone scandalized. No one had ever seen a woman's legs in public before."

"What's 'scandalized' mean?" Sophie whispered to Fiona.

"It's like shocked right out of their Sketchers," Fiona whispered back.

Miss Odetta turned from the Victorian mansion to gaze down at the Corn Flakes. Sophie tugged at her sundress to make it look longer.

"I understand we are looking at party dresses today."

"Mama and I are just getting ideas," Sophie said. "Ma'am." She wondered if Fiona's friends could get demerits slapped on them too.

"Smithfield is the place to do that. You will see every kind of garment from a Colonial ball gown to a Roaring Twenties flapper dress. The possibilities are endless."

They visited the Isle of Wight Museum, which was set up in a country store from the early 1900s. There were displays of cheese wheels and thread and shoes and cake boxes and washboards. They followed Miss Odetta to some sassy dresses that hung on the wall.

"The forerunners of the miniskirt," Miss Odetta said. "Vintage 1921."

Some had fringe, others sequins, and still others were draped with feather boas that must have left some poor ostrich naked. All of them were straight, falling from the shoulders to the knees in one long line. They didn't do much for Sophie's imagination.

But Darbie ran right up to them, arms outstretched—until Miss Odetta told her a lady didn't touch antiques. Still, Darbie stood there with her hands clenched behind her back, the sequins sparkling in her eyes.

"I ADORE these!" she said. "Aren't they just CLASS?"

"And just a little out of our price range, Darbie honey," Aunt Emily said.

Senora LaQuita put her hand on Aunt Emily's arm. "I can design this for Darbie," she said, trilling the "r" in the way Sophie loved.

Darbie looked at her aunt, biting her lower lip.

"I don't know what to say," Aunt Emily said. "That's such a nice offer."

"Say yes," Maggie said. "My mother wouldn't offer if she didn't mean it."

"Well—if that's what you want, Darbie."

"I do! These were MADE for me!"

"That's one, then," Miss Odetta said. "Shall we continue?"

From there it was decided by the Corn Flakes that they would each choose a dress from the time period that, as Fiona put it, "spoke to them." It was just what secret agents would do to conceal their identities from an enemy mob like the Fruit Loops, Sophie was sure.

As they twirled and giggled and squealed through the antique shops and the art galleries, Maggie decided she liked the dresses the Victorian girls wore. Fiona went for a Civil War look with ruffles and a full skirt. Miss Odetta Clide nixed a hoopskirt, but she agreed that they could use Fiona's dress money to have Maggie's mom design one for her.

When Sophie stood for five minutes in front of a painting of a Colonial family, gazing at the young girl in the gold dress with lace around the scoop neck and sleeves that flared out deliciously at the elbows, Mama whispered to her, "I'll see what I can do, Dream Girl."

When they got back to Poquoson, it was too hard to go their separate ways, and they wanted to share their news with Kitty so she wouldn't be left out. Their faces were long as they pulled into Fiona's driveway.

Boppa met them and told Miss Odetta Clide she might need to go inside and do some damage control, since he had been with Fiona's little brother and sister all day. When she was gone, Boppa said, "These girls are going to go into mourning if we don't let them have a sleepover tonight. What do you say, ladies? I'll make them go to bed early."

Mama smiled. "So you're afraid of her too, huh, Boppa?"

Within the hour, the Corn Flakes had returned with pajamas and sleeping bags and Kitty, and they were busily writing down script ideas when they heard a knock at Fiona's bedroom door. They were afraid it was Miss Odetta telling them to turn out the light. But it was Boppa, smiling his soft smile and wiggling his dark caterpillar eyebrows and running his hand over the top of his bald head.

"Anybody up for some dancing lessons?" he said.

"Dancing lessons, Boppa?" Fiona said as they all skittered after him down the hall to the door that led out to the deck.

"I hear you're going to a dance. You've got the dresses taken care of—now you need to learn how to dance."

Boppa had the picnic table scooted out of the way with a boom box on it, and there was a string of white lights twinkling in the May night.

"I know you kids THINK you know how to dance," he said.

"I don't," Maggie said.

"But I'm going to teach you some real dances. We're going to start with the bop."

"I like that word!" Kitty said, giggling. "I want to bop!"

"Come on then," Boppa said. He poked the play button and held out his hand to Kitty. She plunked hers right into it just as a man on the CD started singing about a hound dog.

"I know this song!" Kitty squealed. "My grandma taught me how to play it on the piano!"

"This is Elvis Presley, ladies," Boppa said. "The King of Rock 'n' Roll. Come on — grab a partner."

Before the song was over, Sophie and Fiona had the bop down, and Darbie and Maggie, while they were still slamming into each other at times, were getting close.

After that Boppa taught them to waltz and then cha-cha. The waltz was Sophie's favorite — she could imagine herself in the gold dress with the flared sleeves, sweeping across the floor — but she was doing more stumbling than sweeping.

"Help me, Boppa!" she said, after she stepped on Fiona's foot for the thirtieth time and Fiona refused to be her partner until her bruises healed.

"Miss Odetta Clide, do you waltz?"

They all looked up to see Miss Odetta in the doorway, arms folded. "Of course I waltz. Every well-trained lady knows how to waltz."

"Then please do me the honor of helping me with a demonstration."

Boppa held out his hand to Miss Odetta. Kitty giggled. Maggie blinked like an owl. Fiona slithered down onto the picnic table bench.

But when Miss Odetta Clide slid her hand into his and placed the other one on his arm and they began to move in a smooth one-two-three, one-two-three across the deck, all mouths fell open. "That is class," Darbie whispered.

Boppa and Miss Odetta were floating, looking directly into each other's eyes like they didn't even have to be aware of the feet that carried them in swooping circles across the ballroom floor.

*Agent Shadow lifted her eyes from the skirt of her golden dress to the face of the Unknown Dancer and let him take her hand. Gracefully they swished past the awestruck crowd. "I must remember to keep my mind on the mission at hand," she told herself. But just then, she couldn't remember what it was.*

# Five

For Sophie, time spun in a waltz of its own after their dancing lesson.

On Sunday, Dr. Peter reminded the girls that their Bible study would start Tuesday. Sophie felt a twinge again—the kind she used to feel when she forgot a homework assignment.

*I'm going to read my Bible and pray every night from now on,* she thought.

But Sunday night there was homework, and Monday after school she went fabric shopping with Mama. When Sophie headed for the pattern books at Jo-Ann Fabrics & Crafts, Mama said, "We won't be needing those, Dream Girl. Senora LaQuita told me she would teach me how to design my own patterns." She gave Sophie a wispy Mama-smile. "It's time I learned anyway. Who knows, maybe I can whip up something like they sell at Rave for Lacie."

"Anybody can make Band-Aids, Mama," Sophie said.

They found gold taffeta and brown shimmering lace, and Sophie was so thrilled she barely noticed the Fruit Loops or the Corn Pops all day Tuesday.

What did get her attention was Kitty.

Kitty giggled a lot that morning, more than usual, and it was a different kind of giggling. She laughed when things weren't even funny—like when Gill lost a filling out of her tooth, right into the burrito Maggie gave her from her lunch. Kitty's voice was shrill, and the laughter didn't get to her eyes.

When they went out to the playground during the second half of lunch period to rehearse for their film, Fiona put her hands on her almost-hips and said, "All right, Kitty, you're hiding something. What is it?"

Kitty's eyes got as big as cereal bowls. "How did you know?"

*It's a good thing Kitty doesn't try to be a REAL secret agent*, Sophie thought.

"Because you've been acting mental all day," Darbie said.

Kitty sank down to the ground and leaned against the fence, knees pulled into her chest. "You're all going to be mad at me when I tell you—and you're probably gonna kick me out of the Corn Flakes—but I never wanted to agree to that pack thing anyway."

"What pack thing?" Maggie said.

Sophie nodded. "You mean the 'pact'? About the boys?"

"Yes," Kitty said. "I hate the Fruit Loops, but I like other boys—nice boys—and I found one. And you can't make me not go to the dance with him!"

She burst into the tears Sophie had been expecting. Maggie reached into her backpack and handed Kitty a tissue.

"You don't mean some boy asked you?" Darbie said.

"And you said yes?" Fiona said.

Kitty nodded as she blubbered into the wadded-up tissue.

"I'm scandalized," Fiona said.

Sophie sat down next to Kitty. "Who is he?" she said.

"Nathan Coffey," she said, although from the other side of the tissue it sounded at first like "make some toffee."

"Which one is he again?" Darbie said.

"Curly hair. Braces," Fiona said. "Wears a Redskins hat."

"Remember I told you his dad is in my dad's squadron," Kitty said. "We even went camping with them last summer." She looked up, face streaming and miserable. "I didn't know I had a crush on him before."

Maggie said, "How can you have a crush on somebody and not even know it?"

"All right, let's not all go off our nut here," Darbie said. She sat down and pulled Fiona with her. Maggie squatted beside them.

"You're not in love with Nathan, Kitty," Fiona said, her face serious and sage.

"We're going together," Kitty said. She poked her chin into the tops of her knees.

"Where are you going?" Maggie said.

"I think that means they're boyfriend and girlfriend," Sophie said.

"And THAT means you're breaking the Corn Flakes pact," Fiona said.

Darbie shook her head. "You're making a bags of it, Kitty, I'm telling ya."

Kitty looked at Sophie with panic in her eyes. "Are you going to throw me out?"

"No!" Sophie said, before Fiona could jump in with something Sophie knew she would have to apologize for seven hundred times later.

"If she goes, I go," Maggie said. She even stood up.

"She's not going!" Sophie said.

Kitty flung herself at Sophie's neck and cried until the bell rang, while Fiona and Darbie folded their arms and looked everywhere but at Kitty.

On their way to class, Fiona pulled Sophie back. "What is the point of having a pact if you can just break it and nothing happens?"

"I don't know," Sophie said. "But Dr. Peter will."

Fiona's eyebrows came together. "I thought he was going to talk about the Bible."

"Stuff like that is in the Bible," Sophie said.

There was another Jesus-twinge. *I'm coming back*, she prayed. *Honest, I am.*

It was so much easier to remember to talk to Jesus when Dr. Peter was around. And just as Sophie had expected, he had the Bible study room fixed up so that everybody said some form of "Wow!" when they walked in.

"Everybody" consisted of Sophie, Fiona, Darbie, and Harley and Gill from the Wheaties.

"I didn't know you went to church here, Harley!" Sophie said.

"We don't," Gill said. "Not yet anyway." She always talked for the husky Harley, who just smiled that eyes-disappearing-into-cheeks smile a lot. "Your mom told my mom about this at a PTO meeting, so she's making me try it."

"I don't want anyone to come because her mom makes her," Dr. Peter said. "But I am going to ask you to give it an honest try. Two sessions. Then if you would rather do something else with your time, I'll tell your moms they should let you." Dr. Peter clapped his hands together and nodded toward the beanbag chairs that were set in a circle, each one a different color. "Choose a seat, and let's get started."

Sophie picked the purple chair and flopped into it. Beside each beanbag was a Bible in a matching color.

"This is class," Darbie whispered to her.

"A lady doesn't whisper," Fiona said.

"I don't know about a lady," said Dr. Peter. "But members of this group don't HAVE to whisper—at least not in here."

"Define this group," Fiona said.

"We're going to do that over time," Dr. Peter said. "But I will tell you this: you wouldn't be here if you weren't ready to get closer to God." He wrinkled his nose so that his glasses worked their way back up closer to his sparkling eyes. "Unless your mom made you come."

"It's cool so far," Gill said. Harley gave him a thumbs-up.

"You all got the packet I sent you, telling you what we're going to be doing?"

Heads bobbed.

"So, any questions before we get started?"

"I have one," Fiona said. She resituated herself in her hot pink beanbag. "Sophie says the Bible talks about stuff like what we're dealing with right now with a friend of ours. I just don't see how that could be true, since the Bible was written, like, a million years ago."

Sophie was sure Miss Odetta Clide would say a lady didn't talk to the Bible study teacher like that. But Dr. Peter grinned at Fiona.

"I like a challenge," he said. "Bring it on."

Fiona straightened up tall, and then looked at Gill and Harley. "You guys have to promise you won't tell anybody at school about this."

"What is said in here stays in here," Dr. Peter said. "That's one of the ground rules. But we aren't here to vent about people either."

"This isn't venting. Here's what happened."

Fiona told him all about the pact and Kitty's breaking it, with Darbie and Sophie adding details, and Harley and

Gill looking as if they were hearing about the worst kind of traitor.

"So," Fiona said when they were through, "how can the Bible tell us what to do about something that probably never happened back then?"

"The Bible is full of stories about betrayal," Dr. Peter said. He rubbed his hands together as if he couldn't wait to get into one.

"Oh," Fiona said. "So what's the answer?"

"What's the question?" Dr. Peter said. He looked at the Wheaties. "Do you two mind if we explore that?"

Gill was obviously into the whole thing, which meant Harley was too.

"The question is—" Fiona looked at Darbie.

"Why would an eleven-year-old girl be wanting a boy-friend?" Darbie said.

"So much that she would break the pact," Sophie put in. "We made a promise to each other that we wouldn't go to the dance with a boy—any of us."

"Did Kitty agree to the promise?" Dr. Peter said.

"Yes!" Fiona said. "She pinkied up like the rest of us."

Dr. Peter looked bewildered. Sophie and Darbie linked pinky fingers, and he nodded. "Gotcha," he said.

"But then today she's telling us she never wanted to make the promise in the beginning," Darbie said.

Dr. Peter ran his finger up and down his nose. "Something is really strong in her to make her break a promise. Maybe the Bible can show us what that something is."

"No way," Gill said.

"That's what I'm thinking," Fiona said.

"Don't take my word for it," Dr. Peter said. "Let's go in."

Sophie was squirming in the purple beanbag, but Dr. Peter's eyes were still dancing, the way they did when there was a juicy problem to solve.

"Turn to Ecclesiastes 3—that's in the Old Testament, Fiona. There you go." Dr. Peter glanced around the circle as they thumbed to the right place. "This isn't the most uplifting book in the Bible, but I think you'll like this part. Now, I want you to close your eyes and imagine that you have come to a wise teacher, someone you look up to."

Sophie chose Dr. Peter and pictured him in her mind with a beard down to his chest and wearing a long robe that touched the tops of his rope sandals.

"Imagine you have come to this teacher with your question about Kitty, and you know he or she will give you the right answer."

"What's the question again?" Gill said.

"What is so strong in Kitty that she would break her pact with her friends? What does she think is so important that she would do this? Now picture yourself asking this wise person that question. Hear it coming out of your mouth. Be aware of how you're sitting and what you're feeling. Be there."

Sophie was already there, sitting at Dr. Peter's feet, looking up at him with begging eyes, wanting so much to know the answer before they lost Kitty to some boy who would never be as nice and loyal to her as the Corn Flakes were. She could even feel the knot in her throat.

"Now," Dr. Peter said, "I want you to hear these words as if they are coming from the teacher's mouth—the answer to your question."

"'There is a time for everything,'" he read, "'and a season for every activity under heaven: a time to be born and a time to die, a time to plant and a time to uproot, a time to kill and a time to heal, a time to tear down and a time to build.' "

He went on to read about weeping and laughing, mourning and dancing, scattering and gathering, hugging and not hugging. Sophie listened, waiting for the part where she would have the oh-I-get-it feeling. So far what he was reading was only making the knot in her throat bigger, and she didn't know why.

" 'A time to search and a time to give up' " Dr. Peter read, " 'a time to keep and a time to throw away, a time to tear and a time to mend.' "

She heard an impatient sigh from Fiona.

" 'A time to be silent and a time to speak, a time to love and a time to hate, a time for war and a time for peace.' "

It was quiet, except for the sound of someone trying not to cry out loud.

"You okay, Loodle?" Dr. Peter said.

"No," Sophie said. She smeared her arm across her wet eyes. "Everything is changing. It doesn't ever stay the same. Next year we'll be in middle school, and all the Corn Flakes might not be together. And it might be harder, and I might start doing bad again and get the camera taken away. And maybe Kitty really will decide a boy is better than us, and she'll go away because it's her time to do that."

"That's what those verses mean, isn't it?" Darbie said. "That there's a time for every different thing."

"When is my time to kill?" Fiona said brightly. "There are a few Fruit Loops I'd like to take out."

Dr. Peter grinned. "I doubt that time is now, so hold off."

Harley and Gill looked disappointed.

"Sometimes change is hard," Dr. Peter said, looking at Sophie. "Especially when you like things the way they are right now. It's okay to feel bad over that for a while, as long as you know another time will come with its own set of good things."

"So let me get this straight," Fiona said. "It's Kitty's time to start liking boys."

"That could be part of it," Dr. Peter said.

"I'm not in that time yet," Fiona said.

"Me either," Sophie said.

Harley and Gill were shaking their heads. "I'm not ever having that time," Gill said. "No way."

Dr. Peter cocked his head at Darbie. "You want to tell us what you're thinking?"

"I'm thinking it seems to me it's a bit early for Kitty to be having this time," Darbie answered.

"I definitely don't like this pairing-up thing in the sixth grade," Dr. Peter said. "But there's nothing wrong with discovering that there is more to boys than nose-picking and smelly socks."

"That's so FOUL!" Fiona said.

Darbie was studying Dr. Peter's face like she was following a map.

"So how do we know when it's OUR time?" she said. "When it's okay to really like a boy and maybe want to dance with him or something."

Fiona looked at Darbie in horror.

"That's a great question," Dr. Peter said. "You'll know it's your time for boys when being around them takes you closer to God, not farther away." He rubbed his hands together. "And getting closer to God is what we're going to learn how to do, using the Bible as our guide."

*I wish Kitty were here*, Sophie thought as she flipped through the Bible to the next verses Dr. Peter called out. *I'm not sure she's close to God at all.*

Kitty always bowed her head and closed her eyes when the Corn Flakes prayed together, but Sophie wasn't sure it was always God she was thinking about.

Right now, she was pretty sure it was nobody but Nathan Coffey.

# Six

Over the next few days, Sophie was more and more sure she was right about Kitty's concentrating on Nathan and not God. When the Corn Flakes met before school and between classes and during lunch, and even when they got together outside of school to rehearse for filming their movie—*Secret Agents at the Ball*—all Kitty could talk about was her "boyfriend."

"If he's your boyfriend," Fiona said to Kitty on Thursday in the hall, "why aren't you ever with him?"

"I'm with him!" Kitty said. Sophie wasn't surprised to hear Kitty's voice winding up as she continued. "We talk on the phone every night, and he writes me notes, and this Sunday my family and his family are going to the beach."

"But that's not really a date," Maggie said.

"So?" Kitty folded her arms up under her green poncho. "We're still going to be together."

"Just don't be holding hands or any of that," Darbie said.

Kitty turned a guilty red, like she'd already been considering it. The very thought made Sophie's own palms go sweaty. *Ew*, she thought.

But at least Kitty's liking Nathan wasn't as bad as Anne-Stuart and B.J. going after Jimmy Wythe. The day of the spelling bee in Mr. Denton's class, B.J. actually shoved Anne-Stuart into a bookcase so she could stand next to Jimmy.

Sophie tried not to grin too big at Fiona when B.J. missed the first word Mr. Denton gave her, which obviously happened because B.J. was so busy playing with the belt loops on Jimmy's khakis that she didn't even think about it.

"Opportunity without the *t*," Fiona whispered to Sophie. "How could she make a lame mistake like that?"

When B.J. had to sit down, Anne-Stuart wasted no time in getting as close to Jimmy as she could, whispering who-knew-what into his ear, while on the other side of Jimmy, Ross and Ian — the moon-faced twins — both looked like they were going to explode if they weren't allowed to laugh soon. Jimmy's cheeks practically turned purple, Sophie noted. *Mine would too if Anne-Stuart was that close to ME with her drippy nose*, she thought. Sophie didn't blame him for misspelling *his* next word so he could get away from her.

*I think "B.J." stands for "Boy Jumper,"* Sophie thought. As soon as the bell rang, B.J. was on Jimmy's trail, unzipping his backpack and sticking a note inside.

*Even if I liked Jimmy as much as she does*, Sophie told herself, *WHICH I DON'T — I wouldn't be all in his space all the time.*

In Ms. Quelling's class, when Jimmy said hi to Sophie on the way to his table, she ducked behind *Traditional Spanish Food* — after she smiled back.

It was Friday morning before Sophie noticed that Darbie was being unusually quiet. When Maggie had to tell her twice that the bell had just rung and she needed to get to class, Darbie said that she hadn't heard it. But when Darbie didn't go to the restroom with the Corn Flakes between first and second periods—which she *always* did—Sophie got the feeling that she was keeping something from them.

"Does anybody know what's wrong with Darbie?" she said from her stall.

"Is something wrong with Darbie?" Kitty said from the next one.

Fiona was at the sink washing her hands. "How would you notice, Kitty? All you do is look at Nathan all the time."

Kitty's giggle bounced off the tile walls. "He's cute!"

"Yeah, we know," Fiona said. "You have it written all over your notebooks."

"Does she really, Maggie?" Sophie said.

"Maggie's not here," Fiona said. "She already left."

"Without US?" Kitty said.

*Come to think of it*, Sophie mused, *Maggie has been acting funny too. But not nervous-strange like Darbie. More like sad-strange.*

As they headed for the social studies room, Sophie wondered if Maggie was strange because Darbie and Sophie and Fiona were all going to Bible study and she wasn't. Sophie slipped into their table just as the bell rang and leaned over to Maggie in the chair next to her.

"Do you want to start going to Bible study with us on Tuesdays?" she said. "It's way cool. I bet your mom would let you."

Maggie looked up from the back of the notebook she was doodling on and gave Sophie a droopy-eyed smile. "I'll ask," she said.

Sophie was pretty sure Maggie wasn't cheered up.

At lunch Sophie wolfed down her peanut butter and pickle sandwich and watched Maggie push her red beans and rice around in their container and then pass it on to Harley.

"Those guys are watching us," Kitty said.

"What guys?" Fiona said.

Kitty pointed to a table on the other side of the Corn Pops, where Jimmy, Nathan, and Vincent immediately lowered their heads and examined their milk cartons.

"Check out the Corn Pops," Fiona said. "They thought Jimmy was looking at them."

Anne-Stuart and B.J. were giggling and going blotchy red. Even Julia rolled her eyes at the boys' table, although she quickly returned her attention to Colton, who was sitting next to her, tying her ponytail in a knot.

"If anybody else did that, she'd deck them," Fiona said. "Right, Darbie?"

"Huh?" Darbie said.

"I knew you weren't paying attention." Fiona drummed her fingers on the tabletop. "All right—what's up with you? Come on, you have to tell us. We're your best friends."

"Sophie, I believe we have a date."

Sophie jumped, nearly knocking Ms. Quelling's soda can out of her hand. Sophie had forgotten she had lunch detention for daydreaming in class that day.

"Yes, ma'am," Sophie said.

She got up and whispered to Fiona behind her backpack, "Find out what's wrong with Darbie."

Although Sophie had to sit in Ms. Quelling's classroom for only fifteen minutes, it felt like seven hours before the bell rang and she darted out into the hall to meet Fiona and Kitty.

"What did you find out?" Sophie said.

"Nothing!" Kitty, of course, whined.

"She said we'd be mad at her if she told us," Fiona said. "I said we'd be madder if she DIDN'T tell us, but she still wouldn't spill it." She nudged Sophie with her elbow. "I bet she would have if you'd been there."

"Go talk to her, Soph," Kitty said.

"Where is she?" Sophie said, heading farther up the hallway at a faster pace.

"Look in the arts room—she SO didn't want to be around us," Fiona said. "She's acting like Kitty before she told us about Nathan—"

"Not Darbie!" Sophie called over her shoulder. "She's the one that came up with the pact in the first place!"

"I know what's wrong with Darbie."

Sophie turned around. Corn Pop Willoughby stood there, talking out of a small hole she made in the side of her mouth.

"I heard y'all talking," Willoughby said. "I know why Darbie thinks you'll be mad at her."

Sophie's thoughts flipped back and forth. *Listen to her, because you need all the information you can get. Don't listen to her, because she's a Corn Pop. Listen to her. Don't listen to her.*

Willoughby grabbed Sophie's wrist and pulled her toward the wall. The rest of the sixth graders surged past them. "Ross told me that Ian said that Darbie told him not to tell anybody because all her friends would be mad at her."

Sophie shook her head while she tried to sort that out. "Tell what?" she said.

"That she's going to the dance with Ian."

"Nuh-uh!"

"Yuh-huh. I know because I'm going with Ross, and he knows because Ian is his twin brother. Well, you knew that."

Sophie stared at Willoughby, whose very round hazel eyes quickly surveyed the crowd behind them. She drew in closer.

"Don't tell Julia and them that I'm going with Ross, okay? They think he's a geek, and they'll be telling me that every minute." She tightened her mouth hole. "I don't think I care what they think anymore, but I can't tell them that. You know how mean they can be."

But the Corn Pops were the farthest thing from Sophie's mind.

Finding Darbie—that was the only thing she could think about.

# Seven

Sophie rounded a corner and saw Darbie coming out of the girls' restroom. When Darbie dived back in, Sophie dived in after her.

"When did he ask you?" Sophie said.

Darbie scowled at Sophie in the mirror. "Who's the blaggard who told you?"

"That's not what matters!"

"Yesterday," Darbie said. "And don't be asking me why I said yes because I don't know. He took me by surprise—I never thought any boy would ever be looking at me."

"I didn't think you WANTED them to look!"

"I didn't! Until yesterday when he asked me." Darbie's face softened as she turned to face Sophie. "It's different just talking about it, and actually having it happen. I don't know, Sophie. It just made me feel special."

"A BOY made you feel special?"

Darbie nibbled at her thumbnail. "It's different for me. Nothing special ever happened to me growing up in Ireland. It was all about keeping from getting hit in the head with a brick."

"Do you think it's your time to like boys?" Sophie said.

"Maybe it is." Darbie was almost whispering. "But I'm not thinking more about Ian than I am about God. I even thanked God last night for Ian's asking me. But I still want to be a Corn Flake." Her face scrunched up into a knot. "You let Kitty!"

Sophie didn't even hesitate. She put her arms around Darbie's neck. "We'll let you too," she said.

Darbie—who wasn't the hugging kind—clung to Sophie and whispered, "It's nice to have a boy liking you, Sophie. Just wait till it happens to you."

But Sophie was sure that was one thing she was never going to experience.

The next morning, Sophie and Fiona talked alone together as they walked to meet the other Corn Flakes on the playground.

"It isn't our time," Sophie said. "That's all there is to it."

"It's our time to be best friends forever," Fiona said. "I don't see how any boy could be as amazing to hang out with as you are."

"That's how I feel about you!" Sophie said just as they joined Darbie, Kitty, and Maggie at the fence. Sophie continued. "Could you even imagine one of the Fruit Loops doing a film with us?"

"Sure," Fiona said. "It would be a horror film."

Darbie and Kitty started giggling.

"They would make fantastic monsters," Sophie said. "We wouldn't even have to give them masks!"

"All they would have to do is be themselves." Fiona shuddered. "It would be so heinous nobody would watch it."

Darbie and Kitty collapsed against the fence.

But Maggie didn't seem to be enjoying the moment. She dug into her backpack and produced one of Senora LaQuita's breakfast burritos wrapped in paper.

"Anybody want this?" she said.

"I'll have a taste," Darbie said.

"How come you're not eating it, Maggie?" Fiona eyed her suspiciously. "You hardly eat anything anymore."

Maggie shrugged. "Not hungry."

Maggie looked as if she were about to pull imaginary covers over her head.

"Are you coming to Bible study with us tomorrow, Maggie?" Sophie said quickly.

"I wish I could go!" Kitty wailed. "My dad won't let me though. He says the next thing you know, somebody from the church will be at our door asking for money."

"*What?*" Fiona said to her.

But Sophie stayed focused on Maggie. "Will you come?" she said.

"Yeah," Maggie said. "My mother said I could."

"That is so cool!" Sophie knew her voice was squeaking, but somehow she had to make up for the way Maggie's was thudding. "And Saturday we have fittings at your house."

"Yay!" Kitty said. "Party dresses!"

"I thought you were wearing one of your sisters' hand-me-downs," Darbie said.

Kitty wrinkled her little china nose. "I am—but Maggie's mom said she would—what's that word, Mags?"

"Alter it."

"Yeah—she said she'd fix it any way I wanted! I'm gonna ask her to make it shorter."

"Then we have LOTS to look forward to," Sophie said. She nodded at Maggie until Maggie gave her a grudging nod back.

"What's going on over there?" Darbie said.

Sophie swiveled around in time to see B.J. picking herself up from the ground and wiping off the seat of her red Capris with slapping hands. Her cheeks matched the color of her pants as she bore down on Anne-Stuart like a cornered Siamese cat.

"Uh-oh," Fiona said. "Trouble in Corn Pop world."

Over by the swing set, B.J. had her fists balled up as she took a step toward Anne-Stuart—whose hands were poised like feline claws as she met B.J. head-on.

"There's going to be a catfight," Darbie said.

Julia stood watching Anne-Stuart and B.J. with a smirk on her face, raking her thick hair back as if she wanted a better view.

"Do you think they're fighting over Jimmy?" Kitty said.

"I know they are."

For the second time in just a few days, Willoughby was suddenly there behind them, talking out of the side of her mouth like a ventriloquist. Fiona arched an eyebrow at her, but Darbie inched closer.

"So—tell us," she said.

Sophie had to admit she was interested too. They all gathered in as Willoughby whispered, "Julia told me that B.J. told her that she asked Jimmy to be her date at the dance, only Jimmy said no."

"Okay, he's way smarter than I thought," Fiona said.

"Then Julia told me that she told B.J. it was probably because Anne-Stuart already asked him. So B.J. got all mad and went looking for Anne-Stuart, only Anne-Stuart was already mad at B.J. because Jimmy told HER no, and she thought it was because B.J. already asked him, when she KNEW Anne-Stuart liked him."

"But didn't Anne-Stuart do the same thing to B.J.?" Sophie said.

"That's just the way they are," Willoughby said. "They do stuff like that to each other all the time. I don't even know why they're friends."

Fiona blinked at her. "So why are you friends with them?"

Willoughby switched the mouth hole to the other side of her face. "I'm thinking about not being friends with them anymore, only I have to find just the right way so they won't turn on me and make my life a total nightmare."

Sophie was about to nod when several shadows fell across them.

"Hi," Jimmy Wythe said.

Sophie stared up into his very blue eyes.

"This is where you say hi back," Willoughby whispered to her.

"Hi," Sophie said.

"What are they doing NOW?" said somebody else. It was Vincent. The other three boys were loitering behind them. The round-faced twins flapped their hands in a wave for a fraction of a second at Darbie and Willoughby. Nathan grinned at Kitty, flashing his braces, and then looked at the ground while his ears went crimson. Sophie was sure Kitty was going to pass out.

"They're fighting over you," Fiona said to Jimmy. "Go figure."

"Fiona!" Kitty said. "Rude!" Sophie glared at Fiona.

"That's okay—I don't get it either," Jimmy said. "They're like bees swarming around me all the time."

"You hate it then," Fiona said.

"Ya think?" Vincent said. His voice went from way-low to way-high and back again. "We had to stuff Jim in his locker just now because we heard them coming down the hall."

"No, you didn't," Fiona said.

"Yeah, we did. Ask these guys."

They all nodded.

"You are awesome," Fiona said. She put up her palm and Vincent high-fived it. Sophie could only stare.

"So," Vincent said, crossing his arms and tucking his hands into his armpits. "What is it you guys do when you're out here? Are you acting stuff out?"

Kitty giggled herself over to Nathan. Sophie expected to see the tips of his ears start smoking any minute.

"You promise you won't tease us?" Kitty said. She pointed her pert little nose up at him.

"We won't," Vincent said. "Unless you're cooking up ways to bug guys."

"We hate that," Ross and Ian said together.

"Are you insane?" Fiona said. "No—we're rehearsing for our next film. We do our own video productions, write the scripts and everything."

"What kind of video camera you got?" Ian said.

Sophie looked at Maggie, who knew all the numbers and letters that formed the answer to that, but Maggie was halfway behind Kitty, her eyebrows hooded over her cheekbones.

The bell rang, backpacks were hitched back up onto shoulders, and everyone moved toward the building.

"Are you going to be in social studies today?" Jimmy said. He was at Sophie's elbow. His voice was husky compared to the other boys, especially compared to the Fruit Loops who still sounded like girls.

Sophie was sure this was where she was supposed to say yes, but it was hard to get it out. The word squeaked through mouse-like.

"Are you?" she added.

Jimmy smiled his big white-toothed smile that went farther up one side of his face than it did on the other. "We're doing our culture presentation," he said.

"What's it about?" Sophie said.

"You'll see. It's a surprise—nobody knows except Ms. Quelling."

"Okay," Sophie said.

He smiled again, and then shrugged and said, "Well, I gotta go." And he hurried off to the same place she was going.

"I know why he said no to B.J. and Anne-Stuart." It was Willoughby—again.

"Because he doesn't like them?" Sophie said.

"Partly. And partly because he likes somebody else." Willoughby smiled as if she were completely pleased with herself and skipped on.

Sophie was left to stare after her. *It's like everybody was in all their right cubbyholes when I got up this morning,* she thought. *And then some giant came along and dumped them all out, and now nobody's where they were before.*

Uneasiness seeped in.

*It's definitely something I'll have to keep my eye on, thought Agent Shadow. Something like this could throw me off my focus, which isn't boys. Well, it's partly boys—but just the Fruit Loops Mob, who we must take down once and for all at the ball. THAT is our mission.*

*The secret agent adjusted her special see-all glasses and swept her eyes across the hallway. That little wavy-haired girl would bear watching. There was still the possibility that she could be a spy for the Corn Pops Organization. Or connected with the Fruit Loops Mob.*

*And Agent Shadow must find out what had occurred that was driving Owl back into her shell. No matter how relationships seemed to be shuffling around, she had a job to do.*

It was hard to concentrate on anything else but that job. She was so into Agent Shadow during language arts that she left the class at the end of the period not quite sure what Mr. Denton had just taught. But she was no closer to figuring out what was wrong with Maggie, who didn't answer the note Sophie had slipped to her on her way to the pencil sharpener. Toward the end of the class Maggie had gotten a bathroom pass and was gone for a long time.

Yet even Maggie faded into the background of Sophie's thoughts when Jimmy and his group entered the social studies room after class had started, ready for their presentation.

They were all dressed in black pants and white shirts with billowy sleeves and boots that went up to their knees. When they first dashed up to the front of the room, the Fruit Loops started to snicker — until one by one each boy in Jimmy's group pulled from his leather belt a real-looking sword, painted gold and gleaming in the sunlight through the window.

"Dude!" Colton said. "Are those real?"

"No! Now just watch," Ms. Quelling said.

She didn't have to tell anyone twice. For the next ten minutes the five boys — Vincent, Nathan, Ian, Ross, and Jimmy — swash-buckled back and forth across the front of the classroom, jumping up on Ms. Quelling's desk to engage in swordplay, clacking their weapons together, doing somersaults to avoid being run through. It was like watching a dance.

At the end there was a burst of applause, and Jimmy and his group took a bow, swishing their swords over their heads. Even the Fruit Loops whistled through their fingers and clapped like apes.

All the Corn Pops sat on top of their table, swaying and tossing their heads and looking at one another with bulging eyes.

"They're swooning," Fiona said to the Flakes.

"Look at Anne-Stuart," Darbie said. "She's all but hysterical, that girl."

By then B.J. was up on her knees, waving her hand, very obviously at Jimmy. Anne-Stuart leaned in front of her, flailing a tissue.

"I hope that's not used," Fiona said.

Sophie put her hand up to her mouth to stifle a giggle.

"Sophie!" Kitty whispered beside her. "He's looking at you!"

"Who?"

Darbie put a hand on each side of Sophie's head from the back and pointed it toward the line of musketeers at the front. Jimmy Wythe rose from his final bow and smiled his crooked smile at Sophie.

"He's not the only one looking," Fiona said. She jerked her head toward the Corn Pops' table, and Sophie heard Kitty gasp.

Not only Anne-Stuart and B.J., but Julia too stared at Sophie as if their very eyes were swords. Sophie could almost feel them slicing right into her brain, where they clearly left their message: *you will live to regret this.*

# Eight

"You need to watch your back, Soph," Fiona said after class.

"Better yet, we'll be watching it FOR you." Darbie's dark eyes narrowed. "It's going to take all of us—Fiona, me, Kitty, and Maggie."

"Where is Maggie?" Kitty said. "She went to the bathroom AGAIN last period, and she didn't come back."

Maggie didn't come to arts class either. When she didn't show up in the cafeteria, the Corn Flakes downed the contents of their lunch boxes and went to the office.

"Maggie's mother came and got her," the lady at the counter told them. "She wasn't feeling well."

"Was she throwing up?" Kitty said. "I hope not—that's the worst."

"Poor Mags," Darbie said.

The pixie-faced lady smiled. "I'm not sure what was wrong, but it's sweet that you girls are so concerned about your friend."

"Of COURSE we're concerned," Sophie said. "She's one of us."

"We still need to practice if we're ever going to get this film done," Fiona said as they hurried out to the playground.

Sophie nodded in a vague way. *Why would Maggie leave school without telling us?* she thought. *That's not the Corn Flake way.*

When they got to their place by the fence, Fiona said, "Let's set up the scene. Kitty, you stand over there and pretend you're powdering your nose, only you're really looking behind you in the little mirror. Then—"

"There they go," Darbie said, pointing. "Acting the eejit again."

They all glanced nearby where Anne-Stuart and B.J. were walking backward. Fiona groaned. "Their picture is next to 'acting the eejit' in the dictionary," she said in a low voice.

Sophie had to agree that the Corn Pops—at least, Anne-Stuart and B.J.—were putting on their worst display yet. They were walking backward to face Jimmy and Vincent, who both were looking over their heads, down at their toes, everywhere but at the two girls.

"You were SO awesome with that sword," Sophie heard Anne-Stuart say.

"You made it look, like, so REAL," B.J. said, placing her shoulder in front of Anne-Stuart's. "My heart was beating, like, ninety miles an hour."

Anne-Stuart replaced B.J.'s shoulder with her own. "It was the best sword fighting I ever saw. You were, like, professional."

"Like she knows so much about swordplay," Darbie muttered.

"They're acting like Vincent wasn't even there!" Fiona whispered. "They're just totally blowing him off."

At that exact moment, B.J. wedged her way between the two boys, putting her back in Vincent's face and elbowing him out of the conversation.

"That's totally heinous!" Fiona hissed.

Kitty went wide-eyed as she looked at Fiona. "You LIKE Vincent, don't you!" she said into Fiona's ear.

"Shhh! They'll hear!" Sophie whispered.

Fiona was shaking her head hard. "I mean, I like him," she hissed at Kitty, "but not like a boyfriend or something. I just think they're being jerks to him."

Vincent didn't look that hurt to Sophie. He stopped long enough to keep B.J. from stepping on him in her attempt to snatch Jimmy away from the hold Anne-Stuart had on his other arm. Then he grabbed the back of Jimmy's T-shirt and dragged him around the two girls and away from both of them.

"Hello! Rude!" B.J. shouted after him.

"HE's rude?" Fiona whispered. "What about THEM?"

Again, it didn't seem to bother Vincent. In fact, he didn't look back as he steered Jimmy the ten steps to the Corn Flakes. Sophie looked behind her to see if Nathan or the twins were there waiting for him, but there was only the fence. When she turned back, Jimmy and Vincent had stopped just in front of her. The two Corn Pops, of course, were so close behind them they nearly ran up the two boys' calves.

B.J. whipped off the hooded shirt she had tied around her waist and wrapped it around Jimmy's chest from behind, using the sleeves to tug him backward.

"You're not getting away that easy!" she said. She had her chin tucked in and her eyes slanted down. To Sophie, she looked like a cat with a mouse in its claws.

Jimmy, who up to that point had been looking bewildered, lifted both his arms and wiggled from B.J.'s trap. When Anne-Stuart leaped in front of him, he said, "Vincent and I need to talk to Sophie and Fiona."

"So talk," Anne-Stuart said, with the usual sniff.

"In private," Jimmy said.

Behind him, B.J.'s shoulders sagged until they almost met over her chest. Anne-Stuart looked over her own shoulder at the Corn Flakes as if she were only now noticing they were there — and wishing they weren't.

*You will live to regret this* was once more carved into her face.

"Okay," B.J. said, lower lip hanging down over her chin. "We'll just wait for you."

"What part of 'no' don't you understand?" Vincent said.

"Are you the boss of Jimmy?" B.J. shot back.

Vincent gave her a slow, sloppy smile. "Well, you sure aren't."

Jimmy stepped around Anne-Stuart and looked down at Sophie. There was a pink spot at the top of each cheekbone, and his eyes were shy.

"Can Vincent and I talk to you and Fiona?" he said. He glanced up at Darbie and Kitty, who were openly staring without apology. "I don't mean to be rude — "

"No worries," Darbie said. She jerked her head from Kitty to the two Corn Pops with a splash of hair. "We'll be sure you have some space."

With that she stepped between Anne-Stuart and B.J., dragging a less enthusiastic Kitty by the sleeve, and said, "We would love to talk to YOU privately."

*Remember the Corn Flake rules*, Sophie wanted to call after them as Darbie and Kitty herded them away. There was no telling what might come out of Darbie's mouth if she got good and mad. It could get ugly.

Vincent folded his arms, hands in his pits again, and said, "We wanna ask you something."

"If it's what I think it is," Fiona said, "we don't think you should choose either B.J. OR Anne-Stuart, Jimmy."

"Excuse me?" Jimmy said.

"That's not the question," Vincent said. His voice crackled.

Jimmy gave a soft grunt. "Are you kidding me? They're stalking me." He held up five fingers. "That's how many times B.J. called me last night. My mom finally told her not to do it again—it was, like, nine thirty."

"How many times did Anne-Stuart call?" Fiona said.

"She didn't. She emailed me. Six times."

"Big throw-up," Fiona said. She turned to Vincent. "They're absolutely horrific to you."

He gave an I-don't-care shrug. "This morning Julia comes up to me like she wants to be best friends or something, and then she asks me which one Jimmy likes better—Anne-Stuart or B.J."

"No way," Fiona said. "What did you say?"

"I told her he liked them both the same, which was not at all."

"I bet she didn't like that answer."

"No. She tried to pull my nose off."

"Are you SERIOUS?" Sophie said.

"Check it out." Vincent displayed his profile. "It's, like, an inch longer now."

He grinned, and so did Jimmy.

"That's just WRONG," Fiona said. She looked at Sophie, and they both dissolved into giggles.

"I didn't tell her this," Vincent said, "'cause she might go after my ears next, but Jimmy would rather be tortured than go to the dance with either one of them, even though they asked him about four times apiece."

Jimmy raised five fingers again.

"Nuh-uh!" Fiona said.

He nodded and grinned, and then the pink spots turned to red. He drew a line in the dirt with his heel. Vincent jabbed him with an elbow.

"There's only one person I want to be at the dance with," Jimmy said to the ground. He looked up at Sophie, the red spots covering the sides of his face. "And that's you."

"And I want to go with you," Vincent said to Fiona. "Only I don't dance that good."

"If you're coordinated enough to do stage combat, you can dance," Fiona said. "I can show you some stuff my grandfather taught me—it's not that hard."

"So—is that a yes?" Vincent said.

"Ye—" Fiona stared to say. But she stopped and looked at Sophie.

Sophie herself was gaping at Fiona, chin to her chest. Her heart was racing, and she knew the red places in her own face were starting to match the ones on Jimmy's.

*She's acting like boys ask us out every day!* she thought. *Doesn't she know what just happened? They invited US—not one of the pretty girls—not the popular ones that know what to do around boys. They asked US!*

"I'll only go with you if Sophie goes with Jimmy," Fiona said to Vincent.

All three faces turned to Sophie, but she saw only Jimmy's. His head was tilted to the side, and his forehead was folded into worried wrinkles. She could see that there was a smile waiting on the other side of that anxious expression, if only she said the right thing.

*Darbie was right*, Sophie thought. *I do feel special.*

She tilted her chin up. "Can you waltz?" she said to Jimmy.

"Are you KIDDING?" Vincent said. "He can do ANY dance."

Jimmy nodded. The smile was still waiting.

Sophie sucked in a big breath. "Then I accept," she said.

Jimmy grinned so big she was sure the corners of his mouth were going to disappear into his ears.

"Sweet." Vincent shuffled his feet as if he had run out of things to say, for Jimmy or himself. "We gotta go. See you in class."

"You know it," Fiona said.

The bell rang, and the two boys took off toward the building, bumping shoulders and slugging each other with lazy fists. As Fiona and Sophie headed in the same direction, Fiona clutched Sophie's arm.

"Pretend you don't see them staring at you," she said between gritted teeth.

"Who?"

"Who else?"

Sophie didn't have to look hard to see Anne-Stuart, B.J., and Julia gathered next to the trashcan that held the door open. All six eyes were trained on Sophie like shotgun barrels. But instead of dread, Sophie felt something else pulling her shoulders up straight.

"They're so jealous," Fiona said before they got within hearing range. "And you didn't even have to ask Jimmy—he asked you."

Sophie couldn't smother a grin as she turned her head toward the Pops.

Fiona gave her a rib poke. "But don't look at them! It's totally un-Corn-Flake-like to gloat."

So together they pretended to have important business to attend to on the other side of the door and zoned in on getting through. The Corn Pops didn't make a move—until Fiona went inside just ahead of Sophie.

Before Sophie could get her foot over the threshold, she felt her backpack coming off and something heavy slamming behind her. She tried to turn to the right to see, but she found herself being spun to the left by hurried hands.

Once. Twice. With faces blurring past. When the Corn Pops let go, Sophie staggered and hit the metal trashcan. Its lid clattered off, revealing the smell of rotten banana peels and the sight of Sophie's backpack half buried in garbage.

When she reached out to grab it, she heard Ms. Quelling's voice barking from the doorway.

"Sophie, why are you digging through the trash, child?"

"I'm getting my backpack," Sophie said. She yanked it loose and held it out at arm's length. Stuck to the corner was a wad of green gum. Stuck to the gum was a piece of paper.

"How did your backpack get in there?" Ms. Quelling said.

"You don't want to know," Sophie said.

"Fine. Now go wipe it off in the restroom before you go to class. Mrs. Utley is not going to appreciate that lovely aroma in her classroom." She scribbled out a hall pass on a pink pad and handed it to Sophie. "You are such a bizarre child. I think you're going to graduate from here without my ever figuring you out."

Sophie shook that comment off as she hurried to the girls' restroom, holding her backpack away from her with one hand while she pinched her nostrils with the other. The paper was still dangling from the wad of gum.

In the bathroom, she pulled it off with a paper-towel-covered hand and was about to deposit it, gum and all, in the trash can when something on the paper caught her eye. The writing looked familiar. Only Anne-Stuart made all those curlicues.

Sophie let the gum plop into the garbage can and shook out the wrinkled paper. It was Anne-Stuart's penmanship, all right, *and* her bad spelling.

Dear Julia,

B.J. is making me mad the way she is chaseing Jimmie. She knows I like him and that's the onley reason she's doing it. He dosen't like her and she's always hanging around me, so now he thinks I'm just like her and I'm SOOOO not!!!!!! Tod asked me to the dance and I'm going with him. It mite be kinda fun because you'll be with Colton. Du-uh! Everybody knows you're going out. I thot Jimme and I were going to be until B.J. I thot she was my friend, but your a much better one. She's not the onley one who is out to get me. Those freeks — Soapy and Fiona and them — their trying to get Jimmie away from me just to be hatefull. Like they can. Once he sees that Soapy is WEIRD, then he'll WISH he was with me. If that happens, I'll just break up with Tod.

LOL!! What if B.J. is the only one of us who doesn't have a date at the dance!!!! I don't mean to be meen, but I think she deserves it.

TTFN,

Your best friend, Anne-Stuart

P.S. I know you won't tell BJ about any of this. We can't trust her. Just throw away this note after you read it.

P.P.S. After lunch I'm going to ask Jimmie one more time. Will you please keep B.J. out of my way?

Sophie dropped the note in the trash and went to the sink to scrub her hands.

*Fiona would say that was the most heinous thing she ever read,* Sophie thought. *Anne-Stuart's turning one of her friends against another one. And wishing her almost-best friend would be the only one without a boy to be with at the dance. How grotesque is that?*

She ripped some paper towels from the dispenser and went after a red juice stain on her backpack.

*I can't even imagine doing that to one of my friends. We made a pact, sure, but we ALL broke it—*

Except for Maggie.

Sophie froze and watched her face go pale in the mirror. Kitty and Nathan. Darbie and Ian. Fiona and Vincent. Herself and Jimmy.

Maggie and No One. Sophie left the water running as she turned away from the mirror. It was too hard to look at her own face. *We broke our promise to Maggie. We've left her out. We aren't any better than the Corn Pops.*

Sophie didn't know how long she had stood there leaning against the sink, chasing the same accusations around in her head, when the bathroom door swung open and Willoughby appeared.

"THERE you are!" she said. "Fiona is about to go nuts." She sniffed. "What stinks?"

"I do," Sophie said. "I'm disgusting."

Willoughby brought her nose closer to Sophie.

"No, it isn't you." She reached behind Sophie and held up Sophie's backpack. Water poured from one corner into a puddle on the floor. "It's this. It smells like garbage."

Sophie grabbed the backpack and whirled around to turn off the faucet. Water was creeping dangerously close to the top of the sink.

"I know who did this," Willoughby said.

"Me too," Sophie said.

"And I also know why."

"Me too."

Willoughby squinted her hazel eyes at Sophie. Two tiny lines formed between them.

"Aren't you mad?" she said.

"I'm mad at myself," Sophie said.

"Because of Maggie being the only one who hasn't been asked?"

Sophie felt her eyes bulge. "How did you know that?"

"I heard Fiona telling Darbie and Kitty just now."

"Now everybody's going to know what horrible friends we are!" Sophie could hear her own whine out-Kittying Kitty's.

"I'm not going to tell anybody," Willoughby said. "I swear."

Sophie dragged her backpack behind her, trailing water across the restroom. "I have to go talk to the Corn Fla—my friends."

She turned toward the door, but Willoughby caught her by the strap of her pack.

"There's one more thing you should know," she said. The two little lines were cutting into the bridge of her nose. "Maggie isn't just going to be the only one in your group who won't have a boy. She's the only one in the entire CLASS."

"What about Harley and—"

"Those girls aren't even going at all—they think it's lame—and B.J. just now asked Eddie, in case she can't get Jimmy to go with her."

"I'M going with him," Sophie said miserably. Just ten minutes ago that had made her feel special, like a princess. Now it was the very thing that made her want to escape into a bathroom stall for the rest of her life.

"B.J. doesn't know that yet," Willoughby said. She tucked her poodle hair behind her ears. "But when she does, she ISN'T going to be happy. Trust me."

Sophie wasn't sure she could trust Willoughby—but she definitely knew she was right. Too right.

# Nine

✿ ⌂ ❀

"What are we going to do?" Sophie said when she and the Corn Flakes caught up between science and math. She was afraid she was going to start crying. Kitty already had.

"I don't think we should do anything until we have a plan," Fiona said. "Nobody call Maggie and tell her. We'll think of something by tomorrow."

"We should all pray about it," Darbie said. She looked at Kitty. "You can pray even if you don't go to church."

Sophie didn't feel a twinge this time. She felt a STAB. She still hadn't talked to Jesus.

*I haven't told him one thing in days*, she thought. *I wonder if he'll even listen to me right now. I can't just go back and start asking him for stuff now.*

For once, somebody else was going to have to come up with something. All Sophie could think of between then and the next morning was more heinous things about herself.

She was the one who had said Maggie was "one of us." And then ten minutes later she had told Jimmy she would go to the dance with him—and left Maggie sticking out like a sore toe.

She was the one who was always telling the girls they couldn't be un-Corn-Flake-like to the Corn Pops. But the minute some boy had made her feel special, she had forgotten about one of her own friends.

*There's only one thing to do*, she thought on the bus the next morning, *and that's tell Jimmy I can't go to the dance with him. I'll just hang out with Maggie—and we'll have even more fun.*

But in the next second she knew that wouldn't work. Fiona had said she would go with Vincent only if Sophie went with Jimmy. Sophie couldn't imagine doing that to Fiona, who had already arranged to give Vincent dancing lessons.

"You going to that Bible thing again?"

Sophie jumped. Gill was hanging over the seat in front of her, ball cap on backward.

"It's today," Gill said.

"Yeah," Sophie said. There was another stab. She had offered to take Maggie with her. What if Maggie wouldn't go now because Sophie didn't even act like a Christian—betraying her friend?

"I'm going," Gill said. "Me and Harley. I like that Dr. Peter guy."

"Me too," Sophie mumbled. That was the final stab: Dr. Peter was going to think she was the most awful person on the planet.

Fiona met Sophie as she dragged herself off the bus.

"You can lose the long face, Soph," she said. "Maggie's mom called Kitty to tell her to get Maggie's homework because she isn't coming to school today. That means we have more time to think of a plan. I have an idea." She looped her arm through Sophie's.

Sophie's heart lifted. *You decided not to go with Vincent?*

"I say we ask Dr. Peter about everything today in Bible study."

Sophie sagged. "In front of Harley and Gill?"

86

"They won't tell Maggie. Besides, the one I'm worried about is Willoughby. Have you noticed she's everywhere we are lately?"

Sophie nodded. Maybe Willoughby could come in and take her place and Sophie could just disappear.

Sophie felt heavier as the day went on, although Darbie and Fiona were counting the hours until it was time for Bible class. Sophie just knew Dr. Peter was going to be so disappointed in her—though not more disappointed than she was in herself. That wasn't possible.

"You okay, Dream Girl?" Mama said to her when the three of them climbed into the car after school.

Sophie suddenly wanted to pour it all out to her. She might be disappointed in Sophie too, but she was Mama. She still had to love her.

Dr. Peter had juice and a giant cookie for each of them when they arrived in the beanbag room. Sophie turned hers down.

"You're getting as bad as Maggie," Darbie said.

"I bet that's why she's sick," Fiona said. "She doesn't eat enough."

"I never have that problem." Gill looked wistfully at Sophie's uneaten cookie. "Can I have yours?"

"I feel stress in the air," Dr. Peter said as he pulled his red beanbag closer to the circle. "Anything you want to talk about?"

"We thought you'd never ask," Fiona said. She looked quickly at the two Wheaties, but Gill said, "Go for it."

Fiona picked right up where she'd left off the week before and filled Dr. Peter in. Sophie couldn't look at him. She didn't want to see herself falling from her place in his eyes.

He was quiet for a minute after Fiona was finished.

"Uh-oh," Fiona said. "Even you don't have an answer?"

"I have several," Dr. Peter said. Sophie didn't have to look to see that there was no twinkle on his face. "But this is one of those situations where it's going to make a lot more sense if you figure it out for yourselves."

"If we could do that, we would!" Darbie said. "We've been pounding our brains!"

"I didn't say I wasn't going to help you. I'm going to give you an assignment that I think is going to make it all very clear."

Sophie was glad she could keep her eyes on her Bible. But when Dr. Peter told them to imagine themselves in the story of the rich young man in Mark 10, and Sophie saw that Jesus was in it, she wanted to pull the whole beanbag over her head.

*What if Jesus doesn't want me in his stories, the way I've been ignoring him lately?* she thought.

" 'As Jesus started on his way' " Dr. Peter read, " 'a man ran up to him and fell on his knees before him. "Good teacher," he asked, "what must I do to inherit eternal life?" ' "

"Does that mean go to heaven?" Fiona said.

"Basically, yes," Dr. Peter said.

"Gotcha. Go on."

Sophie imagined herself on her knees with Jesus looking right through her. If there was anybody who needed help getting to heaven, it was her right now.

" *'Why do you call me good?" Jesus answered. "No one is good — except God alone.' "*

That was kind of a relief, Sophie decided.

" *'You know the commandments: "Do not murder, do not commit adultery, do not steal, do not give false testimony, do not defraud, honor your father and mother.' "*

Sophie was pretty sure she hadn't broken any of those, even with Maggie. Still she bowed down even farther in front of Jesus. She couldn't feel this bad and not have disobeyed *some* rule.

Dr. Peter read on. "'Teacher,' he declared, "'all these I have kept since I was a boy.' Jesus looked at him and loved him. 'One thing you lack,' he said. 'Go, sell everything you have and give to the poor, and you will have treasure in heaven. Then come, follow me.'"

Fiona gave a long, low whistle.

"What?" Dr. Peter said.

"MY parents would go straight to you-know-where. They're all about their stuff."

"This guy was too — and, Fiona, we can talk about your parents later. For now, let's continue." Dr. Peter's eyes scanned the page. "'At this the man's face fell. He went away sad, because he had great wealth.'"

Sophie had a hard time imagining herself slinking off sad. If there was one thing she *wasn't*, it was wealthy. She decided to stick around in her mind for the next part. Maybe she was supposed to be somebody else in the story.

"'Jesus looked around and said to his disciples, "How hard it is for the rich to enter the kingdom of God!" The disciples were amazed at his words. But Jesus said again, "Children, how hard it is to enter the kingdom of God! It is easier for a camel to go through the eye of a needle than for a rich man to enter the kingdom of God."'"

Sophie heard herself gasping as she and the disciples looked at one another in dismay. *A camel can't pass through the eye of a needle!* she thought. She knew her face was puzzled as she looked at Jesus.

"'He said, "With man it is impossible to be saved, but not with God; all things are possible with God."'"

Sophie waited at Jesus' knee for him to say something more, to explain how this would help her make things right with Maggie.

But Jesus drifted away, and Dr. Peter closed the Bible.

"No offense," Fiona said, "but that doesn't help."

"It will," Dr. Peter said, "if you do this assignment I'm going to give you." He passed out hot-pink sheets with some words and blanks on them. "I want you to take this home and see what happens. I think you'll be surprised by what you figure out."

"Can we work on it together?" Darbie said.

Dr. Peter wrinkled his glasses up on his nose, and for an awful moment Sophie wondered if he was so disappointed in all the Corn Flakes that he was going to tell them no—they had done enough together. But finally he nodded his head of spiky hair and said, "As long as all of you work to find the right answers."

There was no time to get together that night, so they promised to meet in the morning before school, and they called Kitty to join them. But when they arrived at their secret place backstage in the cafeteria, Maggie was already there.

"Mags!" Kitty said, throwing her arms around Maggie's neck. "Are you better?"

Maggie nodded, but to Sophie she looked worse than she had the last time she'd seen her. She had deep, dark circles under her eyes, and her mouth was in a grim little line. Fiona gave Sophie a look that read, *Do you think she already knows?*

But Maggie didn't say anything about the boys or the dance. In fact, she didn't say much at all. She just sat under an arch of tissue-paper flowers that the fifth grade had used for their spring festival and listened while the rest of the Corn Flakes talked about everything but what they had come to discuss.

The only time Maggie reacted to anything was when the voices of Eddie, Tod, and Colton echoed against the cafeteria walls as they charged through. Maggie scooted herself behind Kitty and buried her face in her knees.

"Today is not the day to bring up anything," Fiona said to Sophie and Darbie after Kitty had followed Maggie to the bathroom.

"She's still sick," Sophie said.

Darbie frowned. "All right—but we better be hoping nobody else tells her."

First period went smoothly, and they knew in second period the Corn Pops were giving their culture presentation, so there wouldn't be a chance for any of them to talk to Maggie. In fact, the Pops were so busy rearranging the room, they didn't even give the Flakes any deadly looks.

*I guess they don't know about Jimmy yet either,* Sophie thought. But that didn't make her feel any better. Just then she would have given up everything she owned if that made any sense for Maggie. *I hate hating myself!* she thought.

"We're going to demonstrate a folk dance the peasants in France used to do," Julia said to the class when all the chairs and tables had been pushed against the walls. "And everyone has to do the dance with us."

"Aw, man!" Gill said, above the groans of everybody else.

"Uh-oh," Fiona said.

Sophie nodded. She had forgotten Anne-Stuart's words until now: *We're going to make the whole class participate.*

"Line up with your partner as I call your names," Julia said. B.J. and Anne-Stuart stood in the middle of the room as if they were ready to enforce Julia's every word. Willoughby stayed at the edge, looking like she wished she'd never heard of any of them.

"Julia and Colton," Julia said.

Colton grinned and went to the spot B.J. pointed out to him.

"B.J. and Eddie. Willoughby and Ross."

So far there were no surprises, but Sophie held her breath. The rest could be worse than heinous.

"Kitty and Ian."

"What?" Kitty whined.

"Darbie and Vincent. Fiona and Nathan."

"She doesn't know as much as she thinks she does," Fiona muttered to Sophie as she went to join Nathan, with Kitty whimpering in their direction.

The Wheaties looked relieved as Julia paired Harley and another Wheatie, then Maggie and Gill. Maggie didn't look any way at all. She shuffled next to Gill, her eyes on the floor.

"Sophie and Tod. Anne-Stuart and Jimmy."

Sophie felt the two red spots burning into her cheeks, but she moved slowly toward Tod. She couldn't make any more trouble with Ms. Quelling. *As long as I don't have to touch him, I can do it*, she told herself.

"Take your partner's hand," Julia said. "And we'll call out the instructions while we do it."

Tod looked as if he would rather hold a deep-sea creature than Sophie's hand. She knew exactly how he felt, but under Ms. Quelling's stern glare, she let him grab the tips of her fingers as if they were jellyfish tentacles. A shiver went through her from head to toe.

Julia called out instructions, but it didn't do much good. B.J. hauled Eddie around anywhere she could get a vantage point to give hate looks to Anne-Stuart because she was dancing with Jimmy. Kitty whined like a terrier every time she passed Fiona, who was only trying to keep Nathan from stepping on her toes. Tod abandoned Sophie altogether and grabbed Anne-Stuart from Jimmy, which sent her into a sniffling tizzy that brought the whole thing to a halt.

Ms. Quelling switched off the CD player and folded her arms. "Fix it, Julia," she said. "Or I'm taking off points."

"All right," Julia said with a sigh. It was obvious she had been enjoying the entire mess. "Everybody get with the partner you're going to have at the graduation dance and we'll start over."

Sophie felt herself going cold. Everyone shifted around, including Jimmy, who slid into place beside Sophie. Nearby, Vincent found his way to Fiona. The Wheaties pulled together in a sulky trio.

Maggie was left standing alone. In a frozen second, her eyes swept the room and came back to Sophie.

"Maggie?" Sophie said.

But Maggie's face crumpled, and she ran for the doorway, knocking Eddie against a table as she went.

"Hey, watch it, wide load!" Eddie called after her.

"Close your cake trap, blackguard!" Darbie shouted at him.

Sophie and Fiona tore for the door, but Ms. Quelling beat them there.

"You stay right here," she said, her face twisted down at them. "I'll call the counselor."

Kitty burst into tears, and Fiona was barely able to hold Darbie back from poking Eddie's eyes out. Sophie could only stare out into the hallway where a shattered Maggie had disappeared.

*I don't think SHE's the one who needs the counseling*, Sophie thought. She wished with all her might for Dr. Peter—and some answers she could understand.

# Ten

Fiona, Darbie, and Sophie were a long-faced, droopy group when they met in Sophie's family room that day after school to work on their Bible study assignment.

"I bet Willoughby was the one who told Julia about our dates for the dance," Fiona said. "I KNEW we couldn't trust her."

But Sophie shook her head. "It doesn't matter who told. We did a terrible thing to Maggie, and we have to take the blame for it."

"I hate it when you're right," Fiona said. She picked up her hot-pink sheet and put it down again. "No wonder Maggie can't eat if she feels like this."

Darbie opened her Bible and unfolded her sheet. "Come on then, enough. Dr. Peter says there's an answer in this Bible story, and we have to find out what it is before we all go mental."

"I just don't think it's in there," Fiona said.

But Sophie had been thinking about the Bible story ever since the dance disaster of second period. Every time Dr. Peter had given her a Jesus story to help her figure out a problem, it had always worked. Sometimes it just took a while to figure out.

"What does the sheet say to do?" she said.

Fiona picked it up again and scowled at it. "It says to answer the question next to each verse below and do, for real, what our answer says."

Darbie craned her neck over Fiona's shoulder. "Mark ten, verse seventeen. 'How did the rich young man get to Jesus?'"

"He ran to him," Fiona said, tapping the page with her eraser. "So—we run to Jesus. But he's not here."

"You imagine he is, in your mind," Sophie said. "That's what I do. Or at least, I used to, before I became a heinous person."

"Can you ever lay off that?" Darbie said. "Jesus already said God's the only one who's good—it says so right here—and he shows us how to be good. That's what we're getting back to. Now get off yourself and let's move on."

Sophie blinked. "So I can still run to him, you think?"

"If YOU can't, nobody can," Fiona said. "You're, like, perfect." She examined the sheet again. "Okay, what does he do when he gets to Jesus?"

"Falls on his knees," Sophie said.

"Then we need to be doing that right now," Darbie said. "We always act everything else out, don't we?"

Fiona was the first one in a kneeling position, sheet and Bible on the floor in front of her, pencil poised. Sophie closed her eyes.

"'What are three things he tells the man that are important?'" Fiona read.

Darbie paused for only a couple of seconds. "Only God is truly good. Know the commandments. Keep the commandments."

"Check," Fiona said. "So far, we already do all this stuff."

"Go on," Sophie said. She kept her eyes closed. Jesus was becoming clearer and her hands, for some reason, were getting sweaty, the way they did when Daddy was about to ground her for an impossibly long time.

"'What did Jesus tell him was the one reason he couldn't get eternal life?'" Fiona read.

"He cared too much about money," Darbie said.

"Wait—there's more." Fiona frowned at the directions. "'HINT: what is separating you from loving God more than anything else? It doesn't have to be money.'"

"Oh!" Darbie said. She had that light-bulb-over-the-head look. "The first day Dr. Peter said we would know it was our time for boys if they didn't get between us and God."

"Anne-Stuart and B.J. are the ones who practically knock each other out trying to get to Jimmy," Fiona said. "They DEFINITELY aren't thinking about God!"

"Today when Julia mixed all the couples up, just to be a control freak," Darbie said. "That wasn't about Jesus."

Sophie didn't say anything. She just looked down at her sweat-sparkly palms.

"What, Soph?" Fiona said. "You don't look so good."

"I think it's talking about ME!" Sophie sank back onto her feet and scrubbed her hands on her thighs. "I used to talk to Jesus all the time, but ever since this whole dance thing started I hardly go him at ALL. He must think I forgot all about him, because I'm always thinking about Kitty all giggling over Nathan, and Darbie feeling special for the first time because Ian asked her, and what to tell Maggie because Vincent and Jimmy asked you and me—"

"Mercy," said a voice in the doorway. "It sounds like a soap opera in here!"

Darbie's aunt Emily bustled into the room with Mama behind her. They perched on the edge of the couch.

"What's wrong?" Fiona said. "You look like we're busted."

"No, you aren't busted," Mama said. "We're just—concerned."

Aunt Emily pulled at a gold hoop earring. "Is your entire class pairing up for this dance?"

"Everybody but the Wheaties," Fiona said. "They aren't even going."

"And Maggie," Darbie said.

Sophie looked down at her hands, but she could feel Mama's eyes on her.

"I see," Mama said, dragging out the "I."

"That's exactly why kids your age are too young for the dating thing," Aunt Emily said. "Somebody gets left out—people get their feelings hurt."

"It isn't exactly a date," Fiona said.

"It might as well be," Mama said. She crossed her arms and drummed her fingers on the opposite arms. "I thought this dance was a bad idea for sixth graders to begin with, but I thought, well, you're so excited about the dresses, and you'll all go together and it will just be a girl thing."

"But it's not turning out that way." Aunt Emily looked at Mama, and they exchanged motherly looks. "I need to talk to Patrick."

"I know what my husband's going to say." Mama turned to the girls. "For right now, let's put your plans on hold."

Fiona had crawled up onto a chair and now stood on her knees. "What does that mean?"

"It means we're going to do what's healthy for you girls," Mama said. She put up her hand. "I know you, Fiona, and I don't want to hear your twenty arguments right now. You can save those for your Boppa."

"Boppa's too busy giving dumb flowers to Miss Odetta Clide," Fiona said when Mama and Aunt Emily had gone back to the kitchen. "He won't care that the Corn Pops AND the

Fruit Loops are going to hate us worse than ever if the dance gets called off."

"The Corn Pops?" Darbie said. "What about our Kitty?"

"There's only one person who might be happy about this," Fiona said, "and that's Maggie." She tried a smile that didn't work. "Maybe this solves our problem, huh?"

Sophie didn't even *try* to smile. "Maggie already knows we forgot all about her when we said we'd go to the dance with boys," she said. "I bet that hurts her more than the Fruit Loops calling her fat."

Their silence said they knew she was right again.

Between that and the fact that Darbie was right too — Kitty was going to dissolve into a puddle for sure if she didn't get to meet Nathan at the dance and act like he was her boyfriend — the girls were very down when they left Sophie's house.

Sophie didn't have any highs to tell at the supper table that night. When she tried to give a low, she had so much trouble picking just one that she burst into tears and excused herself from the table.

"Was it something I said?" she heard Daddy ask as she ran to her room.

*No,* she wanted to cry out, *it was something I said! I said yes, and it messed everything up!*

She had almost stopped "keening" over that, as Darbie would say, when Mama tapped lightly on her door. Sophie *really* didn't want to talk to her, but Mama only said, "Come downstairs. We have a visitor."

Sophie followed Mama down the steps with her heart dragging to her knees.

Senora LaQuita was in the family room, letting a mug of tea get cold on the coffee table in front of her. Mama ushered

Sophie to the chair across from her, and Daddy came in behind her, blocking all hope of escape.

"Senora LaQuita has been telling us why Maggie has been absent from school," Mama said.

For a tiny second, Sophie felt relieved. At least this wasn't about the dance.

"She never eat," Senora LaQuita said. "She say the boys, they call her fat."

Sophie's heart dropped.

"I didn't think it was like Maggie to pay attention to them," Mama said.

Daddy nodded. "She's usually such a little toughie."

Senora LaQuita shook her head, her turquoise earrings jittering against her face. "Never before. But now—the dance—boy asking girl. Now Maggie—she is very upset."

Sophie felt the tears fighting to get out again. "I'm SOOOO sorry!" she said. "I didn't want her to get all hurt like this! We promised her we would all go together, and then boys started asking—and I never thought one would ask me—and when he did I forgot about Maggie because I felt special, and so did Darbie and Fiona, and now I feel like the most heinous person in the world!"

Daddy shook his head a few fast times and crossed his eyes before he said, "Soph, that's not the point. This just confirms what your mother was saying to you earlier—this idea of a dance where boys can ask girls is too much for sixth graders. It isn't your fault that Maggie didn't get asked—but none of this would have happened if the school hadn't put you all in this position in the first place."

Senora LaQuita nodded sadly.

"We're going to talk to the other parents about this thing," Daddy said.

Mama put an arm around Maggie's mom's shoulder. "Meanwhile, we're going to postpone the fittings and give Señora LaQuita time to spend with Maggie."

"She's going to be okay, isn't she?" Sophie said.

"Doctor say she must eat," Maggie's mother said. "Margarita, she is—" She looked at the ceiling as if she were searching for the right word.

"Stubborn?" Daddy said.

Sophie leaned forward, clutching the edge of the coffee table. "We'll make her eat at school," she said, voice squeaking. "And we'll keep telling her she isn't fat."

"Sophie," Mama said. Her eyes were soft. "You aren't to blame that this is happening to Maggie. Just let her know you love her, that's all."

*I can do that*, Sophie thought as she trudged back up the stairs, *but I don't think she'll believe me.*

Maggie was absent again the next day, and Ms. Quelling told the Corn Flakes she'd been told that Maggie was going to be out the rest of the week.

"Has she helped you with your presentation?" she said. "She's not going to be here tomorrow when you do it."

"She got all the recipes for us and she and her mom gave us the ingredients they have at home and she would be here if she could." Sophie took a breath and added, "Ma'am."

"I'm convinced already," Ms. Quelling said. "Sophie, you really ought to consider switching to decaf."

Sophie could almost hear Maggie saying in her matter-of-fact voice, *Sophie doesn't even drink coffee.* Tears sprang to her eyes—yet again.

"Miss Odetta said we could cook at my house tonight," Fiona said when Ms. Quelling had left them alone. "We'll make killer enchiladas and get an A-plus for Maggie."

Then they slumped over their textbooks, and Sophie could see them all trying hard not to cry.

Mama and Daddy dropped Sophie off at Fiona's that night and picked up Boppa and Fiona's mom and dad. That's when she found out the sixth-grade parents were having a meeting at Anna's Pizza.

"They're talking to ALL the parents?" Sophie wailed when they'd left. "I thought just OURS were gonna decide if we could go!"

"We're doomed," Fiona said. She started slapping corn tortillas into a long glass dish.

Darbie went behind her, splattering spoonfuls of sauce into them. "If the Pops' parents are there, don't be surprised if we all have live snakes in our lockers tomorrow."

"I don't care about snakes or lockers," Kitty said. "I just want to go to the dance with Nathan!" She slammed a knife across a tomato, squirting seeds all the way to the refrigerator door.

Miss Odetta Clide was suddenly there, and she calmly took the blade from Kitty's hand. "This food will not be fit to eat if you don't stop attacking it," she said. "A lady does not mutilate her ingredients." She eyed the cheese Sophie was shredding into powder. "In fact, the preparation of a meal can be rather soothing to the soul. Now, shall we start again? Our cooking must be like a dance."

*I'm starting to REALLY not like that word*, Sophie thought.

She tried not to get into Miss Odetta Clide's rhythm as the old nanny floated the tortillas into the dish and poured the sauce, velvet-like, on them. The girls at first only followed her to mock her swirling hand movements and foot glides. But when she put on a collection of waltz music and refused to let them get by with any more slapping and splattering and slamming, lest there be demerits, they eased into the "dance" in spite of themselves.

In the end, they had twenty enchiladas that would have made Senora LaQuita herself proud.

"I bet Maggie would eat one of THESE," Fiona said.

"I wish she was going to be there," Kitty said.

Miss Odetta Clide made that clicking sound with her tongue. "A lady does not wish for things—at least not a lady of faith. She prays for them."

"Dr. Peter SAID we were supposed to get closer to God," Darbie said.

But Sophie was staring at Miss Odetta Clide. Fiona skipped staring and went straight to, "You pray?"

Miss Odetta's eyes seemed to slide right down her nose at Fiona. "Is that such a surprise?"

Nobody said anything.

"I pray every night that your brother and sister will not destroy each other before morning."

*She's better than most of their nannies then*, Sophie thought. *I bet the last four prayed that they WOULD.*

"I guess it's working," Fiona said. "Rory and Izzy are both still alive. Unfortunately."

"I also pray that you, Fiona, will develop a sweeter nature when it comes to your siblings."

"I'm going to start praying for that for my sister," Sophie said.

Miss Odetta Clide nodded. "There is nothing so small that we can't go to the Lord with it. And this situation with Margarita is actually quite large. An eating disorder can be difficult to control once it gets started."

"We'd better get praying then," Darbie said.

She put out her hands and the others latched onto her and one another—except Sophie. Her arms felt too heavy to lift.

"What's up, Soph?" Fiona said.

"I don't know," Sophie said. But she did. She felt so far away from Jesus, she couldn't even get him into her mind.

"If you don't pray, we're really doomed," Fiona said. "God ALWAYS listens to you."

Sophie felt herself caving in like a wet sandcastle. She wasn't sure what she would have said if they hadn't heard the front door open. The Corn Flakes all tore out of the kitchen, and even Miss Odetta Clide moved more briskly than usual.

Mama and Daddy, Boppa, and Fiona's tall, polished parents were all in the entrance hall, smelling like pepperoni and looking as if they'd just been pinched.

"So—what happened?" Fiona said, instead of "Hello."

Everybody looked at Daddy. "Some of us are going to the principal," he said. He pulled his mouth into a tight line. "And some of us aren't. It's still up in the air whether the dance will happen."

"Whether it will HAPPEN?" Kitty was giving new meaning to the word *whine*. "I thought you were just gonna talk about whether we could go with boys!"

"You mean it could get CANCELLED?" Darbie said.

"We're doomed," Fiona said for the third time that night. She looked at Sophie. "We should have prayed sooner."

Nobody had to tell Sophie that. *And now I bet it's too late*, she thought. With every passing second, she felt Jesus slipping farther away.

The next morning, the Corn Flakes, minus Maggie, met under the tissue-flower arch backstage.

"Who spied on parents when you got home last night?" Fiona said.

She, Darbie, and Kitty all raised their hands. Sophie shook her head. She hadn't WANTED to hear any more.

"Some of the parents still think the dance is okay," Kitty said. "Not MINE, though. I hate this!"

"I heard Aunt Emily say that Julia's mom threatened to call the superintendent if the dance was called off," Darbie said.

Fiona grunted. "Figures."

"I hope she does!" Kitty said. "I want to GO!"

Sophie forced herself not to put her hands over her ears. "We're not supposed to talk at school about this whole thing. That's what Mama and Daddy told me ALL the parents agreed on last night."

"Mine too," Darbie said.

Fiona looked as if she tasted something sour. "Most of the time mine barely know I GO to school, and now all of a sudden they're marching to the principal's office."

"But what if B.J. and the Pops know something we don't?" Kitty said.

"We're secret agents, aren't we?" Fiona said. "Nobody said we couldn't listen."

It became obvious the minute first period started that the Corn Pops' and Fruit Loops' parents hadn't told their kids to keep THEIR mouths shut about the dance.

Sophie got a note signed by all the Corn Pops before Mr. Denton had even taken the roll, saying, *Thanks for ruining everything, Soapy.*

The Fruit Loops knocked the Corn Flakes' books off their desks every time they went to the pencil sharpener or the bookshelf, which was every other minute.

After class, Eddie and Colton blocked the doorway to Ms. Quelling's room until the bell rang and made the Corn Flakes late for their own presentation. When they passed out the enchiladas, Julia, B.J., and Anne-Stuart went one by one to the trash can when Ms. Quelling wasn't looking and threw them away, paper plates and all. They made sure the Corn Flakes, however, couldn't miss it.

But it was Kitty who got to Sophie the most. At lunchtime, she didn't show up until long after the other Corn Flakes had already started eating their sandwiches, and when she did, she was quiet and stiff. After taking two bites of tuna salad, she said she didn't feel like rehearsing for their film and left the table to go to the library instead.

"What's up with HER now?" Fiona said.

"Maybe she's just worried about Maggie," Sophie said. "I don't feel that much like practicing either."

"Let's just sit here," Darbie said. "I don't have the heart for it without our Maggie."

"I know what's going on with Kitty." Of course it was Willoughby, sliding into the spot Kitty had just vacated. Her hazel eyes were shiny.

"Don't you think you've spread enough bad information?" Fiona said.

"Excuse me?"

"Nobody can tell whose side you're on anymore." Fiona's nostrils flared. "No thanks—we'll figure Kitty out for ourselves."

"That's fine with me," Willoughby said.

But Sophie could tell by the sting in Willoughby's eyes that it really wasn't fine.

"You were kind of rude to her, weren't you?" Sophie said to Fiona when Willoughby was gone.

"We just can't trust ANYBODY right now," Fiona said. "Just us—that's all. You know what?" She shot up from the table. "I can't sit here. Let's go outside."

They were gathered in a glum knot by their fence with nothing to say when they heard a husky voice clearing its throat. Sophie squinted through her glasses to see Jimmy, with Vincent, Nathan, Ian, and Ross.

"Everybody's dissing you," Jimmy said. His hands were shoved in his pockets, and his eyes dipped at the corners.

"So what else is new?" Fiona said.

Sophie looked at her quickly. Her face was as sharp as her voice.

"Yeah, but I heard they're planning something really bad now," Vincent said.

"We're here to offer our protection," Jimmy said. The guys behind him all nodded.

"Yeah, well, thanks," Fiona said. "But we — "

"Would really appreciate that!" Sophie said.

Fiona gave her a what-are-you-thinking glare.

"There are only three of us right now," Sophie said. "We need all the help we can get."

Fiona sighed. "So what are you going to do, come out here every lunch period and watch us rehearse for our film? That could get pretty boring."

Jimmy shrugged. "You got any roles for guys?"

"We usually play those," Fiona said.

"You COULD be, like, the federal agents we turn the mob over to when we get them. Or you could be counterspies when we write the script," Sophie said. "We're the secret agents."

"Sweet," Vincent said. "I have some walkie-talkies. I'll bring them."

"Before school," Sophie said. "We're gonna get here early to practice."

"We'll be here at zero-dark-thirty," Jimmy said.

Fiona gritted her teeth and said nothing. When the bell rang, she waited for the boys and Darbie to get ahead of them, and then strapped her fingers around Sophie's arm.

"What are you doing?" she said.

"We might need the protection," Sophie said. "You heard Vincent—if the dance gets called off, something really bad could happen to us."

Fiona sniffed through her flared-out nostrils. "We've always been able to handle the Corn Pops before—AND the Fruit Loops—all by ourselves."

"They never had this big of a reason to hate us before," Sophie said.

# Eleven

In science class, Sophie watched, a lump swelling in her throat, as Kitty hunkered without a word over the chapter on bacteria. It was as if she was looking for the cure for some rare disease, and it didn't fit Canary's profile. Agent Shadow would have pointed that out if Sophie hadn't been too stuck to go into spy world.

"Kitty," Mrs. Utley said, a tease playing around her lips, "you feeling all right?"

Darbie and Fiona both gave hopeful laughs. Sophie just held her breath.

"I'm fine," Kitty said in a quivery voice. "Can I go to the restroom, please?"

Sophie could see her squeezing back tears until Mrs. Utley wrote out a pass and Kitty bolted out with it balled up in her fist.

"I'd hate to see her when she isn't fine," Fiona said.

Darbie flicked her eyes toward the Corn Pop table. "I bet it's one of them."

"Why wouldn't she tell us then?" Fiona said.

"Because we can't be trusted."

Fiona and Darbie stared at Sophie. "What are you saying?" Darbie said.

Sophie looked at Maggie's empty chair, the lump now potato-sized in her throat.

Fiona gave a long, ragged sigh. "I wish you'd get off that, Soph. We didn't mean to leave Maggie out. I want to tell her I'm sorry—but you're flagellating yourself."

Sophie felt her face going hot. "For once, would you talk like a sixth grader?"

Fiona's neck rose up out of her hunched shoulders. "Excuse me?" she said.

"She doesn't know what 'flagellating' means." Darbie's eyes shifted from one of them to the other. "It's like you're beating yourself with a stick, Sophie."

"She didn't have to be so rude about it," Fiona said.

"I'm not being rude!" Sophie knew her voice was squeaking. "Everything's confusing enough as it is, and you're just making it harder."

"Actually, now that I think about it—you're the one who's made it all harder."

"ME?"

"Well, no, not you—your parents. The dance would still definitely be happening it if weren't for them. Maybe Kitty IS mad at you—about THAT."

Sophie's mouth dropped open. "Boppa and your parents feel the same way!"

"So do mine," Darbie said. "Only—"

"Only what?" Sophie watched Darbie sweep the tabletop with her hand.

"Only, your mum and dad DID start it. I don't like Maggie being hurt either, but does that mean I have to give up something that's special to me? I wasn't the one who did it to her."

109

"Me either," Fiona said. "This is the first time I ever got excited about a DRESS. And I already started giving Vincent bop lessons!"

Sophie stared at them, mouth still open. What had just happened?

"Ladies." Mrs. Utley's chins were wobbling above them. "I thought you weren't in the crazy half."

"I think the whole class has gone mental," Darbie said to her.

"If you're going to go down with them," Mrs. Utley said, "just discuss it AFTER you've finished your assignment, all right?"

*Who am I going to discuss it with?* Sophie thought. *Who's left that understands?*

Darbie and Fiona went back to their work, stiff as sticks. Kitty returned from the restroom, with her eyes puffy and her face blotchy, just before the bell rang, and when it did, she didn't give the Flakes a chance to corner her. She fled as if she had a pack of wild dogs after her.

*I might know how she feels*, Sophie thought. She mumbled something to Darbie and Fiona about having to catch the bus and hurried for the front door, but when she got outside, Mama was there, standing in a patch of sunlight talking to the principal.

Sophie froze. Even when somebody poked her in the spine, she barely flinched.

"Why does your mother have to stick her nose into our business?" said a hot-breathed voice into her ear.

*I don't know*, Sophie wanted to say to B.J. *I don't know anything.*

B.J. suddenly jerked her hand up and called out, "Hi, Mrs. Olinghouse!"

The principal gave an automatic smile, said something in a low tone to Mama, and strode off toward the buses. Mama held out her hand to Sophie.

*I hope she doesn't start in*, Sophie thought. *I already yelled at Fiona, which is bad enough.* She wasn't sure she could hold back with her mother—and Mama had grounding power.

*Maybe I should just be grounded for life*, she thought to herself. *Then I wouldn't be messing things up all the time.* She could barely drag one foot after the other as she went to her.

"Did you forget that this was your day with Dr. Peter?" Mama said.

Sophie had, and now that Mama was leading her toward the old Suburban, she wasn't sure how to feel. Dr. Peter was the perfect person to talk this out with, but if he was disappointed in her, she wasn't sure she could stand it.

She was still trying to decide when she followed him into his room. But after one look at his eyes searching hers from behind his glasses when they sat down on the window seat, she blurted out everything as if she were avoiding torture. The whole time, she was searching *his* eyes for glints of disappointment.

There weren't any. Instead, he ran his hand across the top of his spiky curls. "This is a tough one, Loodle," he said. "What is Jesus saying about it?"

Sophie wanted to plaster one of the pillows on her face. "Nothing."

"Because—"

"Because I haven't been talking to him."

"Because—"

There were suddenly tears to be blinked away. "Because I don't think I can go to him now!" she said. "I've been away from him so long, he won't want to hear me anymore!"

Dr. Peter handed her a tissue and waited while she blew her nose. She was feeling as drippy as Anne-Stuart. Dr. Peter leaned toward her with firm eyes.

"Listen to me carefully," he said. "God is ALWAYS there for you, no matter how long it's been since you even thought about him. Jesus is the way to him, and that way is always available. Are we clear?"

"No," Sophie said.

"Why not?"

"Because I can't make myself go back to him. I'm too ashamed."

She needed another tissue then.

"Did you and the Corn Flakes do your assignment?" Dr. Peter said.

Sophie nodded.

"And did you figure out what stands between you and God? Because that's what this whole thing is about, you know. Something is getting in the way."

"It isn't money, like that guy in the story," Sophie said. "And it isn't Agent Shadow — even being her doesn't make me feel any better."

"New film character?" Dr. Peter said.

"Yes."

"Secret Agent?"

"Uh-huh."

"Let's investigate a little further then." Dr. Peter scrunched his neck down and looked over his shoulders as if at that very moment someone might be spying on them. After humming a few bars of the *Mission Impossible* theme, he said, "My sources tell me that a number of things can get between a girl and God —"

He started ticking off his fingers. "Popularity?"

"No."

"Grades?"

"Nope."

"Parents?"

"Not anymore."

"Fashion?"

Sophie looked down at her nearest-thing-to-Colonial-style skirt that no Corn Pop would be caught DEAD in. "I don't THINK so!" she said.

"Boys?"

Sophie hesitated, but then she shook her head. Boys might have gotten between her and Maggie, but they didn't separate her from God.

Dr. Peter pulled all his fingers back in. "Then I think there's only one answer, Agent Loodle. The thing that's keeping you from going to Jesus—is you."

"ME?!"

"I think Jesus wants to say to you, 'Sophie, leave behind all your mistakes and your shame and just hang out with me.'" He shrugged. "He's probably tried to tell you that himself, only you weren't listening."

"I'm standing in my own way?" Sophie said.

Dr. Peter lowered his voice. "Let me tell you a little agent secret: most of the people who come to see me are doing that."

Sophie looked down at the tissue and tore a hunk out of it. "I don't know how to stop doing it."

"You've come to the right place," Dr. Peter said. "It's really pretty easy. You just need to stop believing that you have to be close to perfect before you can talk to Jesus."

"You don't think he's disappointed in me?" Sophie said.

"He's already forgiven you because he loves you. Love is always where it starts with God. Now you have to accept that and get back to talking to him."

"Like now?"

"That would be good, yeah."

Sophie bowed her head, but then she looked up at Dr. Peter again.

"Do you think you could come with me?" she said.

"Sure, I can put in a good word for you." Dr. Peter folded his hands. "Shall we?"

As he prayed, Sophie had never seen Jesus more clearly in her mind. His eyes were kinder than ever, and when she asked him—okay, begged him—to show her what she was supposed to do about her Corn Flakes, she felt a little inkling of hope.

Sophie was transporting the salad dressing bottles from the table back to the refrigerator after supper when the phone rang. Daddy answered it, said "Uh-huh" a couple of times, and hung up, jaw muscles twitching.

"Mrs. Olinghouse?" Mama said.

"Lacie," Daddy said, "why don't you take Zeke upstairs?"

"Busted," Lacie murmured to Sophie as she steered Zeke toward the door. The potato lump reformed in Sophie's throat.

"What did she tell you?" Mama said to Daddy.

"She said she appreciated us all coming in to talk to her today, and that she understood our concerns, but—"

"They're going to go ahead with the dance," Mama finished for him.

"You got it."

They both turned to Sophie, but before they could even get their mouths around their words, Sophie said, "It doesn't matter. I'm not going."

Their eyebrows lifted as if they were pulled up by the same string. But neither one of them seemed as surprised as she was.

*I don't know where that came from!* Sophie thought. *Was that Agent Shadow talking?*

No—this decision could ruin the whole film and maybe even push the Corn Flakes further away from her.

But it might also show Maggie that Sophie loved her more than a dress or a date—and that was where it had to start. If Dr. Peter was right, love was where it always started.

Mama and Daddy were gazing at each other. Slowly their eyes moved to her.

"You were right," Sophie said. "This is too much for sixth graders. It's messed everything up, and I don't want to have anything to do with it."

"All right," Daddy said, "who are you, and what have you done with Sophie?"

Mama gave him a hard jab with her elbow and looked at Sophie with a shine in her eyes. "We're proud of you, Dream Girl. And I'm still going to finish that dress."

Sophie wasn't sure she could stick to her decision if she saw that gorgeous piece of gold and lace, much less put it on. And there were even harder things than that to face now—like Fiona—and Darbie—and Kitty.

*First thing tomorrow before school, before we even practice,* she decided.

And then she talked to Jesus some more.

# Twelve

❋ ⌂ ✺

By the time she finished her homework, Sophie had a plan. She was nervous, but, as she told herself, "I have to get this out of the way." She took a deep breath and called Maggie.

Senora LaQuita told her she didn't think Maggie would come to the phone.

"Please—just ask her?" Sophie said. Her voice was barely squeaking out.

Sophie heard Maggie's mom call out something in Spanish—twice—three times—until finally a frail voice said, "Hello?" sounding more like a pin-drop than a thud.

"Maggie?" Sophie said.

"I'm only taking the phone because my mom is making me," Maggie said.

Sophie's hand tightened around the phone until her fingers went white. "I just want to say, please come to school tomorrow. I'll protect you—I promise."

There was a heavy silence. Then Maggie's words dropped with close to their usual clunk. "I don't care if I ever go back to that school again—but my mom's making me do that too."

"Meet us on the playground early, okay?" Sophie held her breath again.

"Whatever," Maggie said. And then she hung up.

*Love is where it starts*, Sophie reminded herself. *I sure hope Dr. Peter is right.*

When Mama dropped Sophie off at school—earlier than the bus—the next morning, Darbie and Fiona were waiting for her on the sidewalk, and they half dragged her to their spot backstage.

"Are we glad to see you!" Fiona said as she finally let go of Sophie under the flower arch.

"We thought you'd still be mad at us after yesterday," Darbie said.

Fiona hooked her elbow around Sophie's neck. "I wish we hadn't had that fight—especially since the dance is going to happen anyway."

Darbie nodded soberly. "You can't help what your mum and dad do."

"I'm not going," Sophie said.

She could feel Fiona's arm going stiff around her neck.

"You're not going to the dance?" Fiona said.

"Aunt Emily said I can go," Darbie said. "I just can't dance with only Ian the whole night." She shook her head. "Sophie, your parents really ARE strict."

"They didn't tell me I couldn't go. I decided myself."

Fiona let go of her completely. "WHAT?" she said. "But what about your dress?"

"I can use the dress in our film."

"What about Jimmy?"

"I'll just tell him the truth: the whole thing is messed up, and Maggie doesn't want to be my friend now because of it, and maybe Kitty either."

Sophie lowered her eyes. She'd said what she knew was right to say, but she didn't want to hear what Fiona and Darbie

117

were going to say back. Maybe if she didn't look at them, the words wouldn't come out of their mouths.

"Sophie! You guys! You gotta come right now!"

Sophie turned around in time to see Willoughby burst through the curtains in a billow of dust.

"Why?" Fiona said. "If this is some kind of trick—"

"They've got Maggie on the playground—she needs you. Come on!"

Without asking who "they" were, Sophie charged off the stage, through the cafeteria, and out the back door. Darbie and Fiona were right behind her.

"I told Maggie to meet us out here!" Sophie cried. "I told her we'd protect her!"

"We'll take care of those Corn Pops!" Fiona said.

Willoughby ran ahead and led them around the corner of the school to the area where the trash Dumpsters stood. At first Sophie didn't see anyone, until Willoughby stopped and motioned for them to look between two of the giant green boxes. It wasn't the Corn Pops they saw. It was the Fruit Loops.

Tod was sitting on top of one of the boxes, dangling his legs as he looked down. Colton had his back to them, facing Eddie, intent on doing something that obviously cracked up the other two. Their faces were exploding with hysterical laughter. When Fiona yanked Colton back by his shirt, Sophie saw why.

There was Maggie, with Eddie's arms wrapped across her chest from behind, and she had what looked like a donut stuffed halfway into her mouth. It was hard to tell which was bulging more, her cheeks or her eyes, as she coughed and choked.

Colton held a Krispy Kreme box over his head as he stumbled into Darbie. Fiona made a dive to catch her before she careened into the side of the Dumpster, Sophie hurled herself straight at Eddie, and Maggie and hung with her whole weight on Eddie's arm.

"Dude!" he shouted.

He let go of Maggie, but before Sophie could even reach for her, she felt her own arms being pulled behind her back. It wasn't Colton who was doing it. It was B.J.

"Get off me, you little *eejit*," Darbie cried — because Anne-Stuart had leaped onto her back like a spider monkey.

Fiona had both hands entwined with Julia's, pushing her back, obviously to keep from being slashed by her fingernails. As Sophie watched in horror, Julia spit into Fiona's face.

But that wasn't the worst of it. Maggie was on her hands and knees, spewing out pieces of donut and rocking as if she were going to throw up any second. Sophie took two steps toward her and ran smack into Tod — who had apparently come down from on high.

"Going somewhere?" he said. His whole face seemed to come to a point just inches from hers. And then it was gone as he twisted her around, latched his arms around her, and picked her up. "Dude, we gotta get rid of the garbage around here. It's starting to smell."

Eddie was up against the dumpster with Colton standing on his shoulders. Tod plunked Sophie into Eddie's arms, and Eddie lifted her up to Colton as if she were one of the donuts.

"Watch this!" Colton said. He flipped Sophie over and held her upside down. There was no decision to be made about what to do — screams ripped out of her and she banged her fists against anything close enough to reach.

Sophie looked around frantically as her head began to throb. Even upside-down she could see B.J. with Fiona in a headlock, and Anne-Stuart and Julia sitting on Darbie while she clawed at the air and shrieked about eejits. Both her Corn Flakes were putting up a good fight, but the Corn Pops weren't giving in—and Sophie felt herself being hoisted, head still lolling, toward the opening to the Dumpster. Willoughby was nowhere in sight.

"Somebody HELP!" Sophie screamed.

"Wythe here," said a voice above her. "JAMES Wythe."

Sophie curled upward. Jimmy's head appeared above the dumpster, and then his whole chest appeared as he pulled himself up by his gymnast-muscled arms and swung the rest of his body over the side. He dropped past Sophie to the ground and yelled, "Ready, Double-O-Nine?"

Another head popped out of the Dumpster—Vincent's this time—and he reached out and grabbed one of Colton's ears. "Drop her," he said.

"Dude! Let go!"

"Not until you drop her!"

"Don't drop me!" Sophie screamed.

But Colton did, right into Jimmy's arms. He set her down almost as soon as she realized where she was and moved in front of her. Vincent was now sitting on Colton's shoulders, fingers wrapped around both of Colton's ears.

"One move and I pull," Vincent said.

By now Eddie's face resembled a turnip, and he hurled himself at Jimmy. But Jimmy stepped aside, taking Sophie with him, just in time to avoid being plowed down by Eddie's chunk of a body plummeting to the ground.

"What the—" she heard Tod shout, sounding as if he were inside a cave.

Sophie peered around Jimmy. *Make that a bag*, she thought. Ian and Ross were wrapping Tod soundly inside a large cloth sack with a hunk of yellow rope from the bottom of the Dumpster.

"Eddie—get up and do something!" Colton cried, voice cracking.

"I can't!" Eddie said.

It was easy to see why. His ankles were tied together with more yellow rope. Nathan appeared from the other side, dusting off his hands and grinning like he'd just taken a gold medal.

"Good work Double-O-Eleven," Jimmy said. "What is the status of Agent Canary?"

Nathan whipped something black out of his pocket and talked into it. "Canary, this is Double-O-Eleven. Do you read me?"

"Canary?" Fiona said.

Sophie stepped all the way out from behind Jimmy. Fiona was rubbing her neck—and B.J. was long gone. So were Julia and Anne-Stuart. Darbie was frozen in an I'm-going-after-them position, staring at Jimmy.

"Are you talking about Kitty?" she said.

"Canary has the spies in her sights," Nathan said as he returned what was obviously a walkie-talkie to his pocket. "She and Mockingbird will keep a tail on them until help arrives. She'll advise if they head back this way."

"Who's Mockingbird?" Darbie said.

"I don't know," Nathan said. "I thought you did."

Sophie didn't catch the rest of the discussion. She went to Maggie, who was still on her knees, wiping her mouth with the back of her shaking hand.

"Did you throw up?" Sophie whispered to her.

Maggie shook her head. "None of it went down. I spit it all out. They said I would never get skinny—that I was always feeding my cake trap anyway, so they were going to 'help' me."

Sophie knelt down beside her. "I let you down again. I'm really sorry—"

There was no answer. Maggie spit another sugary glob into the dirt.

"Do you hate me now?" Sophie said. "You probably do — but Maggie, I LOVE you, and I'll never hurt you ever again. I'm not even going to the stupid dance."

"Me neither," said a voice above them.

"I wouldn't go if they PAID me," said another one.

Sophie's head came up. Fiona and Darbie were standing over them. Their faces looked ready to crumple.

Nathan's walkie-talkie crackled, and he pawed it out of his pocket. "Double-O-Eleven here. Come in, Canary."

There was more sputtering that Sophie couldn't make out, but it brought a grin to Nathan's — Double-O-Eleven's — face.

"She said the Corn Pops were on their way back here, but Mockingbird and two other agents cornered them at the door." Nathan's eyes crunched up. "Some kind of cereal?"

"Wheaties?" Sophie said.

"Yeah, that was it. Canary has gone to get O."

"O?" Fiona said. "Oh! Mrs. Olinghouse!"

"Are you talking about Kitty?" Darbie said to Nathan. "OUR Kitty?"

While Nathan's ears went so red they looked like Christmas lights, Sophie turned her attention back to Maggie.

"I'm going to protect you," Sophie said. "Even if you hate me — "

"I don't hate you." Maggie sank back and folded her arms around her knees so she could hug them against her. "But you can't be around me to protect me every minute. And people are always going to do stuff like that to me. I'm never gonna be skinny — I'm not made that way, and somebody's always gonna say I'm fat."

"Those guys are slime," Jimmy said.

Jimmy squatted down in front of the Corn Flakes, looking suddenly as if he didn't know where to put the arms that could, as far as Sophie was concerned, do just about anything.

"You aren't fat and besides, even if you were—" Jimmy swallowed, so that Sophie could see his Adam's apple bobbing up and down."—you don't deserve to be treated like that."

Vincent gave Colton's head a shake. "Whenever you need assistance, Agent Owl, just call on us."

"How did you know her code name was Owl?" Fiona said.

"Canary told us," Nathan said. "When SHE came to me for protection."

"From what?" Darbie said.

"From the Corn Pops. They threatened her with bodily harm if she got in the way of these morons. Mockingbird told her this was going to go down, but she couldn't tell YOU agents because the Corn Pops' threat covered you all too."

It was the most Sophie had ever heard Nathan say. He must have realized it too, because his ears turned into Christmas bulbs again.

"WHO is Mockingbird?" Darbie said.

But she didn't get an answer, because "O" rounded the corner of the Dumpster with Mr. Denton and Kitty.

"All right, guys, turn them loose," Mr. Denton said.

"They were saving us from being thrown into the garbage!" Sophie said.

Mr. Denton took a sniff at Vincent. "You really got into it, didn't you? Okay—let's go sort this out."

He nodded for Colton to come with him and waited while Nathan untied Eddie—who had been lying facedown ever since he'd fallen. Sophie could see that he'd been spending the time crying.

"Where's the other one?" Mr. Denton said.

Ian and Ross whipped the bag off Tod. Sophie wasn't sure, but she thought a hint of a smile trailed across Mr. Denton's face.

When they were gone, along with Jimmy, Nathan, Vincent, and the twins, Mrs. Olinghouse turned to the Corn Flakes.

"I want you to tell me the absolute, unvarnished truth about how Julia and B.J. and Anne-Stuart were involved in this."

"You can count on us," Fiona said. "Especially Sophie. She's always honest."

"If your story matches Kitty's and Willoughby's," Mrs. Olinghouse said, "then I think Julia and her friends are in a great deal of trouble. They've had enough chances this year."

"Excuse me," Sophie said. "Did you say Willoughby?"

"Yes, ma'am, Willoughby Wiley. I just talked to her and Kitty. I was surprised she would turn her friends in, and I thought maybe they'd had a falling-out and this was her revenge." She turned her sharp blue eyes on Sophie. "But if you confirm it, I guess I'd better believe it, hadn't I?"

"Willoughby is Mockingbird," Fiona whispered to Darbie and Sophie as they followed "O" into the building. "I'm going to have to get down on my KNEES to apologize to her."

"I know," Sophie whispered back.

"Ahem," Darbie said. She was grinning. "A lady does not whisper."

And Mrs. Olinghouse made it clear that a lady does not threaten or conspire or hold people against their will either. The Corn Pops were suspended for five days.

Except for Willoughby, who made it official when she sat with the Corn Flakes at lunch that day, that she was no longer one of Julia's Pops.

"I think you should be one of us," Kitty said. Then she glanced quickly at the other Corn Flakes. "I mean, if that's okay."

They all looked at one another and nodded, except for Maggie, who was tearing the roll from her sandwich into pieces and not eating it.

"Is it all right with you, Mags?" Sophie said.

"Do I still get a vote?" she said.

"Well, duh-uh—you're a Corn Flake!" Fiona said.

"I don't know if I fit in so much anymore." Maggie let the last chunk of bread drop into her lunch box. "You all have boys liking you—and you're pretty—and you look good in clothes. I'm never gonna have any of that."

"That's a bit of a horse's hoof, I think!" Darbie said.

Maggie looked at Darbie with hopeless eyes. "You wouldn't say that if you were more like me. Any of you."

"But we ARE like you!" Kitty said.

"We're all alike in the important things," Sophie said.

"Yes!" Darbie pulled her eyebrows together. "Tell us what they are, Sophie."

Sophie got up on her knees so she could look right into Maggie's dark, sad eyes. "None of us are perfect," she said. "But we ALL try to follow our rules—like we're all mostly loyal and we don't do bad stuff to people like the Corn Pops even though they do it to us—and we TRY to do the right thing. When we fight, we always make up because—"

Sophie stopped and slid her eyes toward Kitty—whose parents "didn't believe in church." She was pretty sure Jesus would want her to go ahead anyway.

"Because what?" Kitty said.

"Because love is always where it starts with God."

Willoughby stuck her hand up. "If you call Julia and them Corn Pops," she said, "what do you call yourselves?"

Darbie and Fiona and Kitty whipped their heads toward Sophie.

"Willoughby totally helped us," Sophie said. "Of course we can tell her. We're the Corn Flakes."

Willoughby gave a nod that bounced her wavy bob. "Then I want to be one."

Fiona looked at Maggie. "Mags?" she said.

"Yeah," Maggie thudded.

Sophie suddenly felt a little squirmy. "Just one thing," she said to Willoughby. "We're not like some clique. I mean, we have other friends too."

Willoughby looked down the table at Gill and Harley.

"Yeah," Darbie said. "The Wheaties."

"And don't forget the Lucky Charms," Sophie said.

Question marks formed in Corn Flake eyes, until Fiona said, "OH—Jimmy and those guys. But I thought we said no boyfriends."

"They aren't boyfriends," Sophie said. "They're boys who are friends. I think it's our time for that."

"Yes!" Kitty said. "They are our Lucky Charms!" She high-fived Sophie and Darbie and Fiona. And then even Maggie put up her hand and let Kitty slap it—about fifteen times.

*Dr. Peter WAS right*, Sophie thought. *Love IS always where it starts with God.*

They got word later that day from Willoughby, who just seemed to know everything that happened at Great Marsh Elementary, that the Fruit Loops were suspended for the rest of the year. And the dance was cancelled.

"There isn't going to be a dance after all," Sophie told her parents when Daddy got home that night. "I figure you're happy to know that."

They seemed more than just happy. They looked the way they did when everybody finally woke up on Christmas morning.

"We have a surprise," Mama said.

Sophie looked back and forth between them. Daddy was sporting a major grin.

"You wanted a dance," he said, "so you're going to have one—you and the rest of the Corn Flakes."

"At Fiona's house," Mama said. "It's being decorated as we speak."

Daddy nudged Mama. "Don't tell her everything!"

"I'm excited!" Mama said. She was all but clapping her little elfin hands. "Your dress is upstairs, all finished. You need to go get into it—your date will be waiting."

"My date?" Sophie said. "But I thought—"

Mama nodded at Daddy, who was holding up his hand. "Will I do?" he said.

"Are all the dads—?"

"Yes," Mama said.

"And Darbie's uncle Patrick?"

"Yes."

"But what about Maggie?"

"Boppa to the rescue," Daddy said. "IF she can get him away from Miss Odetta."

"Of course she can," Mama said. "This whole thing was Miss Odetta's idea."

"No WAY!" Sophie said.

"There's only one problem." Daddy shuffled his feet. "I'm not a dancer."

Sophie felt a grin spreading across her face. "That's not a problem. I can teach you." She put her arms out. "We'll start with a waltz."

Daddy lifted her so her feet were on his and leaned down to get into position.

"It's one-two-three, one-two-three," Sophie said, and they began to move.

"I want to be the most important guy in your life for a while longer, Soph," Daddy said in a soft voice she didn't even know he had.

"You are, Daddy," Sophie said.

And then she thought, *You and Jesus.*

With that, Sophie decided not to think of a new mission, now that the old one had been accomplished. She just swept across the kitchen, dancing with her daddy.

# Glossary

**a.k.a.** (ay-kay-ay) a cool way of saying "also known as"

**accommodate** (a-KAH-mah-date) make room for something

**alter** (ALL-ter) to fix or change a piece of clothing so it fits better

**astonishingly** (a-STOHN-ish-ing-lee) a word that describes something done so incredibly well that people can't help but be amazed

**blackguards** (BLAG-ghards) very rude and offensive people

**class** (klas) not a group of students, but a word that means something's really cool

**demerit** (di-MARE-it) kind of like traffic tickets for your behavior; if you get too many of them, you are punished

**disdainful** (dis-DANE-full) when you think you're better than someone else, and look at them with so much disgust that you show your feelings on your face

**enchanting** (in-CHANT-ing) something that is so charming and fantastic that it casts a spell on you

**flagellating** (FLA-gel-late-ing) constantly bringing up something you did wrong to punish yourself; kind of like beating yourself up

**flick** (flik) a fun word for "movie"

**foil** (foyl) to keep something from happening, usually through some sort of plan

**formidable** (for-MI-da-bull) a problem so big and scary that there doesn't seem to be any way to avoid or defeat it

**inconsiderate** (in-kon-SI-dehr-ret) not thinking about other people, and doing what you want instead

**irresponsible** (ir-e-spahn-se-bule) not doing the things you're supposed to do, such as chores, coming home on time, or your homework

**keening** (keyn-ing) crying really loud, like when someone dies

**nostalgic** (na-STALL-jick) something old that makes you all mushy inside, so that you want to live in the time period it's from

**resilient** (re-zill-yent) someone who is really tough, and can bounce back quickly from difficult things

**scandalized** (SKAN-duhl-eyzed)what happens after people are totally shocked by something. Sometimes, these people are very mean to the person who is "shocking," and spread gossip about them.

**scornful** (scorn-full) hateful, in a I'm-better-than-you way, and making sure people know how you feel

**steely** (STEE-lee) to look at someone in a cold way, like when you're disappointed in them

**succumb** (suh-come) when you finally give into something more powerful than you

**surveillance** (sir-VAY-lents) to secretly follow and spy on someone closely in order to gather special information on that person

**Victorian** (vic-TORE-ee-an) literally something that was made during the reign of Queen Victoria (1837 – 1901), when everything was really fancy. Victorian homes in America are usually pastel, and have a lot of fancy stuff on the outside.

# Sophie's Stormy Summer

# One

❊ ❥ ✿

"No way would I ever want to be a lifeguard here," Maggie said.

Sophie tilted her head back to look from under her floppy hat at her getting-tanner-by-the-minute friends.

Sophie's best-best friend, Fiona, didn't look up from the miniature hut they were building with dried seaweed sticks in the sand. Instead, she kept poking them in the sand with one hand while she brushed the usual strand of hair out of one eye with the other. "Why not, Mags?" she said.

Kitty wrinkled her made-like-china nose, now spattered with freckles. "I wouldn't want to *be* a lifeguard, but I might want to be *saved* by one." Her dark ponytail bounced as she giggled—which she did at the end of almost every sentence.

"Of course you would," Darbie said with her lilting Irish accent. "If it was a boy lifeguard."

"Gross," Fiona said.

Sophie looked at Maggie, whose dark eyes were going from one of the Corn Flakes to another.

"So why wouldn't you want to be a lifeguard here, Mags?" she said.

All the Corn Flakes sat back on their heels and squinted through the sun at Maggie.

"Because your little brother and sister are always screaming like there's a shark attack twenty four-seven," Maggie said. Her words seemed to make soft thuds in the sand. But Sophie thought being at the beach even made Maggie's matter-of-fact voice sound lighter. "How does the lifeguard know when to save somebody and when not to?"

She nodded toward Fiona's little brother, Rory, and her even littler sister, Isabella, who hadn't stopped shouting and squealing the whole five days they had been at Virginia Beach.

"Izzy and Rory *have* to make all those sounds at the sea-shore because they're little," Sophie said. She had also felt like holding her arms out to the ocean and squealing several times since she and the Corn Flakes had been there, and she was TWELVE. It was as if the waves themselves, tumbling over one another like puppies, were setting her free. Well, that and the fact that she was here with the four people in the whole world with whom she could be herself.

*Sure, we're flakes*, Sophie thought happily. *And we do corny stuff—but we are who we are.*

"At least they're making happy noises for a change," Darbie said, nodding toward Izzy and Rory. "Usually they're shrieking like terrorists." She clapped a sunblock-shiny hand over her mouth and looked quickly at Fiona's mother. "No offense, Dr. Bunting," she said through her fingers. "They're perfectly charming."

Dr. Bunting pulled off her sunglasses and turned to Darbie. "You were right the first time. They are little terrorists."

"What I can't get," Fiona said, "is why they always have to be throwing something—buckets, sand, food—on each OTHER." She sighed out loud. "It's heinous."

136

Dr. Bunting blinked her gray-like-Fiona's eyes and put her sunglasses back on. "If tossing a few Cheetos is the worst those two do before we leave here, it's because Miss Genevieve is the nanny from heaven."

"I thought we were supposed to call her the *au pair*," Maggie said.

"Just call me Genevieve." The blonde, creamy-skinned woman who was on her knees making castle towers pointed a graceful finger at Rory. "Get more of that sand you just gave me," she said to him. "With it just wet enough, we can build anything."

Rory trotted obediently toward the water with his bucket and shovel and Dr. Bunting looked out from under the brim of her white visor. "See what I mean?" she said.

Sophie tried to imagine Fiona's last nanny playing at the beach with Rory and Izzy doing things like dumping seashells over each other's heads. Miss Odetta Clide had handed out demerits if they spilled their milk. True, she had turned out to be less like a steel rod than they'd thought at first, but she NEVER would have gotten on her hands and knees in the sand.

The Corn Flakes—including their newest member, Willoughby—had all been worried about who would take Miss Odetta Clide's place when she married Fiona's grandfather Boppa, and they went off to Europe on their honeymoon for the summer. With Fiona's parents taking all of the girls—except Willoughby, who was on vacation with her family—to Virginia Beach for ten whole days, the choice of a nanny would determine the amount of fun they could have.

Sophie watched Genevieve drip wet sand through her hand to create a castle tower that looked the way soft ice cream piled on top of a cone. The au pair's thick braid hung over her shoulder like a silk rope, and her blue eyes seemed to hug

Isabella as the curly-headed four-year-old tried to dribble sand through her tiny fingers. *I want to be like Genevieve when I grow up*, Sophie thought.

Not that she WANTED to—at least not right now. Here—building a little beach hut out of dried seaweed with her best friends, she didn't have to think about anything scary, like starting middle school in two months ...

"Okay," Sophie said out loud. "Everybody tell their favorite part about being at the beach so far."

Fiona pushed a stubborn strand of golden-brown hair behind one ear as she poked the sticks into the adobe-colored sand as if she was doing math. "I liked it when we dug those giant bowls in the sand and climbed in there, all of us together."

"We KILLED ourselves laughing over things that are funny only to us," Darbie said.

"Was that your favorite too?" Sophie said to her.

Darbie kept weaving seaweed into the roof of their masterpiece. Her reddish hair and her snapping eyes were as dark as her flesh was white. She was the one most likely to burn like a marshmallow. Sophie liked to think of Darbie running on the beaches of Northern Ireland where she had lived until last year, shouting things like "blackguards"—which Darbie pronounced as "blaggards" and meant people who did evil things.

"My favorite," Darbie said finally, "was when we used those long sticks to write our names on the beach—and the shells were our periods and commas." She grinned her crooked-toothed smile. "At least, the shells we're not taking home by the bucketful to Poquoson."

"I liked pelican-watching," Maggie said. She was just returning to the job site with a bucket full of dried seaweed, her face Maggie-solemn, as if she were doing serious business. "I liked watching them fish."

"I DIDN'T like that part," Kitty said. "We only did that when Genevieve made us wait thirty minutes after we ate before we could go back in the water."

Maggie cocked her head at Kitty, so that her blunt-cut shiny hair splashed against her face just below her ears. "You have to do that," she said. "Or you'll get a cramp and drown."

Sophie squinted her brown eyes through her glasses at Kitty. "So what WAS your favorite?"

"It's too hard to pick," Kitty said. Her curly ponytail bounced on the breeze, and at that moment, Sophie thought, *I want her, I want ALL of us, to stay just like we are. And I want everything we ever do together to be as perfect as it is right now.*

"While you're thinking about it, Kitty," Fiona said, "we need more seashells for furniture."

"Why do *I* have to get them?" Kitty went straight into whining mode. To a certain degree, as Fiona always said, that was just Kitty's usual voice, just like Maggie's dropped out in matter-of-fact blocks, and Sophie's was as high-pitched and squeaky as a caught mouse. But right now Kitty suddenly had an I'm-about-to-cry edge to her voice.

"You don't have to get them," Fiona said, her own voice cheery. "You can just stand there and watch while we do all the work."

"Don't yell at me, Fiona," Kitty said.

"Who's yelling?" Fiona looked blankly at Sophie. "Was I yelling?"

"All right, I'll get more seashells, Kitty," Darbie said. "And you keep making the entrance."

"What entrance?"

"Right here," Maggie said.

She pointed to the sticks, like soft bamboo, that Sophie had laid crosswise between two rows of those stuck upright into the sand. *No offense, Kitty,* Sophie thought, *but we've been making it since lunch. Hello?*

Genevieve hadn't let them go back into the water after they'd eaten their sandwiches because she'd spotted jags of lightning so far away that Fiona said the rest of them would need the Hubble Telescope to see them. But when Genevieve had shown them how to make exotic-looking buildings, their claims that they were going to "go mental" if they couldn't go swimming had faded.

"It isn't rocket science," Fiona said to Kitty. "Just put them in there."

"I'm not stupid, Fiona!" Kitty said. "You always make me feel stupid!"

Sophie could hear the Kitty-tears getting closer, and she crawled over to Kitty and put her arm around her. Kitty usually put her head on Sophie's shoulder when she did that, but Sophie could feel her cringing.

"What's wrong?" Sophie said.

"Is it a sand issue?" Darbie said. "I hate when it gets in my bathing suit—especially right where it's sunburned at the edges."

"No!" Kitty said. "It's everybody being mean to me!"

Dr. Bunting toyed with a gold hoop earring as she studied Kitty. "Define 'mean,'" she said.

"I can't!" Kitty said—and she pulled her sandy hands over her eyes and burst into tears.

Dr. Bunting looked at Genevieve. "Oh, those preadolescent hormones," she said.

Genevieve lifted her chin—chiseled out of pure marble, Sophie was sure—as if she were listening to something.

"Thunder," she said. "Time to move indoors."

"No!" Rory said.

"Yes," Genevieve said.

"Okay," Rory said.

"If you can do that, you can stop a storm, Genevieve," Dr. Bunting said.

"What storm?" Fiona said.

Sophie looked up. The sky was like a moving watercolor picture, all in grays, and the wind was delivering karate chops to the water.

"I felt a raindrop," Maggie said.

"Wasn't that just spray from the ocean?" Darbie said. "Isn't that what it was, Fiona?"

"No," Maggie said. "It's rain."

"Thanks, Mags," Fiona said, grinning. "You're tons of help."

"Everyone pack up what you carried down and let's head to the house," Genevieve said.

"Can somebody else do mine?" Kitty said. "I'm too tired — I can't."

"I will," Sophie said — before Fiona could set her sobbing again.

"You're barely big enough to carry your own stuff, Little Bit," Fiona's mom said to Sophie. "What's the deal, Kitty?"

Kitty dropped onto a cooler and put her face in her hands again. By then, the wind was scattering the beach hut and kicking sand over Kitty's beach tote.

"I'll get that," Darbie said.

Maggie didn't say anything. She just knelt down with her back to Kitty, and Kitty climbed on. Plodding through the sand, Maggie headed up the beach.

"You go ahead with her," Genevieve said to the rest of them.

Genevieve rolled Izzy into a towel like a burrito, handed her to Dr. Bunting, and then put Rory up on her shoulders. Darbie, Sophie, and Fiona hoisted their own burdens on them-

141

selves like pack mules and started for the big wooden house. Its wide windows looked sightlessly down at them as the rain began to slash against the glass.

Sophie had to take off her hat so it wouldn't get blown away, and her hair whipped across her face. A pair of windshield wipers for her glasses would have been nice. But there was something about the sudden storm that prickled her skin with excitement.

"Let's pretend we've been shipwrecked!" she shouted to the girls.

"And that house is our only refuge!" Darbie shouted back.

"The only problem," Fiona cried over the wind-howl, "is that the place is full of pirates!"

Sophie raised a fist above her head. "We have no other choice! We must survive!"

"Help, Kitty!" Maggie cried out. "Help her!"

*Kitty's finally getting into it*, Sophie thought. Kitty was sprawled out in the sand, and Maggie threw herself down beside her.

"Now is NOT a good time to start acting it out!" Darbie called to Maggie.

"I'm not acting! There's something wrong with her!"

Sophie only stared for a second before she dumped her tote and the basket of chip bags and churned her feet in the sand to get to Kitty. She fell on her knees next to her and let her breath go with the wind.

Kitty lay on her back, face gray like ashes. Sophie put her hand on her arm and Kitty winced and her face twisted into a knot, but she didn't pull away.

It was as if she couldn't.

"Please don't touch me," Kitty said. "It hurts. It hurts."

# Two

Fiona was suddenly holding her rolled-up little sister, and Dr. Bunting was on the sand beside Kitty, her white beach top whipping around her body like a flag. Sophie felt Darbie leaning against her, their swimsuits plastered together in the rain as they watched Dr. Bunting run her expert hands over Kitty.

But Maggie didn't move from Kitty's side. The wind flapped her hair against the side of her face, and yet she stayed still as a stone.

"Let's get you into the house, Kitty-Cat," Dr. Bunting finally shouted to Kitty.

"It hurts to move!"

"That's why I'm going to carry you. Up we go."

Dr. Bunting was as lean as the runners Sophie had seen on the sports channel, but she stood up with Kitty in her arms as if she were lifting a bag of sponges. Genevieve shifted Rory onto one hip and took Izzy from Fiona and planted her on the other.

"Heads down, everyone!" Genevieve called out. "Plow right through!"

The two little ones squealed happily. But the Corn Flakes were a solemn group as they plodded after them, faces cowering from the bite of the storm.

When they got to the house, Dr. Bunting and Kitty disappeared. Genevieve led the group inside. "Showers, ladies," she said over her shoulder.

"I want to see Kitty," Maggie said. Her voice was thudding.

Genevieve turned and walked backward. "I know you do. Get showered and I'll find out from the doctor when you can see her."

"I want to see her now," Maggie said.

"Just give it a few—"

"I have to make sure she's okay."

"My mom's a doctor, Mags!" Fiona said. "Of course she's okay."

"I don't think it's as bad as it looks." Genevieve continued to back toward the downstairs hall. "You know our Kitty has a strong sense of the dramatic."

"What does that mean?" Maggie said as the Corn Flakes climbed the stairs to their suite.

"It means Kitty's a drama queen," Fiona said. "Which is our own fault. We made her that way."

"She'll be up making our film with us before supper," Sophie said to Maggie. "You know she will."

"No, I don't," Maggie said. "And neither do you. You didn't see her when she fell down. She went limp—like this."

Maggie demonstrated on the stair landing. *We made HER a drama queen too*, Sophie thought.

"I did that when I had a bad dose of flu," Darbie said.

"Yeah, I bet she's got the flu," Fiona said. "She was sick the week before we came. Her mom almost didn't let her go with us, but since my mom's a doctor she said it was okay."

Maggie looked at each one of them as they spoke, but nothing on her face was moving.

Darbie put her hand up to her mouth. Sophie could hear a laugh bubbling up her throat.

"It's not funny," Maggie said.

"Not that! Look at us!" Darbie said. "We're all in flitters—we look as if we washed up onshore and some old beach bum dragged us in!"

Sophie looked at the four of them and started her own fit of giggles. Their hair was all soaked and matted to their heads, and their suits and T-shirts drooped on them like hung-up laundry.

"Do I look as funny as you guys do?" Fiona said. She ran to the mirrors on the closet doors and shrieked at herself. "I'm hideous!"

"I'm a sea witch!" Sophie squeaked at her own reflection.

Even Maggie's lips twitched as she stared at her wilted self. "I'm taking a shower," she said. "I'm gross."

Clean and combed and equipped with juice boxes and tortilla chips and the homemade salsa Maggie's mom had sent along, the girls were in the big second-floor sunroom watching the ocean whip into a frenzy when Genevieve came in. She looked as if she'd never even been in the storm. She was in jean shorts and a stretchy T-shirt with lime green flip-flops to match.

"Can I go see Kitty now?" Maggie said.

Genevieve smiled at her. "You have a mind like a steel trap. Dr. Bunting's still with her. What's good to eat?"

"What's wrong with her?" Maggie said.

"She's not sure yet," Genevieve said, smiling again and scooping a handful of chips.

"But you know something."

Sophie thought Maggie was right. Genevieve was acting the way adults did when they were trying to change the subject—being all thrilled over something like chips and making their voices cheery.

"Someone's perceptive," Genevieve said. She sighed. "Kitty's running a fever. Mr. Bunting is calling her parents to see if they want to come get her to take her to her own doctor."

"My mom's a great doctor!" Fiona said.

"The best. But she doesn't have all the equipment here to run tests."

"Why do they have to run tests for the flu?" Fiona said.

"It must be a REALLY bad dose," Darbie said.

Maggie shook her head. "It's not the flu."

Genevieve's eyes sparkled at Maggie as she nibbled on the tip of a chip. "You're a doctor now too."

"Doctors don't get all concerned about the flu," Maggie said. "She's bad-off sick."

"She's not that sick, Mags," Fiona said.

"You don't know."

"Guys—" Sophie said.

"You know a lot of stuff," Maggie said. "But you can't know this—"

"Guys—"

"We all get fevers. Darbie—when was your last fever?"

"Guys!"

They all stopped and looked at Sophie. She tried to wind her voice down out of squeak zone.

"Maybe we should just pray," she said. "That's what Dr. Peter would say."

"But first—fill me in," Genevieve said. "Dr. Peter's your Bible study teacher, right?"

Everyone started to talk at once—except Maggie—and Genevieve finally held her hand up to shush them all, and pointed to Sophie.

"You tell, Cuteness," she said.

So Sophie told her everything about Dr. Peter, the Christian therapist her parents started sending her to see almost a year ago when she had been spending most of her time daydreaming. Now she was seeing him only once a month, but Darbie talked to him almost every week because she had a lot of things to deal with—like her father's dying in Northern Ireland when she was just a baby, and her having to grow up with violence on the streets, and then her mother's being killed in a car accident so that she had to come to the United States to live with her aunt and uncle in Poquoson. Dr. Peter was the best, the best, the best at helping kids work out their stuff. He'd even gotten Maggie to start eating again, back at the end of the sixth grade, when nobody else could.

And now, Sophie explained to Genevieve, Dr. Peter had their new Bible study group at church, which they just called their Girls Group, where they were learning how to be close to God by getting to know Jesus—big breath—by studying the Bible and learning that it showed them how to live. All the Corn Flakes went to the class, except for Kitty.

"Her parents don't believe in church," Sophie said.

Darbie lowered her voice to a whisper. "We're not even sure they believe in God."

Genevieve nodded. Not a single smirk or "isn't that cute" had appeared on her face while Sophie was talking.

"Then that's all the more reason to pray for her," she said. "Do you join hands or what?"

They always did, and they did it now, and with Sophie starting they all asked God, one by one, to be with Kitty and not let her be afraid. Maggie just flat out TOLD God that he had to make Kitty better fast.

When they all opened their eyes, Genevieve still had hers closed. Sophie waited until she lifted her eyelids.

"What were you praying there at the end?" Sophie said.

"I don't think you can ask someone that, Sophie!" Darbie said, pronouncing Sophie's name the way she always did, like it rhymed with "goofy."

Fiona grinned. "She's just inquisitive."

"What's 'inquisitive'?" Maggie said.

"I ask a lot of questions." Sophie pushed her glasses up her nose. "Is that okay, Genevieve?"

"It is absolutely okay. There at the end, I was just imagining Jesus."

Darbie practically knocked over the salsa dish. "That's what Dr. Peter taught us to do!"

Genevieve daintily chewed a chip. "I learned it from my grandmother, my mother's mother. It's what got her through some pretty horrible times in her life."

"What happened to her?" Sophie said.

Fiona nodded. "Definitely inquisitive."

Genevieve dusted the salt from her hands over the table and wiped it with a napkin. She made it look like a hand lotion commercial.

"My grandfather—her husband—was Jewish. They lived in the south of France when the Nazis occupied France during World War II."

"Oh," Fiona said. "The Holocaust." She turned to the Corn Flakes. "You know, when Adolf Hitler tried to have all the Jewish people killed."

Sophie found herself inching closer to Genevieve.

"Was your grandmother Jewish too?" Darbie said.

Genevieve shook her head. "No, but she thought what the Nazis were doing was—"

"Heinous," Fiona put in.

"And she refused to abandon my grandfather."

"Was your mother born yet?" Fiona said.

"No."

"Then we know it turned out okay, because if it didn't, there wouldn't be you." Fiona nodded as if that took care of that.

"Depends on what you mean by 'okay,'" Genevieve said. Her smile was turned down at the corners. "They weren't killed, but they went through horrible things that haunted them for the rest of their lives."

Sophie felt Darbie shudder beside her. "Could we not talk about this right now?"

"Actually," Genevieve said, crossing her legs in front of her, "I was thinking we should watch a movie. Who's up for *Ice Age*?"

Sophie didn't catch much of the movie. She was busy in the south of France —

*Huddling with her mother in the dark, wet alley, the young woman trained her eyes to see at least the outline of her father. Her brave father, who had crept out to see if the Nazis were coming. "Father!" she hissed into the eerie mist. "Come back — they'll see you!" But there was no answer, no sign of her papa. "Mama," the French girl who didn't have a name yet said, "put your shawl over your head. Like this. Stay warm." She pulled the rough woolen shawl over her mother's head and tried not to see the frightened look in her eyes. She must stay brave.*

"Sophie, why do you have that beach towel over your head?" Maggie said.

"Leave her alone, Mags," Fiona said. "It's our next film."

It was dark and they were starting *Ice Age* for the third time when Dr. Bunting let them see Kitty.

She was lying very still in the guestroom bed downstairs, just the way she had on the beach. When Fiona bounced onto the mattress beside her, Kitty winced as if Fiona had punched her out.

"She's achy," Dr. Bunting said.

"Like the flu," Darbie said.

Fiona looked at Maggie. "It IS the flu, right, Mom? I told Maggie it was."

"It hurts more than the flu," Kitty said. Sophie could barely hear her voice.

"Bad dose, then," Darbie said.

Maggie, meanwhile, was shifting her eyes between Kitty and Dr. Bunting.

"She has flu-like symptoms—" Dr. Bunting started to say.

But Fiona's father appeared in the doorway, looking tanned from the golf game he must have gotten rained out of, and tall and sort of ropey as if he were all long, tight muscle. "Your dad's on his way, Kitty," he said.

"In this storm?" Maggie's eyebrows were twisted.

"I think your mom would do the same thing if you were sick," Dr. Bunting said. "Hey, why don't you guys keep Kitty company for a few minutes?"

She patted Kitty's hand and made her exit with Mr. Bunting right behind her. Sophie knew there was going to be a no-kids-allowed talk. It made her stomach uneasy.

"I don't want you to leave, Kitty!" Darbie said. "Sophie has a new idea for a flick. You should have seen her dreaming on it when we were watching *Ice Age*!"

"For the second AND third times," Fiona said.

"I'm sorry you missed it," Sophie said. "I know it's your favorite—but OUR film is going to be even better—"

"I don't want to go home," Kitty said.

At least she hadn't lost her whine. *That's probably why she's been thinking everybody's yelling at her*, Sophie thought. *She's been sick the whole time.*

"So beg your mom to let you stay," Fiona said. "My mom will take care of you."

"She's the one who said I have to go home."

"No way!" Fiona said. "Stay right here—I'll take care of this."

Fiona charged for the door, but her dad was already standing there. "It's a done deal, Fiona," he said. "So don't start giving me a five-point proposal."

"Let me just ask this one thing," Fiona said. "Why won't Mom take care of her? Will it interfere with her tan?"

Sophie sucked in a breath. She could picture herself talking to Daddy in that tone. She could also picture being grounded until she was in college.

But Fiona's father just said, "Step into my office and we'll discuss it."

Fiona turned to the Corn Flakes and gave them a thumbs-up as she followed him into the hallway.

"Do you think she'll get him to let me stay?" Kitty said in her tiny voice. "If I go home, I'm going to miss everything!"

"No worries," Darbie said. "We won't have a bit of fun without you."

"I know I won't," Maggie said. Sophie could tell she meant it.

"It isn't fair!" Kitty said—and once again she started to cry. But it looked like it hurt to do that, and so she cried even harder.

"It's okay, Kitty," Sophie said. She got as close to the bed as she could without touching it. "We're only going to be here four more days. That'll give you time to get well so you can be in the film. We're all going to be French—what do you want your name to be?"

Kitty blinked. "Danielle. I always wanted to be called Danielle."

"I'll write that down in the book," Maggie said.

"I was Antoinette when we did our Williamsburg movie," Sophie said. "But I need to pick another name because this takes place during World War Two, so Antoinette couldn't still be alive—at least, I don't think so—"

Kitty just watched her.

"We prayed for you," Sophie blurted out.

"It still works, even if you don't go to church," Darbie said. Then her face got blotchy-red and she gave Sophie a "Do something!" look.

Sophie didn't have to because Fiona came back in looking like something was pinching her face.

"My mom says we have to let Kitty sleep," she said.

"I'm not leaving," Maggie said.

"What if we're really quiet and we just sit here with her?" Darbie said.

Sophie didn't say anything. She knew Fiona. It wasn't just that she'd lost the battle with her parents. Something was very, very wrong.

# Three

Kitty's father arrived, still in his U.S. Air Force uniform, and when he walked into the house, Sophie felt like they should all jump to attention. The Corn Flakes followed him silently into the bedroom where he scooped the sleepy Kitty up in his beefy arms, ignored her whining to please let her stay, and told the Buntings he was sure she was going to be fine. He barked when he talked.

Only when they were gone and Maggie and Darbie were asleep did Fiona whisper to Sophie, "He told my dad he came to get her because he didn't want my parents to have to be taking care of her while they were on vacation. But my mom said she made him take her because she's sure Kitty has something worse than the flu."

Sophie propped herself up on her elbow. "Like what?"

By the glow of the nightlight, she could see Fiona rolling her eyes. "She said she was not at liberty to say until the test results confirm her suspicions."

"What does that mean?"

"It means she knows, but she's not telling because if she's wrong she'll look stupid."

"Oh." Sophie flopped back onto her pillow. The wind was still slapping the windows with rain, making the night as dismal as she felt. "It's not the same without Kitty."

"But, Soph—we have to try to have fun."

"Right," Sophie said. "Maggie's never even been to the beach before—and Darbie never went on a vacation her whole life, ever."

"Fun is what Corn Flakes do."

And the Corn Flakes did try. They built more beach huts and made necklaces out of shells that already had tiny holes in them. They made the best one for Kitty.

They tossed around ideas for their film and Fiona wrote them down in the Treasure Book. Sophie was Sofia, and Maggie was Marguerite, and Fiona was Fifi, and Darbie was Daphne. But they named Kitty Danielle, just as she wanted.

For the rest of their vacation, they filmed everything they did on Sophie's video camera so they could show it to Kitty when they got home. But when the camera was off, every time anybody brought up Kitty's name, they deflated a little, like air slowly being let out of a balloon.

Maggie asked Dr. Bunting at least four times a day whether she'd heard anything from Kitty's parents. Dr. Bunting always said no news was probably good news.

On their last day at the beach, the Corn Flakes were down at the water, saying good-bye to the ocean, when Maggie said, "Hey, Sophie. Your little brother's here."

Sophie whirled around to see six-year-old Zeke, dark brown hair sticking up in spikes, tearing down from the beach house with Izzy and Rory hot on his trail. Genevieve strode calmly behind them. Lacie, Sophie's fourteen-year-old sister, was standing on top of a sand dune, her hand forming an awning over her eyes.

"I see she's back from her mission trip," Fiona said. "Are you ready for her to be the boss of you again?"

Sophie didn't answer, because the sight of her sister made her want to run — not away from her, but to her. *I missed her!* Sophie thought. *I actually missed her!*

She started toward the dune, but Zeke hurled himself at her and took both of them down to the sand, squealing like piglets.

"Sophie! I got a new Spider-Man and it's got a wall he can climb up and I can make him do it and I didn't mean to use up your whole purple marker and Mama said I should say I'm sorry and I am and Lacie brought me a drum from Mexico and Daddy says I can play it on all the days that don't end in *Y*—"

Sophie did a few more rolls in the sand with him before he suddenly bolted up and took off with Rory. Lacie stood over her, her dark-like-Daddy's hair pulled up into a fashionably messy bun. She looked like while she was away she'd stretched upward and inward, and in some places outward. She reached down a hand to pull Sophie up.

"I won't hug you 'cause I'm all yucky now," Sophie said.

"Are you kidding me? I haven't seen you in three weeks!"

Lacie pulled Sophie into a hug and then held her out by the shoulders to look at her. Her deep blue eyes sparkled. "You haven't grown any. I guess you're always going to be a peanut. So, how ARE you?"

Sophie could only stare at her. Where was the *real* Lacie?

Darbie, Maggie, and Fiona were also gazing at Lacie as if she were an extraterrestrial. They had talked Sophie down from a furious-with-Lacie fit more than once.

"I'm good," Sophie said. "Where's Mama and Daddy?"

Lacie pointed toward the beach house, and slapping at the sand on her arms as she ran, Sophie headed that way. She could hear the other three Corn Flakes behind her, squawking as if it were *their* parents who had just arrived. Everybody loved Mama. And everybody understood Daddy, which was basically enough.

Daddy met her on the wooden walkway and picked her up for a hug. He held on to her longer than usual. It made Sophie glance toward the porch, where Mama—who everyone said was a grown-up version of Sophie—was listening to Dr. Bunting. Sophie's stomach tied in a knot. Mama's eyes were puffy, like she'd been crying. Hard.

"Dream Girl!" Mama said. She flung out her arms to Sophie and the other Corn Flakes, although when Maggie stepped up for her turn, she refused the hug and just said, "Something's wrong."

"Sit, ladies," Dr. Bunting said. "Let's talk."

Maggie didn't sit.

Sophie squeezed into the chair with her mother. Fiona hiked herself up onto the low railing. Only Darbie selected her own chair, where she curled up into a ball.

*I don't think we want to hear this*, Sophie thought.

"Okay, girls, here's the deal," Dr. Bunting said. She ran her fingers through her short-cut hair and pushed up the sleeves of her shirt. "And I want you to hear me out before you start asking questions." She looked right at Fiona. "Or jump to any conclusions."

"About what?" Fiona said.

"Exactly my point. The doctors have done tests, and Kitty has been diagnosed with what's known as ALL—acute lymphoblastic leukemia—"

"Kitty does NOT have leukemia," Fiona said.

Dr. Bunting put up her hand without looking at Fiona. "It's a very serious form of cancer that happens in children sometimes, BUT—" She waited while Fiona closed her mouth. Darbie sat up straight in her chair, and Maggie doubled her fists like she was going to take Dr. Bunting down.

"BUT—two-thirds of the children diagnosed with leukemia go into remission."

"What does that mean?" Maggie said.

"Remission means they don't show any signs of having leukemia anymore."

"Then that's what's going to happen for Kitty," Fiona said.

"That may very well be true with the kind of treatment Kitty is going to get at Portsmouth. It's one of the finest military hospitals in the country."

"What happens if she doesn't get that remission thing?" Maggie said.

Dr. Bunting folded her arms. "Then they'll keep treating her."

Maggie looked like she was digesting something she hadn't bothered to chew. Mama hugged Sophie close to her. "The best thing we can do for Kitty is pray for her and let her know that we love her."

"She can still play with us though, right?" Fiona said. "They'll start medicating her, and she'll be able to have the rest of summer vacation, right?"

Sophie looked up at Fiona. There was a look Fiona sometimes got when she sounded like she knew what she was talking about, but she really didn't. She had that look now.

"Eventually she will," Dr. Bunting said. She tilted her head toward Daddy, who was standing off to the side, rubbing the back of his neck. "How much detail do you want me to go into?"

"I know everything I want to know," Darbie said. She was gnawing hard on her lower lip.

"Then I think that's plenty," Mama said. "I promised your aunt Emily we would pay attention to that."

"But there IS more you have to tell us," Fiona said. "Just not now. Which means it isn't bad, because if it was bad, you'd give it all to us right now. I know how you are."

Fiona's mother looked at Mama. "You want her? You can have her."

"Oh, no, not a chance," Daddy said. "She's more trouble than my three put together." He grinned at Fiona. But Sophie didn't see a grin in his eyes. There was no room in there with the sadness.

Mama volunteered to pack Sophie's stuff up for her. Maggie, Darbie, and Fiona trailed after her to get their own things together, Fiona explaining in eleventh-grade vocabulary words what "two-thirds" meant for Kitty.

But Sophie didn't follow. She wandered back down the wooden walkway that led from the house to the beach, draping her towel around her shoulders like a shawl.

*Sofia hung her head as she dragged her bare feet along the edge of the Mediterranean Sea, the heat of the sand biting at her soles. What difference did it make? Her friend Danielle was sick. She asked, "Why did God let this happen?" Something tugged at Sofia's shawl. When she looked up, she saw —*

Genevieve fell into step beside Sophie. "That's always the question when something bad happens," she said. "You want to talk about it?"

Sophie dragged her toes as she walked, digging into the darker sand that hid beneath the soft golden part. She never talked about God except to Dr. Peter, not about the hard things, anyway. She could count on him not to tell her she was the worst person on the planet for not being sure God knew what he was doing.

She looked sideways at Genevieve. She didn't *look* like she was about to whip out a rule book or anything.

*If she did,* Sophie thought, *I'd just go right down, right here, just like Kitty did.*

She squeezed her thoughts together so the memory wouldn't get through, but there was her friend in her mind—all pale and limp and hurting because she had a terrible disease.

"Why don't we just walk?" Genevieve said. "Walking is also good."

"What about the brats? I mean—Rory and Izzy." Sophie hunched up her shoulders. "Sorry. Fiona always calls them that so I hear it all the time."

"I think of them as puppies, myself," Genevieve said. "As soon as I get them housebroken and through obedience school, they'll be very nice pets."

"Are you serious?" Sophie said.

Genevieve's green eyes were shiny. "No, but it sounded good, didn't it?"

Sophie had to smile at her. She was kind of like Dr. Peter, only taller, and prettier, of course. Maybe she COULD tell her—

"You can have them back now!"

It was Lacie, dragging herself out of the ocean with Izzy and Zeke clinging to her like koala bears and Rory hanging off her back, all making little-kid beach sounds.

"Slacker," Genevieve said to Lacie with a grin. "It's time for me to take them back up to the house anyway."

"Not yet!" Zeke said.

Rory turned to him, his small face serious. "We don't say no to Genevieve, dude."

Genevieve ushered them up the dune. Lacie pulled a towel out of her bag, which she'd parked on the beach, and wrapped it around her chest.

"You okay, Soph?" she said.

"No," Sophie said. "Kitty has leukemia."

"I know. Dad told me."

"She's really sick."

"Well, yeah, she is." Lacie shook her head like a wet dog. "But you have to have faith. God will take care of her."

Sophie studied her sister while Lacie sat down and knocked water out of her ear. There really was something different about her now, Sophie thought as she joined her on the sand. Before they'd both left on their trips, they were getting along a LITTLE better than they used to, but Lacie had still been saying things like, "You better start acting normal before you go to middle school, Sophie."

But Sophie hadn't wanted to scream once since Lacie had arrived that day. Sure, they had said only about three sentences to each other, but that was still a record.

Sophie watched the sand slide back and forth across her toenails. There was only one way to find out if Lacie had really changed, and besides, if she didn't ask *somebody*, she might scream anyway.

"Why do you think God let this happen to Kitty?" Sophie said.

Lacie set about untangling her bun. "I kind of asked the same question when I was in Mexico. Why is he letting all those little kids be poor and hungry and sick?"

"Was it awful?" Sophie said.

"You don't even want to know. Seriously, Soph—our garbage cans at home have better food in them than what those poor people are eating."

"But why? Doesn't God care about them?"

Lacie loosened her hair with her fingers and dug in her bag until she pulled out a comb. "Of course he cares about them. Somehow it's part of his plan. That's what I learned down there."

Sophie felt her eyes bulging. "God PLANNED for Kitty to get sick?"

"See, that's the thing. We can't go there. We have to pray for God to show us what to do about it. It's like, don't ask 'Why,' ask 'What next?' That's what the people in our village did."

"Even if Kitty's parents won't even let her go to church?"

Lacie pulled a clump of wet hair out of the comb. "You definitely need to make sure Kitty accepts Jesus Christ as her Lord and Savior and gives her heart to him."

It sounded to Sophie like Lacie was reciting the alphabet. She wasn't even sure she knew what Lacie was talking about.

Lacie put the comb down. "We should probably pray for Kitty's soul right now."

"Her soul?" Sophie said. She pulled a narrow panel of her hair under her nose like a mustache. "Why don't we pray for God to make her better?"

"It's more important for her to be saved."

"Yeah — like go into that remission thing."

Lacie sighed and put her hands on Sophie's shoulders. "I've seen it up close and personal now, Soph. It doesn't matter how awful your life is. If you have a personal relationship with Jesus Christ and you believe he is the Son of God, you can handle anything. But if you don't — "

"What?" Sophie said. "Then God doesn't care about you?"

"I didn't say that — "

"I don't believe it!" Sophie scrambled up, scattering sand as she stomped her foot. "I don't believe God won't take care of Kitty!"

"Chill, Soph, okay? Maybe you aren't ready for this conversation — "

"I HATE this conversation!"

Lacie shook her head. "Nope. Definitely not ready."

Sophie wadded up her fists. "I thought you changed—but you didn't. You're still—"

"What?" Lacie said, squinting up at her. "Trying to help you?"

"You're not helping!" Sophie cried. "So just don't try!"

She ran for the dunes, kicking sand out behind her.

But she wasn't quite sure what she was running from.

# Four

Everything seemed different to Sophie when she got back to Poquoson. The grass was so un-beach-like, and after living in a beach house that her whole HOUSE would have fit inside one and a half times, her room felt like it had shrunk. Mama still made brownies and called her Dream Girl and tucked everybody in at night. But somehow it seemed to Sophie as if everything had gone on without her while she was away, and she couldn't quite join in again.

It *was* good to be back with Mama and Daddy, when Daddy wasn't saying things like, "Pinch-hit for Lacie on the dishes tonight, would you, Soph? She has volleyball practice." Or youth group. Or babysitting. Or worse, afterward, when he'd say, "Way to take a hit for the team."

It was even pretty good to be with Zeke, except when she found out he had not only emptied her purple marker, but the light blue and the lime green too. Her three favorites.

Lacie was another thing all together. Sophie stayed away from her as much as she could so Lacie wouldn't try to tell her that Kitty wasn't going to get *any* help from God if she didn't do whatever it was Lacie had said she better do. It wasn't hard to avoid her sister, because she was always off doing all the things that kept her from doing her chores. Sophie was taking a lot of hits for the team.

Mostly, it was hard to get used to not having her Corn Flakes with her every second. One night Sophie even woke up and whispered, "Fiona? Are you hungry?" before she realized she was in her own bed.

It helped to think back and giggle over the outrageous things they'd done at the beach. But whenever Kitty danced across her mind-screen, Sophie stopped giggling and started thinking about leukemia and how heinous it sounded, even though she didn't know exactly what it was. And about Kitty looking so tiny and too-white lying on the sand.

*Sofia drew her shawl over the lower half of her face, darting in and out of alleys with the Nazis close behind. She couldn't let them catch her, not before she found Papa and got him to safety. The things they might do to him—*

The problem was, Sophie didn't have a clue what the Nazis were going to do to her if they caught her or what the south of France looked like or even if there *were* any alleys there. Fiona always got that kind of information for the Corn Flakes.

Sophie knew what she really needed to do, of course, and late one night after three days of milling around the house and sighing and having Mama make suggestions that didn't sound fun, one night she decided to do what Dr. Peter had taught her. It was time to imagine Jesus and tell *him* what was going on with her.

It was hot upstairs in their old house, even with the air conditioner humming its heart out, and Sophie kicked off the covers and stared at the paste-on stars that glowed on her ceiling. They all were in the proper constellations. Fiona had seen to that.

"Okay, God," Sophie whispered before she closed her eyes, "I'm scared to talk to you because what if I wait for an answer like I always do, and then tomorrow or the next day or the next day after that you find a way to tell me Lacie was right — that if Kitty doesn't do all that stuff Lacie said then something bad is gonna happen to her that Lacie never did tell me because she said I wasn't ready."

Sophie took a breath and whispered lower, until she almost wasn't speaking at all. "I don't even know if *I'm* doing all that stuff Lacie said — like accepting Jesus as my Lord and Savior — it was like it was all one word and I didn't understand it. I just thought I had to talk to you and try to act like you, because you're the only God and you love me and I love you."

It was getting harder to talk. Sophie closed her eyes and gathered up the picture of her Jesus with the kind eyes and the face that never twisted all up because she was dreamy and silly and weird and a lot of times wrong.

He was there. He was always there. She could always talk to him. Dr. Peter had taught her not to imagine him talking back, the way she had her imaginary film characters do. He said Jesus would do his own talking in his own way, if Sophie would only wait.

It had always happened before —

"Is it wrong that I have questions about what you're doing?" she asked out loud. "I only have two: Why did you let leukemia happen to Kitty? And is it true that you won't take care of her if she doesn't get 'saved'? And Jesus, I'm not exactly sure I know what that means, so would you explain that? I guess that's three questions.

"And I don't care what Lacie says, even though she went on that mission trip, I'm going to ask you: Would you please make Kitty well? Would you make sure she has one of those things that two-thirds of all leukemia kids get? That's five questions. Is it too many? I love you. Thank you. Amen."

Sophie knew there wouldn't be answers right away, especially since she had given Jesus an entire list. She *did* expect the light feeling she usually got when she went to him, like he was now carrying all the stuff she'd been lugging around.

But the feeling wasn't there. She was cold now and she pulled her pink bedspread up to her chin and shivered.

*I wish Fiona was here*, she thought. *We'd sneak into the kitchen for cold pizza.*

*Sofia could hear her stomach growling. She had been running from the Nazis for so long, she hadn't eaten in days. What COULD she eat? Creeping like a shadow down the steps toward the subway, in case the Nazis were following, Sofia stole up to a trash can. 'The food in the trash cans is better than what the poor people are eating,' her sister had told her. Lifting the lid without making a sound, Sofia peered inside. The smell of garbage assaulted her nose and she had to force herself not to slam the lid back down. Even as she replaced it, she saw an empty Corn Flakes box. But behind her, something moved in the darkness. There was no time to go back for the box in hopes of a few crumbs. She scurried back up the steps, pulling her shawl tightly around her—*

She woke up later with Mama pulling the bedspread off her.

"Aren't you hot?" she said.

"Can we have Corn Flakes tomorrow?" Sophie said.

She heard Mama chuckle in the dark. "You can call them in the morning, Dream Girl," she said.

Having her friends over the next day was, as Darbie put it, "Class!" That was the highest form of "great" in her vocabulary. Willoughby was still away, and, of course, they didn't have Kitty—but with what Fiona knew about the Nazis and Marseille, the city in the south of France on the Mediterranean Sea, they could still plan their film, which they did over the next three days.

There was a special process to make a Corn Flakes production come together. Sophie always took care of Step One, which was to discover the perfect characters and the most excellent mission from one of her daydreams.

Step Two was Fiona's job, which was to do the necessary research to make it totally real. She had already checked that one off.

Step Three: As they talked about the production—the characters, script, setting, and props—notes were made in the Treasure Book. No one but Maggie did that, and nobody else touched the gel pens.

They were now on Step Four: deciding what the story would be. That was Sophie's favorite part, because they didn't just sit at a table and write it—how boring would that be? They chose their characters and played out the story until it told itself, and Maggie wrote it down as they went, usually with Fiona making sure she got it all in there. At that point Kitty was always starting to nag Maggie about her favorite part, the costumes Maggie and her mom would make for the film. But, of course, Kitty wasn't there. Nobody else brought it up.

For practice, they dried out the ends of the old bread that Mama usually saved for the birds and gnawed on them while they hid between the garage and the line of azalea bushes. Maggie said, as she chewed, that she didn't think it had to be *that* real.

Then they barricaded themselves behind the boxes and trunks in the attic to hide from the Nazis, until even their shorts were soaked with sweat and Mama made them come out and drink about three gallons of water.

By then it was time for Step Five: defining roles and casting the extra parts.

They gathered in Sophie's room, with Maggie sitting at Sophie's desk ready to fill in the names next to the roles, which she had written neatly on a page in the book. Sophie figured it probably took Maggie ten minutes to print each one precisely.

"We need Nazis," Maggie said.

"I don't think I can be one of those," Darbie said from her place on her tummy at the end of the bed. "They're absolute blaggards."

"I'll do it," Maggie said. "But I'll have to change my name. I don't think a Nazi can be called Marguerite."

Fiona plopped onto one of the cushions against the wall in the library corner of Sophie's room. "I'll be one too, even though they were evil and heinous and killed over six million Jews. Six million! Do you have any idea how many that is?"

"Can the Nazis in our movie get what they deserve?" Darbie said, kicking her feet back and forth. "Can't we reef them?"

"We can do anything we want," Sophie said. "That's why I love making movies." She sat up straight in the middle of her bed and wafted a hand in the air. "Sofia can lead her mother to safety while the brave and bold Daphne takes them down."

Maggie frowned. "That means we have to change the script. It'll mess it all up."

"We'll ad-lib," Fiona said. "You know—make it up when we get to that part."

Maggie gave a grunt and made a note of that. "Next is Sofia's mother. Who's gonna play her?"

"Willoughby can when she comes back," Sophie said.

"What about Kitty?"

They all looked at Fiona.

"Kitty can't." Maggie's words were thudding harder than usual.

Fiona rolled her eyes. "My mother always gives the worst possible scenario when she talks to patients' families, so if something bad happens they can't come back and say she didn't warn them. She told me that herself." She picked up another cushion and hugged it. "It isn't going to be that long until Kitty will be home. Go ahead and make her the mother—Danielle."

"But you don't know—" Maggie started to say. Someone tapped on the door.

Mama poked her curly head inside the room.

"I was just wondering if anybody wanted to go see Kitty with me tomorrow. She can have visitors now."

The Corn Flakes wriggled, squealing, into a group hug, and even Maggie smiled. Mama suggested they put together a basket of things Kitty might enjoy—which meant a major trip to the store and a complete raid of the house. By the time they were finished, Mama's huge basket was bulging with markers, very cool paper, CDs for the portable player Lacie put in there on loan, hair thingies, a stuffed kitten that purred when you squeezed it, and a kit for making jewelry that Sophie had gotten for her birthday. Kitty had gone nuts over it at Sophie's party.

Not only *that*, but they managed to stuff in granola bars, juice boxes in Kitty's favorite flavor—strawberry kiwi—and little bags of Mama's amazing brownies.

"THIS is class!" Darbie said the next morning as Daddy loaded the basket into the old Suburban, because nobody else could lift it alone.

"You better get a wheelchair for this thing when you get there," Daddy said.

Sophie was so excited, she actually clapped her hands.

But the closer they got to Portsmouth, the less anyone talked—except Fiona, who chattered on the way she did on those rare occasions when she was a nervous wreck.

"I hope they let us all go into her room at the same time," Fiona said, "because Mom said they might limit the number of visitors she can have at once, but we can always ask her sisters to leave if they're all in there. She has like four or five. Let's see, there's Karen, Kayla—"

"Fiona," Mama said as they pulled into the parking lot, "take a breath."

That was when Sophie realized she'd been *holding* hers.

It felt, as Fiona put it, "disconcerting" to be in a hospital. Everything was stainless steel and too clean. *So sick people won't get sicker*, Sophie thought. She was feeling a little nauseated herself. They had to have special passes to get in since it was a military hospital, and somehow that made it even more disconcerting.

But nothing caught Sophie's breath and held it like the sight of Kitty, sitting up in the middle of a bed that had more cords and knobs than the space modules she'd seen at NASA, where her dad worked.

Kitty let out a little half-scream and reached out her arms for hugs—which were hard to give because there was a tube hanging from one of her arms that led to a bag of liquid stuff on a pole. Sophie didn't want to know how it was attached to Kitty.

They each gave her a careful squeeze and then backed off as soon as they could get free to stare at things they had seen only on TV. Except Fiona, who said, "What's all this for?"

"I don't know." Kitty giggled. "They told me, but I didn't exactly get it."

"I bet I can figure it out," Fiona said.

Sophie was watching Kitty carefully. She didn't look any worse than she had when she left the beach. And she wasn't whining—yet. And she seemed ecstatic to see them, which Fiona said was the happiest you could get.

"All right, Kitty," Darbie said, hands on hips. "Are they decent to you here?"

"I can have anything I want! Well, almost anything. I wanted to order a pizza, but they wouldn't let me do that. Oh, and my nurse on the day shift is really cute." She giggled again. "His name is Sebastian."

*Talking about a cute boy. That's a very hopeful sign*, Sophie thought.

Maggie, who had up till now been standing with her arms folded, taking a full survey of Kitty, said, "Do you still hurt?"

"Not as bad. They're giving me medicine." She pointed to the bag on the pole.

"What's its name?" Sophie said.

"I don't know!" Kitty said.

"It has to have a name if it's going to live in here." Sophie turned to the Corn Flakes. "Any suggestions?"

"I want it to be a boy," Kitty said.

"Figures," Fiona said.

Darbie smiled her crooked-toothed smile. "I think it should be Hector."

"No!" Kitty wailed.

"Percival!"

"Maurice!"

"NO—give it a cool name!" Kitty was whining. Definitely a good sign, in Sophie's opinion.

"Joe," Maggie said.

They all looked at Kitty.

"Is that cool?" she said.

"No doubt," Darbie said.

"Okay. Joe."

Fiona picked up what looked like a remote. "This works your bed, Kitty."

"It does?"

"Yeah, watch."

Fiona pushed a button, and the foot of the bed began to rise. She pushed another one, and the head came up. Kitty was slowly being folded into a mattress taco.

"I don't think you're supposed to do that," Maggie said.

"I told you I can do almost anything I want here," Kitty said. "Except be with you guys."

Her lower lip trembled, and Sophie could see what was coming.

"We brought you a basket, Kitty!" she said.

"Roll the bed down, Fiona," Darbie said, "so we can give it to her."

Maggie and Darbie hoisted the basket up beside Kitty, but she didn't even get a hand into it because the Corn Flakes pulled out each item and held it up to her and explained it—all at the same time. Kitty giggled through the whole thing and said thank you about a hundred times. When she sniffed at one of the packages of brownies, Fiona said, "You want me to open it?"

"Let's open them all!" Darbie said. "I'm not ashamed to mooch!"

"Not right now," Kitty said. "I'm getting kinda tired."

"I'll fix the pillows—"

"Let me do the bed thing—"

"I can hold this tube deal up for you—"

"You want some covers?"

Kitty sank against the pillows and sighed. Her eyelids drooped over her eyes.

The Corn Flakes stood on each side of the bed, looking at her.

"Should we go?" Sophie whispered.

"We probably should," Darbie whispered back.

"I have to have an operation."

They jumped as if Kitty had leaped off the bed.

"They're going to operate on me," she said.

"What kind of operation?" Maggie said.

Darbie nudged her. "You don't have to talk about it if you don't want to, Kitty."

"They're going to put me to sleep and put a thing in my chest. When I get better from the operation, they'll put medicine in the chest-thing and they won't have to keep sticking things in my arms."

"You'll be asleep," Fiona said, as if she performed surgery herself daily. "It won't even hurt."

Kitty opened her eyes and looked at her, looked at all of the Corn Flakes.

"I'm scared," she said.

All the way home, Sophie held back something hard that was pushing against her chest from the inside, while everyone talked about everything but Kitty. As soon as she got her bedroom door closed and flung herself across the bed, Sophie's chest broke open and let the sobs and the tears come out.

It wasn't long before she felt her mother joining her on the bed and stroking her hair.

"It's hard, isn't it, Dream Girl?" she said.

"You know what, Mama?" Sophie said into the bedspread.

"What?"

"There's nothing in that basket that's going to make Kitty better."

# Five

"Did Dr. Peter go on his vacation yet?" Sophie said the next morning on the way to church.

Daddy grinned at Mama. "Is that the fifth time or the sixth time she's asked us that since we got up today?"

"Sixth," Lacie said. "And counting."

Mama turned around in her seat and gave Sophie a look that knew things. "I hope he's still around, Soph," she said.

*What if he's not?* Sophie thought. *I need him to be there! I need him, God, okay?*

It was one of those instant-answer prayers. Dr. Peter was waiting for her at the door to the Sunday school room.

"Sophie-Lophie-Loodle," he said.

It was his special name for her, and it almost made her start crying again. He motioned her over to the little niche by the water fountain. Behind his glasses his usually twinkly eyes were soft, and they drooped at the corners. He ran a hand over his short, gelled curls.

"I heard about Kitty," he said. "I'm so sorry."

"Me too," Sophie said.

"How are you doing with it?"

"Not good at all."

"Let me guess." Dr. Peter wrinkled his nose to scoot up his glasses. "You're feeling anxious and confused and you want to cry every other minute."

"Yes!"

"That's not doing 'bad,'" he said. "That's doing normal. This is a really hard thing to deal with. Of course you're going to feel that way."

Sophie swallowed hard. "But is it normal to be sort of mad too?"

"You think? I'm mad myself. A twelve-year-old suffering like that? It doesn't seem fair."

"I feel madder than that. I want to know why God let this happen." She moved a little closer to him so she could lower her voice. "Do YOU think it's because Kitty doesn't go to church and Bible study?"

One of Dr. Peter's eyebrows twitched. "Did somebody tell you that's the reason?"

"Lacie sorta did."

Dr. Peter glanced at his watch. Sophie had never seen him do that before when they were talking.

"You have to go, huh?" she said. "I didn't mean for us to, like, have a session right now—"

"No, no! I'm glad you asked me. I just want to make sure I talk to somebody before Sunday school starts." He leaned a hand on the wall, above his head, and looked at Sophie with serious eyes. "Kitty doesn't have any control over whether she gets to come to church, so if you think God is punishing her because she doesn't, I don't think that's true." He watched the door to Sophie's Sunday school room close and then glanced down the hall toward the high school room. "I wish I could have you come to my office tomorrow, Loodle, but I'm leaving for vacation right after church. Tell you what—"

He pulled a pen and a pad out of his pocket. The pad was shaped like a lily pad, and the pen, of course, had frog's feet sticking out both sides.

"I'm going to be gone for two weeks," he said as he wrote. "I want you to promise me you'll do two things while I'm away."

"Anything," Sophie said. She could already feel herself getting lighter.

"One—you'll read this Bible story and put yourself in it. You know how."

"Promise."

"And two—you won't stop imagining Jesus every day and listening to the answers. Do what he says, even if it hurts."

"If it HURTS?" Sophie said.

"It just might mean a few sacrifices. Nothing you and God can't handle together." He gave her a smile, and to Sophie it looked a little wobbly. "You can do anything God asks you to do, Sophie. You've proved that—and I think that's why he's asking more from you." He pressed the paper into her hand and whispered, "You can do it."

As she watched him hurry down the hall to the high school room, she sure hoped he was right. It was a heavy thing to even think about doing this without him.

So after church, Sophie dragged a little as she climbed the stairs to her bedroom. A Post-It note was stuck to her pillow.

Soph,
Come to my room, K? We need to talk.
Lace

Sophie sniffed. *SHE might need to talk to ME, but I don't need to talk to HER.*

But how many times in the last year had Lacie invited her into the room next door? Besides, Sophie wanted to set her straight about Kitty now that she'd seen Dr. Peter and *really* knew what she was talking about.

Pulling herself to her full but not very impressive height, Sophie went to Lacie's door, all prepared to knock, but the door was already open.

"Hey, Soph," Lacie said from her cross-legged seat in one of her bowl-like green papasan chairs that swiveled in circles. "Wanna sit?"

It wasn't an order, so Sophie parked herself in the other one, legs sticking straight out above the floor, ready to take off if things got ugly.

"You're still mad at me, aren't you?" Lacie said.

"Yes," Sophie said.

"Well—I don't blame you."

Sophie stared. "Are you serious?"

"Yeah. I messed up at the beach the other day when I was talking to you about Kitty needing to be saved and all—and I wanted to say I'm sorry."

Sophie only nodded at first, since this was *so* un-Lacie-like. She even studied Lacie's freckled face for signs that she might change her mind or add a "But—"

"So—do you forgive me?" Lacie said.

"Sure," was all Sophie managed to say. This was like talking to a stranger she'd known her whole life.

Lacie wiggled to a straighter position in the chair. "What I said wasn't wrong, exactly; it was HOW I said it. Kip said I needed to—"

"Who's Kip?"

"Hello? My high school youth director that took us on the mission trip. He's like Dr. Peter in your Bible study group thing."

Sophie wanted to correct her with the fact that there was *no one* like Dr. Peter, but she held back. So far, Lacie was being pretty decent.

"Anyway, I told Kip what I told you and that you were mad at me about it, and he said that the way I presented it to you probably turned you totally off."

"You mean 'has she accepted-Jesus-Christ-as-her-Savior?'"

Lacie let out a husky laugh. "Is that the way I sounded?"

"Yes."

"No wonder you were mad at me! See, I got so used to saying it over and over on the trip, so — well, whatever — I was TRYING to say that I really want to see Kitty know Jesus like a friend and see that he's the Way."

"To getting well?"

"To living the life he told us about in the Bible and getting to go to heaven — someday. You know, like, when she's an old woman."

Sophie squirmed in the bowl-chair. "But what about now? What about her getting better so they don't have to keep treating her and she can come home and all that?"

"Um, Soph?" Lacie leaned forward so far the chair almost tipped over. "They told me to say I don't know — which is good, because I don't."

"Who's 'they'?"

"Kip. And Dr. Peter."

"Dr. Peter! MY Dr. Peter?"

Lacie looked like she had a gas pain. "Yeah. He came into the high school room and talked to Kip and then Kip AND me, and they said — well, what I already told you."

Sophie felt her eyes narrow. "Did you just apologize because they said you had to?"

"No! I'm totally serious! I'm the one who decided to say I was sorry. They just said to make sure you knew—"

"Got it." Sophie twisted a strand of her hair around a finger as she thought.

"You aren't going to do that mustache thing, are you?" Lacie said.

"No," Sophie said. "I only do that when I'm confused. I'm just thinking—"

"Uh-oh." Lacie grinned and settled back in the chair. If Sophie hadn't known better from past experience, she would have thought Lacie was actually relieved that Sophie didn't storm out of the room.

"I was thinking that if we're not going to figure out why Kitty got sick," Sophie said, "then we have to ask Jesus what to do to help her and listen to what he says and do what he tells us."

Lacie was nodding, the way teachers nodded when it looked like a kid was getting some big math concept. "How do YOU talk to Jesus?" she said.

"I imagine him."

"Go figure."

"But I don't put words in his mouth."

"Right. I have a hard time just sitting there praying, so I write him letters in my journal—WHICH is hidden."

"I'm not gonna go looking for it, if that's what you mean," Sophie said.

Lacie looked startled. "I didn't mean you. I was talking about Zeke. He gets some really bad ideas from Rory."

"Oh," Sophie said. "Yeah."

It was suddenly as if she had run out of things to say. Usually, if she wasn't in an argument with Lacie, they didn't talk this much.

"I don't want to boss you around or anything," Lacie said finally.

"You don't?"

"No. This is just a suggestion. Are y'all still doing a film about the Jews running from the Nazis?"

"Yeah," Sophie said carefully.

"Well, while you're planning this film, maybe really think about the Jews—they had to have total faith or they would have just gone nuts with the fear. So I'm thinking that could kind of help you with the Kitty thing—I don't know. Just a thought."

"Oh," Sophie said. "Thanks."

She climbed out of the chair and went for the door. Lacie twirled her chair around to face her. "Whatever you want me to do for Kitty, just let me know, okay? I'd hate it if it was one of my best friends."

"Thanks," Sophie said. And she left in what could only be called a state of shock.

Darbie's aunt Emily called that afternoon to invite them over for a cookout. Mama said she could hear Darbie shouting in the background that the rest of the Corn Flakes and their parents were going to be there.

"Let me see," Daddy said to Mama when they got in the car, "do I have everything I need for an afternoon with the Corn Flakes? Earplugs. Tranquilizers. Are the Buntings' two little ones going to be there?"

"No," Mama said. "Just Fiona. We're dropping Z-Boy off to stay with Genevieve."

"Oh, then I didn't have to pack the shin guards after all."

"Da-dee," Sophie said.

"What? What did I say?"

Sophie had everything *she* needed for an afternoon with the Corn Flakes, which was a mind full of the film. She'd called Maggie to make sure she was bringing the Treasure Book and plenty of gel pens.

Darbie, Fiona, and Maggie had a quilt spread out on the grass down by the Poquoson River where Darbie lived with her aunt Emily and uncle Patrick. They were fully equipped with assorted bags of chips, a small cooler full of every juice and soda made and, of course, the Treasure Book. Maggie already had the pen poised for action.

"We totally HAVE to do this film!" Sophie called out as she ran toward them. She slid to a stop on the quilt, narrowly missing Darbie's grape juice box. "You're not gonna believe this, but Lacie gave me the idea."

"No way," Maggie said, as if that were a fact.

"Way. She even invited me to her ROOM." Sophie whipped out the Post-It note from her pocket.

"Let me see that," Fiona said. She took the paper and studied Lacie's handwriting. "She's up to something, guaranteed."

"And maybe she isn't," Darbie said. "Maybe she's just decided to stop running your life."

"Anything's possible, I guess," Fiona said.

"Not that," Maggie said.

Darbie peered over Fiona's shoulder at the note. "So what idea did she give you?"

Sophie got up on her knees. "She said our film could be about the Jewish people having FAITH because that was the only way they got through all the horrible stuff that was happening—just like we have to for Kitty."

Darbie pulled her knees up to her chest and hugged her legs.

"Something's wrong," Maggie said.

"I think that's a class idea—if OUR Jews get to escape."

"Of course they will," Fiona said. "They won't be part of the ones that got killed."

"How'd they kill them?" Maggie said.

"Do we have to go there?" Fiona said. "Some of them got away—Genevieve even said so. Let's concentrate on that." She leaned back on straight arms. "If we're doing this film sort of about faith and all that, God has to take care of them, right?"

"Then why didn't he take care of ALL of them?" Maggie said.

Sophie's stomach went into a square knot. "We can't ask 'Why,' because we don't know," she said. "We have to ask 'What next?'"

"That's what my mum always taught me," Darbie said. "When they threw eggs at me in the street because I was Catholic—"

"They threw EGGS at you?" Fiona said. "That's just heinous."

"What's that other word for *heinous*?" Maggie said.

"Devastating," Fiona said.

"Instead of asking why God let them do that," Darbie went on, "my mum told me we had to figure out how I was going to behave with love."

Darbie sank her chin onto her knees. They all got quiet.

"Does it make you sad to think about your mom?" Sophie said.

Darbie nodded like she couldn't talk just then.

"Okay—enough with the sadness," Fiona said. She took one last slurp from her soda can and stood up. "Let's get to work."

When they took off for the house, Sophie followed at an I-don't-want-to walk. All of a sudden she wasn't so excited about this film anymore.

Maybe believing that God was *somehow* there wasn't as easy as it sounded. Darbie was still devastated about her mum. Kitty was still having an operation on top of everything else.

Maybe it was just too hard.

# Six

✻ ⬠ ✺

Maggie and her mom left the next morning to visit relatives in Miami. Sophie could imagine Senora LaQuita dragging Maggie to the car, because she didn't want to leave with Kitty so sick. But her mother did promise she would help them make costumes for their film when they returned, just like always. Sophie tried to act as though that was great news.

After breakfast, Sophie went outside and hid behind the azalea bushes by the garage and tried to imagine she was hiding from certain discovery.

*Sofia was glad she hadn't brought her mother this far, that she had left her in the safe house where the sympathetic Frenchman—who had a mustache and wore a blue silk scarf around his neck—said he would keep her mother from harm. "But you must be back before dawn," he had told Sofia.*

*With danger crawling up her spine like icy fingers, Sofia crept carefully along the wall. She must stay out of the light—she couldn't make a shadow. The Nazis were just across the street, standing guard outside the very building where her father was hiding beneath the floorboards.*

*I have no choice, she thought. I have to find a way to sneak in there and beg Papa to come with us. We have people who will help us escape to America. She crept along a few more inches, and then a few more, each step slower than the last. But what if they catch me? she thought. What if they drag me off to a concentration camp?*

*In spite of the perspiration that had formed like little beads across her upper lip, Sofia shivered. She didn't know what could happen in those camps, and she was afraid to find out. Whatever it was, she did know it was heinous. Worse than heinous. Devastating. And to avoid this kind of fate for herself and her family, Sofia would risk her life—*

"Soph?"

It was Mama's voice, but it took Sophie a few seconds to realize she was calling from her Loom Room above the garage. Mama's voice came from the upper window.

"Fiona called. She wants you to come over. I told her I'd take you."

Sophie leaned against the wall and wiped the sweat off her upper lip. She had never been relieved to have somebody interrupt a pre-film daydream before, and she called up, "Okay. Thanks."

*Fiona's been on the Internet since Sunday*, she thought. *I bet she knows ALL about how evil the Nazis were by now.*

Mama pulled the Suburban into the circular driveway at Fiona's, which was one of the biggest homes Sophie had ever been in where somebody actually lived. Dr. Bunting and Fiona waved them over to the deck that sprawled along the whole side of their house. Sophie knew that Fiona's mom never came home for lunch unless somebody needed stitches or had a fever of 102.

Sophie had a sinking feeling in her chest, the kind she used to get as a little girl when she'd agree to go to somebody's birthday party and then realized on the way there that she really didn't want to go.

"Hey, you two," Dr. Bunting said to Sophie and Mama. "I came home for lunch so I could talk to Fiona, and when she said you were coming over I thought I'd catch you too."

Sophie could feel the sweaty-lip-thing happening again, but tiny beads of sweat also broke out on her forehead this time.

Dr. Bunting shook hands with Mama—most of the time Mama hugged everybody—and said, "Do you want me to send in for some iced tea?"

Mama said no to the tea. She had a little wrinkle between her eyebrows.

"So, I want to talk with you all about Kitty," Dr. Bunting said. "I've been keeping in close touch with her parents, and they want you to know that Kitty got through her operation just fine—no problems."

"Does she have that thing in her chest?" Sophie said.

"Yes—it's called, well, something big and long, but we'll just call it a CVC."

"What's the long name?" Fiona said.

"I'll cover that later," her mom said. She rolled her eyes at Mama. "Soon they'll start her on chemotherapy, which is the treatment for leukemia."

"They'll put the medication in through that CVC," Fiona said.

"Right. The chemotherapy is a mixture of several drugs that will kill off the leukemia cells in her blood and her bone marrow."

"And that will make her have that remission thing?" Sophie said. Her mouth was so dry; she wished Mama had said yes to that iced tea, even though she didn't even *like* the stuff.

"We-e-ell," Dr. Bunting said. "This is only the first round of chemotherapy. She'll get several rounds at different times, and it usually takes a while for a patient to go into remission. All her blood counts have to return to normal so her blood can do all the good things it does for your body, including keeping you from getting infections."

"So it takes, what, three, four weeks?" Fiona said.

"I wish that were the case." Dr. Bunting sat up and folded her hands on the tabletop. "It usually takes at least a year of treatment, usually longer, for remission to occur."

"A YEAR?" Sophie said.

"But that's the worst-case scenario, right?" Fiona said.

"No," her mom said. "That's the best case. For most kids, you're looking at two years."

"Bless her heart," Mama said. The little wrinkle had gone deeper.

"Unfortunately—" Dr. Bunting stopped and looked from Sophie to Fiona as if she were deciding whether to go into this part or not.

*Don't tell us*, Sophie wanted to say. *Only please do—and don't make it really bad.*

"With most medicine for illness, once you start taking it you start to feel a little better pretty quickly. You know, like when you take an antibiotic for an ear infection."

"Right," Fiona said. "I hear a 'but' in there though."

Dr. Bunting nodded. "But with chemotherapy, you feel a whole lot worse when you take it. See, when you kill off the leukemia cells, you kill off a lot of the good ones too, so you run the risk of other infections, and you can get nauseated and vomit, and—you usually lose your hair."

Fiona pulled her head back. "Like, she'll be bald?"

"She could be. Not everybody experiences hair loss, but we always tell patients it's a possibility so they can prepare themselves. That's the least painful of the side effects, but it seems to be the hardest thing for people to deal with, especially girls."

"Does it grow back?" Sophie said. She was almost whispering.

"Oh, yes. She may even have a thicker head of hair when it does."

"In two years?" Sophie said. Kitty would be about to start high school by then. The Corn Flakes would be Lacie's age.

*Two years of throwing up and getting infections and going around with no hair?* Sophie thought. *God—this is SO not fair! Why would you—*

She had to put out a mental foot and trip that thought because it was way too hard. Dr. Peter said—what did he say about that? She couldn't even remember now. All she could see on her mind-screen was Kitty, hearing this same news in that hospital room in Portsmouth. It was a sure thing that even Sebastian the cute nurse hadn't been able to keep her from sobbing for days.

"Does Darbie know yet?" Sophie said.

"I just got off the phone with her aunt before you got here," Dr. Bunting said. "Emily's mother has had cancer so she understands about chemotherapy. She's going to explain it to Darbie. You two have any questions?"

"Yes," Fiona said. She folded her hands on the table just as her mom was doing. "What are the chances of Kitty going into remission BEFORE most people do?"

"I have no idea, Fiona," Dr. Bunting said. "I can't make a guess, okay? We just have to wait and see."

In Fiona's room, Sophie curled up in the overstuffed striped chair by the window. Fiona squeezed in beside her.

"Okay," Fiona said, "this is totally wretched. Not to mention the fact that my mother talks to me like I don't know anything. Hello! I make straight A's." She got to a position where she could look straight at Sophie. "I think we have to be positive about this. Kitty COULD only need a year of chemotherapy—maybe less, which is what I know my mom is thinking, only she won't say it because that's the way she is. And Kitty might NOT lose her hair. And what's a little throwing up? There are worse things."

Just then, Sophie couldn't think of anything worse than the entire situation.

"I say we just think positive and keep praying and get on with our film," Fiona said. "I found TONS on the Internet." She squirmed out of the chair. "I'm gonna call Darbie. There are only three of us, but we're the brains of the Corn Flakes anyway, right?"

But Aunt Emily said Darbie couldn't come over and when Fiona, of course, asked her why, she said Darbie needed some quiet time.

"Who needs quiet time in the summer?" Fiona said to Sophie. "We'll get enough of that when we have to do homework again."

"Then let's not work on the film by ourselves," Sophie said. "We can't leave EVERYBODY out."

*I can't hear anything else that's awful today*, Sophie thought. *I think I need some quiet time too.*

Evidently, Darbie needed a lot of it, because over the next several days when Sophie called her, Aunt Emily always said Darbie couldn't talk right then. The third day, Sophie finally found out why.

Mama got off the phone with Aunt Emily and said Darbie had gotten really upset over the things that were happening to Kitty, and it started her thinking about her mom and all the other people she'd lost. Aunt Emily said she could get together with the Flakes again, as long as they didn't talk about Kitty or work on their movie. She said the Holocaust was too disturbing for Darbie right now.

"That's okay with me!" Sophie said. "Fiona isn't going to like it though."

But Aunt Emily had obviously thought of that, because she said that she and Mama would take the three girls to do some fun things until Darbie felt better.

Her first suggestion wasn't the most "fun" thing Sophie could think of, but at least she and Fiona could be with Darbie. The next day, they went to the mall to shop for school clothes.

Darbie loved to shop, so that made it better. She led them on a lively journey from Old Navy to Limited Too to Gap, collecting bags full of skirts and tops and ponchos and shoes. Aunt Emily said Darbie never got to have nice clothes in Northern Ireland, so she just kept smiling and pulling out her credit card.

Sophie and her mom usually shopped at less expensive stores, so Sophie acted as Darbie's fashion adviser and brought things for her to try on in the dressing room. Dr. Bunting had given Fiona money, which Fiona said she was saving until they got to the bookstore.

"They don't have school clothes at the bookstore," Sophie said.

"I know," Fiona said.

By lunchtime, Darbie was so loaded down, Aunt Emily had to take her bags to the car while the rest of them got a table at the food court and dug into wonderfully greasy Chinese food.

"I have a feeling the Chinese don't eat this stuff," Mama said as she fished for a piece of chicken with her chopsticks. "But isn't it great?"

"Uh-oh," Darbie said.

Mama jumped and put her hand on Darbie's arm. "What is it, honey? You okay?"

"I WAS—until I saw THEM."

Sophie didn't have to ask what she was talking about. Just two tables over, the Corn Pops—the rich, popular girls from school—were arguing over who was going to sit where.

B.J., Anne-Stuart, and Julia, the Queen Bees. Each one of them had more bags than Darbie, and their voices grew louder and louder.

"Charming," Mama said. "Just ignore them, girls."

Nobody else in the food court was ignoring them. They couldn't.

B.J. could have been heard inside the movie theater at the other end of the mall. She tossed her buttery-blonde bob at the end of every sentence. Julia sat rooting through a shopping bag, seemingly unaware of the other two Corn Pops as she flicked her long auburn hair out of her eyes. Standing with her arms folded across her chest and a pout on her face was skinny Anne-Stuart, glaring at B.J.

"I totally called this seat first!" B.J. said, with a hair-flip.

"Like you ALWAYS do," Anne-Stuart flipped back— although her silky white-blonde hair was up in a bun with the ends sticking out perfectly in all the right places.

*Here it comes*, Sophie thought.

Julia looked up and seared them both with a green-eyed glare. "You two are acting so immature," she said. "Who CARES where you sit?"

Sophie turned to Fiona and rolled her eyes. She knew that Fiona knew that Julia knew exactly *why* they cared. Whoever sat at Julia's right hand was second in command.

Fiona grunted. "Without Willoughby to pick on, they're fighting for their lives."

"When is Willoughby ever coming back from holiday, any-way?" Darbie said. She called all vacations "holidays," which Sophie liked, only she could never remember to say it herself. "We hardly had a chance to get to know her and she was gone."

"I'm looking forward to getting better acquainted with her," Mama said. "She seems like a sweetheart. I don't know how she ever got mixed up with those three."

"Kitty was a Corn Pop too once," Fiona said.

Sophie glanced at Darbie and kicked Fiona under the table. Still, she had to wonder how Willoughby was going to feel when she got back and found out about Kitty. Willoughby laughed at the smallest thing and made it funny for everybody else, even if they didn't get it.

*There's nothing funny about leukemia*, Sophie thought.

"Oh, look at this show," Darbie said.

Sophie looked at the Pops and shared disgusted looks with her fellow Flakes. Three high school boys were loping through the food court, and Julia and B.J. and Anne-Stuart were fol-lowing their every trying-to-be-macho move with their eyes. Sophie expected B.J. to start drooling any minute.

"Give me a break," Fiona said. "They're, like, four years older than us. As if the Pops had a chance."

"Chance to what?" Mama said. She looked horrified.

"I don't know," Fiona said. "THEY don't even know."

The boys draped themselves over the McDonald's coun-ter, obviously unaware that the Corn Pops even existed. Immediately, Julia, Anne-Stuart, and B.J. whirled back to their tables and dug through the purses that exactly matched their outfits. Julia produced a compact and fluffed some blush onto her cheeks. Anne-Stuart slathered on lip gloss, and B.J. went after her eyelashes with a mascara brush.

"Cosmetics?" Darbie said.

"That's makeup, all right," Fiona said. "Like it's really going to get those three boys to look at them."

"Hello?"

They both looked at Sophie.

"Just because they talk about us behind their backs," Sophie said, "that doesn't mean we should talk about them."

"You're always so good, Sophie," Darbie said. "Now of course I feel like a complete bogey."

"I just want to say this," Fiona said. "I don't think we're going to have to worry about them anymore. After all the trouble they got into at the end of last year? They're gonna keep WAY far away from us."

Sophie did give the Pops once last look though. Even without the makeup, they looked so much older than they had two months ago. Sophie didn't know exactly what it was, but it wasn't the kind of older she wanted to be.

# Seven

Mama and Aunt Emily took Sophie, Fiona, and Darbie on several day-trips—to Norfolk to see the botanical gardens, to Charlottesville for a tour of Jefferson's Monticello, and back to Virginia Beach. That took Sophie's mind off Kitty during the day, but it was still hard when she was in bed at night, watching the shadows on her ceiling. She couldn't help wondering what it was like for Kitty in that hospital room, chasing shadows of her own. Even for Sophie it was impossible to imagine.

So when Fiona begged for Sophie and Darbie to spend the night at her house one Thursday, Sophie practically held her breath for the whole hour it took for Aunt Emily finally to make the decision to let Darbie go. She just made Sophie and Fiona promise they wouldn't talk about Kitty's sickness or rehearse for their film.

"What ARE we gonna talk about then?" Fiona said to Sophie before Darbie arrived.

They were sitting in the breakfast nook eating some kind of dip Genevieve had whipped up and served with little triangles of toasted pita bread. Genevieve called it hummus. Sophie didn't ask her what was in it. It tasted really good and she didn't want to ruin it by finding out it was made from something gross.

"I mean, that's what the Corn Flakes DO," Fiona went on. "We make films and we help each other with problems."

Dr. Bunting hurried into the kitchen, and Genevieve slid a zip-up lunch bag toward her on the counter.

"Tell them about camp," Dr. Bunting said.

"Mom, I'm not going to tell them about camp because I'm not going," Fiona said. She finalized that by stuffing an entire pita triangle into her mouth.

Fiona's mother barely glanced at her as she adjusted her collar. "You go every year, Fiona."

"Not this year," Fiona said with her mouth full.

"You should have told your father that before he wrote the check."

Fiona dunked another piece of pita into the hummus like she was trying to smother it.

"Nobody asked me," she said.

Dr. Bunting finally looked at her. "I thought you loved that place. All the horses and tennis courts and sailboats—it's better than Disney World."

"I just can't be gone for three weeks this summer," Fiona said.

Sophie's hand froze halfway to the dip bowl. *Three weeks? Three weeks without Fiona—right NOW?*

"What, Fiona?" Dr. Bunting said. "Do you have some agenda we don't know about?"

"You don't know anything about what I do." Fiona muttered it so low her mom didn't appear to hear it. Her mother flung the lunch bag over her shoulder by the strap and glanced at her watch.

"Your father already paid the tuition and it's nonrefundable," she said, halfway out the back door. "You'll be fine. Nice to see you, Sophie."

Sophie could only stare at Fiona.

"I'm not going," Fiona said. "She just doesn't know it yet."

She dropped the piece of pita into the hummus and scraped her chair away from the table. She was out of the kitchen in three steps, but not before Sophie saw tears filming her gray eyes.

Fiona never cried.

Several seconds later, Sophie heard Fiona's bedroom door slam way down in the west wing of the house.

"Should I go after her?" Sophie said to Genevieve.

Genevieve slid into the chair Fiona had just vacated and tucked her feet onto its edge.

"I'd give her a few minutes," Genevieve said. "She's had a couple of meltdowns since Kitty got sick. She always seems to want to calm down by herself." She smiled a little. "I don't know if she'd actually leave a mark on anybody, but I wouldn't chance it."

"Fiona has meltdowns?" Sophie said. She could feel her eyes widening. "I'm her best, best friend, and I never saw one."

Genevieve toyed with her thick braid. "I have a feeling it's because you three aren't allowed to talk about Kitty when you're together, so it gets all bottled up inside. Plus you can't work on your movie, so there goes that outlet. I'm not questioning Darbie's aunt. I can just see that it's hard for you and Fiona."

Sophie put her hands behind her head and pulled her hair into three sections.

"You want me to braid it for you?" Genevieve said.

"Are you serious?" Sophie said.

"Sure," she answered. "You have great hair." Genevieve went into the small bathroom around the corner and came out with a comb and a ponytail holder. She pulled up a chair behind Sophie and started in.

"It does kind of feel like we're, like, stuck," Sophie said.

"You don't do meltdowns, do you?" Genevieve said. "I don't either."

"Nuh-uh. I mostly get into a daydream so I don't have to think about it. Only—that's not working so good lately."

"It's tough to dream your way out of something like this."

Sophie could feel the comb making even panels of hair, and Genevieve pulling them tight in a way that felt firm and neat.

"I could always do it before, no matter what was wrong," Sophie said.

"It's scary when it doesn't work, isn't it?"

"You think?" Sophie picked up the ponytail holder from the table and stretched it in and out with her fingers. "I promised Dr. Peter I would imagine Jesus every day, but I'm scared to do that too. I know that's lame, but—"

"It doesn't sound lame at all. He might end up telling you something you don't want to hear."

"That's totally it!" Sophie said. "Because then I'd have to do whatever he showed me to do, and if it's something like—well, I don't know—like, if it's hard, I don't know if I can do it. Dr. Peter said it might actually hurt."

Genevieve was quiet for a moment. Sophie could feel her getting farther down the braid.

*Now she probably thinks I'm a loser*, Sophie thought. *There probably isn't anything she thinks is too hard. She tamed Izzy and Rory, didn't she? They're in bed this very minute.*

"Remember my telling you about my grandmother?" Genevieve said.

"Hello? We made our whole film script about her!"

"You might want to put this in then." Genevieve held her hand out for the ponytail holder and snapped it into place. Sophie got up on her knees in her chair to face her.

Genevieve looked over Sophie's head as if she were seeing her old grandmother right there in the air. "Every time I had a problem I didn't think I could face, she'd say"—Genevieve shifted into a French accent—"'Gennie, as long as you do what God tells you to do in love, it won't be impossible. It might be difficult, but it won't be impossible.'"

Genevieve pulled her eyes back to Sophie with the memory still shining in them. "She said it in French, of course. It loses something in the translation—it was so beautiful. Anyway—she was right. It's gotten me through some really tough times."

Sophie stroked her new braid. "I didn't think anything was hard for you."

Genevieve grinned. "That's FUNNY. Everybody gets something that's too hard for them. Otherwise, why would we need God?"

"Oh," Sophie said.

The doorbell rang, and Sophie heard Fiona's bare feet slapping on the ceramic tile.

"That's probably Darbie," Sophie said.

"Let the games begin," Genevieve said. "I'll bring you guys some smoothies."

Sophie went for the door, and then she stopped. "I like talking to you," she said.

Genevieve nodded the way one grown-up nodded to another.

"I totally feel the same way," she said.

Sophie, Darbie, and Fiona managed to find things to do—like painting designs on each other's toenails and drinking smoothies with Genevieve and braiding each other's hair. Darbie's was too short for a French braid, so they put hers in tiny ones all over her head. The effect was good for fifteen minutes of giggling. There was no evidence of Fiona's meltdown.

But when Sophie woke up in the middle of the night, Fiona wasn't laughing. She was sobbing into her pillow.

Sophie sat straight up in bed, heartbeat throbbing in her neck. "What's wrong?" she said. "Fiona?"

"I don't want to go, Soph," she said in a broken voice. "I don't want to go to camp."

Sophie scooted closer so she wouldn't wake up Darbie, who was conked out on the other side of her in Fiona's king-size bed.

"Is camp heinous?" Sophie said.

"No. I just can't leave you—and Darbie—and Kitty. You guys need me. I'm the one who makes you see that Kitty's gonna be okay. Without me, you'll believe every worst-case scenario my mother tells you."

Sophie squeezed Fiona's hand. "I promise I won't." She glanced over her shoulder at the sleeping Darbie. "And you don't have to worry about her. Aunt Emily probably won't even let her near your mom."

"Pinky promise?" Fiona said.

She crooked her little finger, and Sophie hooked hers with it.

"I take the solemn oath of the Corn Flakes," she said.

Fiona sighed, and in another minute she was asleep. Sophie closed her eyes. All she could see was Kitty, who had nobody to link pinkies with.

Fiona left for camp the following Monday. Sophie guessed that all the meltdowns in the world weren't going to change the Buntings' minds. With Fiona gone—and Maggie, and Kitty, and Willoughby gone too—Darbie and Sophie clung together. They sat glumly at each other's houses, staring at movies they'd already seen and lying on blankets in their backyards, flipping aimlessly through books and turning down every offer Aunt Emily made for yet another day-trip. Sophie was pretty sure she would have offered to fly them to Hawaii if the idea appealed to them.

It didn't.

By the Wednesday after Fiona left, Aunt Emily insisted that Darbie go to Richmond with her for the day.

"She thinks Darbie needs a change of scene," Mama told Sophie the night before.

"I think she needs to talk about Kitty," Sophie said. "Like we do here. It's scarier when you don't talk about it. Everything gets all weird in your mind."

Daddy muted the baseball game on the TV.

*Uh-oh*, Sophie thought. *This is serious*.

"That makes good sense, Soph," he said. "When did you get to be so smart?"

Even *that* coming from her father didn't do much to cheer Sophie up. She didn't feel smart. She just felt lonely — lonelier than she had in a whole year.

# Eight

Sophie was so desperate the next morning that she decided to clean up her room. She was hanging up the dress she'd worn to church two Sundays before when she felt something crinkle in the pocket. She knew before she pulled it out that it was the piece of paper from Dr. Peter's lily pad with the verse for a Bible story written on it.

She felt a guilty pang.

*I promised him,* she thought. *Dr. Peter will be coming back and I haven't done anything I told him I'd do.*

So she pulled out her Bible and settled herself on the floor, where the sun made a square on the rug, and leaned against her bed facing the window. "Luke 5:1–11," the paper read. She thumbed through the thin, tissue-like pages.

There was Dr. Peter's handwriting in front of her, almost like he himself was waiting. No way was she going to disappoint him. He had taught the Girls Group to read the Scripture as if they were actually in each story. Sophie skimmed through the verses and decided that she needed to imagine herself as Simon Peter, even though she was a girl. She knew it wouldn't work if she didn't jump right in the middle of things.

Puffing her chest out to get the feel of big fisherman's muscles, she read out loud.

"'One day as Jesus was standing by the Lake of'—some huge word—'with the people crowding around him and listening to the word of God, he saw at the water's edge two boats, left there by the fishermen, who were washing their nets. He got into one of the boats, the one belonging to Simon, and asked him to put out a little from the shore.'"

*This is where I come in*, Sophie thought. She drew in a breath and could almost smell the fish-scents, just like at Virginia Beach when they went to get crabs at the fish market. She tried to see herself as Simon, pulling his wet fishing nets from the water to help Jesus. In her mind, Sophie/Simon let the boat drift away from shore.

"'Then he'—Jesus—'sat down and taught the people from the boat.'"

Sophie squeezed her eyes shut tighter. Sophie/Simon's heart would be beating really fast, and his hands would get sweaty—right there next to the real-live Jesus.

"'When he had finished speaking, he said to Simon, "Put out into deep water, and let down the nets for a catch."'"

Simon/Sophie wanted to roll his eyes, but he couldn't—not in front of this man. He had a feeling you just didn't do that. Sophie read Simon's answer to Jesus out loud: "'Master, we've worked hard all night and haven't caught anything.'"

And then his heart almost stopped and something took over his words as if it were somebody else talking. "But because you say so, I will let down the nets."

Sophie was almost sweating herself as she imagined Simon nodding to the other fishermen. They probably grumbled that they'd been fishing all day without catching anything—that it would take a miracle. Or a new career. Sophie answered them herself. "Get over yourselves. He said do it—so do it."

She continued to read the Bible. "'When they had done so, they caught such a large number of fish that their nets began to break. So they signaled their partners in the other boat to come and help them, and they came and filled both boats so full that they began to sink.'"

Simon/Sophie was shouting orders until his throat went hoarse, telling the other fishermen to grab on and get the catch to shore. He had never seen so many fish, all silvery and slithery and flipping over and under one another. He hadn't known there were that many in the whole lake—maybe even in the whole ocean.

"'When Simon Peter saw this,'" Sophie read, "'he fell at Jesus' knees and said, "Go away from me, Lord; I am a sinful man!"'"

*Don't send him away!* Sophie wanted to shout—until she remembered she was supposed to *be* him. She held her breath as she read on.

"'Then Jesus said to Simon, "Don't be afraid; from now on you will catch men." So they pulled their boats up on shore, left everything and followed him.'"

Sophie closed the Bible on her lap, but she kept her eyes closed. The sun turned the darkness behind her eyelids red.

*I would've gone too*, she thought. *I imagine Jesus' eyes all the time, and I'd go anywhere if I could see him in PERSON. Simon was right there WITH him, for real—of course he went.*

Who wanted a fishing business anyway? She was supposed to do whatever Jesus told her to do. Would it really be *that* hard? Obviously he'd give her everything she needed to do it. Simon had enough fish there to sell and keep his family going for a couple of years.

"Okay!" Sophie said. "I'm getting it."

"Hey, Soph," Lacie called from her room. "Are you hogging the phone again?"

"No!" Sophie said.

"Then who are you talking to?"

"Dr. Peter," Sophie said.

"Oh—naturally—silly me."

Sophie waited for Lacie to yell to Mama that Sophie was finally losing it, but she didn't.

*I totally get it,* Sophie told Dr. Peter, in her mind this time. *I'm not gonna wait and do a bunch of other stuff if Jesus says to follow him right now.*

Something told Sophie to imagine Simon again, standing there with all the fish he'd ever imagined he could catch, and then some. She imagined how he felt when Jesus said, "Okay, now leave it all here and come with me."

And Simon did.

*Yikes!* Sophie thought. *I wonder how HIS kids felt when they found out he'd just LEFT. What were THEY supposed to do with all those fish?*

She put the Bible away and plopped down in the middle of the bed where all the clothes she'd planned to put away were piled. She stuck her swimsuit bottoms on her head, just because.

What *would* Dr. Peter say if she could talk to him?

Sophie grunted. That was easy. He'd tell her to ask Jesus to show her what it meant, and then wait.

*I'm sick of waiting,* she grumbled to herself.

But she did it anyway. And she prayed.

*Whatever I'm supposed to do for Kitty, I'll do it,* she told his kind eyes, *even if I have to leave—well, not fish, because I don't even have any—but I'll leave everything you want me to if it'll help Kitty.*

She kind of hoped he'd ask her to leave middle school before it even started or run away from the Corn Pops or something like that, but that wasn't much of a sacrifice. Okay, so it wasn't a sacrifice at all.

Besides, how was that going to help Kitty? Sophie decided it was a good thing she didn't have to figure out what *would* help her on her own, because nobody was telling her what Kitty needed. Nobody was saying *anything* about Kitty.

The day was promising to drag itself right into a pit when Mama poked her head in the doorway to hand her the phone. She looked straight at the swimsuit bottoms on Sophie's head but she didn't say anything.

When Sophie heard Willoughby's voice on the other end of the phone line, she squealed.

Willoughby was there in ten minutes. Sophie remembered to pull off her headdress before Willoughby arrived. Then it took twenty more minutes to fill her in on everything that had happened while she was away. The more Sophie told her, the bigger Willoughby's hazel eyes grew, but everything else on her seemed to be shrinking. By the time Sophie was finished, even Willoughby's short, nut-brown curls were drooping.

"I can't BELIEVE this is happening to Kitty. I bet she's crying every minute." Willoughby nodded wisely. "She's always been a crier—and a whiner—but I love her anyway."

"We ALL do," Sophie said. "It's driving me nuts not being able to do anything to help her. I just sit here."

Willoughby got up from Sophie's bed and crossed to the dresser where she picked up Sophie's brush. She perched on the pile of pillows behind Sophie and went to work, pulling the brush through Sophie's hair.

"Everybody wants to do my hair all of a sudden," Sophie said.

"That's because your hair is super thick," Willoughby said. "I KNOW it's gotten thicker while I was gone."

"Nuh-uh!"

"Yuh-huh! If there's anything I know, it's hair. My aunt's a stylist. She owns her own shop."

"Are you serious?"

"She goes to hair shows all the time and comes back with all these killer styles she can do. Too bad I have such lame hair."

"I like your hair!" Sophie said.

"Julia and them never thought so. They were always calling me 'Poodle' and some other names I won't even tell you."

Sophie tried to turn to look at Willoughby, but she had a firm grip on Sophie's hair so she couldn't move her head.

"And they were supposed to be your friends?" Sophie said.

"They just kept me around so they could pick on me," Willoughby said. "Only I never saw that until you guys came along. Being a Corn Flake has, like, saved my life." She giggled. "I love that name—the Corn Flakes. I'm gonna put your hair in all small braids and then put them up in a bun. It'll be cool."

Sophie settled in for what sounded like it was going to take all afternoon. She couldn't help thinking about what the Bible was telling her to do. Arranging her next words carefully, she said, "Do you go to church?"

"We used to when I was little, before my parents got divorced," Willoughby said. "Then my dad stopped taking us because he said he could barely get us all out the door for school five days a week, much less on Sundays too."

"You live with your dad all the time?" Sophie said.

"Yeah, my mom left town," Willoughby said—as if she were merely pointing out that someone had left the room. "You have any bobby pins?"

"I have clips in that box on my dresser," Sophie said.

"Hold this." Willoughby handed her the end of a long, thin braid and stretched for the dresser.

"Do you still believe in God?" Sophie said when she was back to the job.

"Are you kidding me? I pray every night. Tonight I'm gonna pray for Kitty, like, big-time." And then Willoughby giggled, for no apparent reason, which was one of the things she did a lot. Sophie always thought it was the way a poodle might laugh—but she didn't say it. She didn't want Willoughby to think she was like the Corn Pops.

"I'm praying for her too," Sophie said. "I just want to know what she needs so I can do it for her."

"Why don't you ask her?" Willoughby said. Sophie could tell she had several of the clips pressed between her lips.

"She's having her chemotherapy right now, so she's probably really sick. Mama says Dr. Bunting—you know, Fiona's mom—will let us know when it's okay to call her. Except I promised Fiona I wouldn't really listen to her mom, because she always tells us the worst thing that could happen."

"So we could write Kitty a letter," Willoughby said. "This is going to be so cute."

"The letter?" Sophie said.

"No, your hair." Willoughby giggled again.

"You mean, just write to her and ask her to, like, make a list of everything she needs?"

"Why not? My dad always says—" Willoughby made her voice go low and man-like—"'How are you ever going to find out anything if you don't ask questions?'" She went back to her own bubbling tone. "That's why I always ask so many. Julia hated that. She was always telling me to shut up."

"Stop for a second while I get some paper," Sophie said.

She wrote the letter to Kitty while Willoughby finished her hair creation. When they took the letter downstairs to show Mama, she stopped the mixer and stared at Sophie.

"Oh, my Dream Girl," she said. "You look so grown up."

Her eyes turned down at the corners, and for a moment Sophie was afraid she was going to start crying, right in front of Willoughby. She got even more afraid when Mama read their letter, and her eyes got all swimmy.

When Mama finished it though, Sophie saw her swallow a couple of times before she looked up at them. No tears.

"So—can I have a stamp so we can send it to her?" Sophie said.

Mama shook her head, and Sophie's heart started a downward plunge.

"Let's not send it," Mama said.

"But Mo-om—"

"Let's take it over to her house. This is the kind of thing her parents will want to deliver right into her hands."

# Nine

❋ ⌂ ◉

Before Mama took Sophie and Willoughby over to the Munfords' that night, Lacie wrote a Bible verse on paper for Kitty and decorated it, even though Sophie told her Kitty had never read the Bible. Zeke made a picture to put in the envelope too. It was a purple dinosaur, which was Zeke's specialty at the moment, but he assured Sophie that Kitty was really going to like it.

Armed with a fat packet, they drove to Kitty's house. Sophie had never been there before, and she didn't expect what she saw when they walked in the back door.

"This is a zoo," Willoughby whispered to her.

Four of Kitty's five older sisters were there, and Sophie wouldn't have been surprised if the other one was just lost in the chaos.

There were dishes overflowing the sink and nothing in the drawers or cabinets, which Sophie could tell because they all were hanging open. Clothes were piled up on the dining room table, although it was hard to say whether they all were clean, dirty, or some of both. The tangle of plants in the bay window looked like there was a drought going on.

Three of the girls—Sophie knew their names all started with *K*, but she didn't have a clue who was who—were lounging in the living room watching *Oprah* and passing around an almost-empty bag of sour-cream-and-onion potato chips. When the fourth K, who let Mama and Sophie and Darbie in, said, "We've got company," the rest of them startled up from their seats, and one of them even said, "It's not Dad, is it?"

When they saw that it wasn't, they assumed their previous positions and went back to *Oprah*.

"We're supposed to have the place cleaned up and dinner started before the Colonel gets home," said the girl who let them in.

Sophie had heard Kitty talk about her dad as "the Colonel." She'd also told them he'd had his promotion for six months before she learned that it wasn't spelled K-E-R-N-E-L.

"And you are?" Mama said to the sister who was actually speaking to them.

"I'm Kandy," she said.

"Nice to meet you, Kandy," Mama said. "The girls have written a letter to Kitty, and we thought someone could deliver it when they go to the hospital."

"Sure," Kandy said. "Kelly's going tomorrow—she can take it. Kelly! I'm putting this on the table! Take it to Kitty!"

"Uh-huh," Kelly said. She never took her eyes away from the television.

Sophie watched with horror as Kandy stuck their letter under a pair of jeans that was hanging off the end of the dining room table.

Mama watched her, and Sophie prayed that God would come down and sweep up the envelope and stick it back into Mama's hand—or at least that Mama would think of retrieving it herself.

Instead, Mama stepped farther into the living room and planted herself in front of the TV. Three pairs of glazed eyes came into focus on her.

"Ladies," Mama said in her soft voice, "I have met your father, and I have to say that I personally wouldn't want to be on the receiving end if he walked through that door right now."

"He'd definitely bust a blood vessel," said the K-girl in the reclining chair. "But we don't even know where to start. Mom does everything around here—"

"And now that she's at the hospital with Kitty all the time—" The one on the floor spread out her hands and shrugged.

"It just so happens that I know how to do this kind of thing," Mama said. She gave them her wispy smile. "So what do you say we get to it? I'll give the orders."

They all looked at her as if she couldn't order them out of a wet paper sack, but Sophie knew better. Within five minutes Mama had Kandy and Karen folding laundry, Kelly doing dishes, and Kayla helping her mix up a meat loaf. Mama even unearthed thirteen-year-old Kendra from a back bedroom and got her to start vacuuming. She sent Sophie and Willoughby into the living room to pick up all the clutter and dump it into a laundry basket.

Make that three laundry baskets.

"My dad would ground us forever if we let our house get this messy," Willoughby said, "and I've got two brothers."

By the time Colonel Munford got home, dinner was on the table instead of the laundry, which was neatly tucked into drawers, and the living room and kitchen were ready for military inspection—if he didn't look too close. Which he didn't.

Sophie watched Kitty's father glance around. He said, "Good job, girls," and leaned wearily against the wall, rubbing the top of his nearly shaved head.

"He doesn't look so tough to me," Willoughby whispered to Sophie.

All Sophie could do was stare. This couldn't be the same man who had carried Kitty out of the beach house. This guy was smaller and sort of scared-looking, and he didn't bark when he talked.

"I bet I have you to thank for this," he said to Mama.

"They did the work," Mama said.

"I can't tell you how much I appreciate it."

Then he didn't say anything else. It looked like it was just too hard to move his mouth.

"How's our Kitty?" Mama said.

He rubbed his head again. "She's pretty sick. My wife won't even leave her room."

Sophie and Willoughby clenched hands.

"They brought a note for her," Kelly said. "I'm taking it to her tomorrow."

"That's nice," Colonel Munford said. "That's really nice."

Mama nodded, lips pressed together. Then she said, "How about if I come by tomorrow and show the girls how to keep the place going? That will be one thing off your mind."

"You don't have to."

"I know—but I want to." Mama blinked several times. "I love Kitty. It's the least I can do."

The Colonel turned to Mama and engulfed her tiny elfin hands in his. Sophie and Willoughby mumbled their good-byes and backed out the door before the adults could start breaking down and leave nobody knowing what to do. Sophie didn't have much confidence in the K's.

"How come they just sit around and don't clean up?" Sophie said on the way home. "I don't get that."

"I have a theory," Mama said. "Maybe if they just stare at the TV they won't think about their sister. If they do something that doesn't really require them to concentrate, they probably imagine all kinds of things."

"I guess you don't have to concentrate too hard when you're dumping out the trash," Willoughby said with the usual giggle.

"I do know one thing for sure though," Mama said. "It's obvious they need a lot of help, and I want to do everything I can for them." She glanced over at Sophie in the seat next to her. "Okay—no more trying to distract you. I understand what Aunt Emily has to do for Darbie, but I'm going to let you help as much as you want to. That's the only healthy way you're going to get through this."

Sophie nodded several times. Maybe Jesus wasn't going to ask her to do something that hard after all.

Over the next four days, everybody got focused on "Mission: Kitty." Lacie got the high school youth group together to mow the Munfords' lawn and wash their cars. They even had a pizza party for the five K's.

"Ken said the girls had a great time last night," Mama told Lacie the next morning.

"Who's Ken?" Sophie said.

"Kitty's father."

Lacie stopped eating her cereal with the spoon in front of her mouth. "Please tell me their mom's name isn't Katie or something."

"Michelle," Mama said.

"That's sad," Sophie said. "I bet she feels left out."

Mama grinned in Lacie's direction "I don't think so. Kendra told me all their middle names start with *M*."

"Don't take me there," Lacie said.

Daddy made up a spreadsheet on his computer so the K's would have a chore schedule. Mama spent two days helping them get rolling with it. She reported that they all fell in love with Zeke, who went with her.

"They'll get over it," Lacie said, and kissed Zeke on the nose.

Mama also made up a bunch of meals the K-girls could pull out of the freezer and warm up for suppers. The best part of that for Sophie and Willoughby was that she got Aunt Emily to come over and help. So they got to be with Darbie again.

After Aunt Emily made Darbie promise she would let her know if she started to get upset, Sophie, Darbie, and Willoughby escaped to Sophie's room to decide what *they* could do for Kitty—since she hadn't sent them her list yet.

"I know what I want to do for her," Willoughby said. "I've wanted to do it ever since I first saw you guys out on the playground."

"And that is ...," Darbie said.

"I want to make a movie."

Darbie hooked her hair behind her ears. "We can't do the Nazis," she said. "Aunt Emily would put me in solitary confinement!"

Willoughby shook the curls that sprang out from the edges of the bandana she had tied around her head. Only Willoughby could look good in something like that, Sophie decided.

"No," she said, "let's make a movie about all the things Kitty is missing—you know—us."

"I love it," Darbie said. "Don't you love it, Sophie?"

Sophie was already pulling her camera off the bookshelf.

Before they started, Willoughby did everyone's hair and went through Sophie's closet and drawers to put together out-fits that would, as she put it, work for the camera.

"There's still a bit of the Corn Pop in you," Darbie said as Willoughby tied the sleeves of one of Sophie's hooded sweatshirts around her neck, because tall Darbie couldn't actually fit into any of Sophie's tiny tops.

"My dad says there's nothing wrong with looking your best as long as it's not all you think about," Willoughby said. "THAT would be the Corn Pops."

When they all met with Willoughby's approval, they set out to shoot. Corn Flakes piled on the bed. Corn Flakes in a circle on a blanket in the backyard discussing stuff. Corn Flakes making lasagna for the K-crew. But a lot of what they wanted to do was impossible because they didn't have Maggie or Fiona.

*I just hope they aren't having too heinous of a time*, Sophie thought.

But she knew nobody was having as heinous a go of it as Kitty. No matter how good it felt to be finally doing something for her, Sophie was still flattened by sadness when she crawled into bed that night. She closed her eyes and brought Jesus into view.

*I mean it*, she prayed to him, *no matter how hard it is, I will do anything you want me to for Kitty. It doesn't feel like what I'm doing is hard enough.*

Usually it took at least a few days for Sophie to see an answer when she really, really asked Jesus a question. But the very next morning, she woke up to what seemed to be the very thing she was asking for.

There was an envelope next to her cereal bowl when Sophie climbed onto the snack bar stool. It had her name on it, but she didn't recognize the handwriting.

"The Colonel dropped it off on his way to the base," Mama said. "It's from Kitty."

Mystified, Sophie tore open the envelope and unfolded the paper.

*Sophie*, it said, *I'm Sebastian, writing exactly what Kitty tells me to. She makes me wait on her hand and foot.*

Sophie felt herself grinning. She could *clearly* imagine Kitty beaming her dimples at the cute nurse while he took dictation with the pink gel pen.

Sebastian's note from Kitty was a numbered list of only five things:

*1. I need more letters from Corn Flakes. I can tape them to my walls.*

"We'll write every single day," Sophie said. "Maybe twice a day."

*2. I need to see my Corn Flakes. I can't have visitors right now because I might get germs — like you guys actually have any! Hello? I might go mental if I don't get to see you SOON. (Sebastian says I already am.)*

Sophie smiled at the paper. The film was going to be *perfect* for that.

*3. I need some school clothes. My mom keeps telling me not to worry about stuff like that because I might not be well enough to start school, but if I don't think about clothes then I'll worry too much about what's gonna happen to me next. (Sebastian says to PLEASE bring me some clothes because he's tired of hearing about it.)*

Sophie paused on that one. She didn't exactly have the money to go to the mall and buy Kitty a new wardrobe. She and the Corn Flakes would figure something out. So far this was actually pretty easy. But that thought popped like a soda bubble when Sophie read the next item.

*4. I want to talk to Dr. Amy again — you know, Fiona's mom. She explains things better than anybody. (Sebastian says what is he, chopped liver?) My mom says I shouldn't bother her because*

*Dr. Amy is way busy—but would you ask her to call me? She's really nice—I know she'll do it if she knows I HAVE to talk to her.*

Sophie put the paper down and swung her legs. *I can't tell Fiona's mom to call her,* she thought. *I promised Fiona we wouldn't listen to her mom tell the worst things that could happen.*

She propped her cheeks on her hands with her elbows on the counter and pretended to study the list. But all she could see was Fiona having a meltdown. But a worse image was listening to Dr. Bunting tell Kitty—whatever it was she might say. In that image, *Kitty* was having a meltdown.

Sophie knew she would scratch that item off with a Sharpie if she didn't move on down the list.

*5. I need some hair—and not a wig, because they look fake. Mine is already falling out. Sebastian says I look cute, but he's just being nice. I look heinous. (Sebastian asked me how to spell that. Like I KNOW! I wish Fiona were here. I wish all of you were here. I love you. I miss you.)*

At the bottom, Kitty had signed her own name. The letters were bravely rounded, and she had put a wobbly heart for the dot. Sophie looked at it until she couldn't see it for the tears.

*Why did you put those last two on there, Kitty?* Sophie thought. *One's too hard, and the other one's impossible. I can't do this.*

She closed her eyes to stop the tears before they splashed into her Cheerios. And there was Jesus, right where she'd left him—when she'd said no matter how hard it was that she would do whatever he said.

"Is that Kitty's list?" Mama said. She poured apple juice into Sophie's glass.

"Yes," Sophie said. "And I have to find a way to give her everything on it."

# Ten

The first two needs on Kitty's list were easy to meet, just as Sophie had thought — especially since, when she and Darbie got to church on Sunday, Maggie was there waiting for them.

"Mags!" Sophie cried and threw her arms around her.

Maggie hugged her back, and Sophie knew she had missed her. Maggie didn't hug that much.

"Get your brain ready, Maggie," Darbie said, "because we have loads to tell you."

That very afternoon they met at Sophie's — Willoughby too — and wrote letters to Kitty so whichever K-sister was going to Portsmouth the next day could take them. They each wrote another one to be opened the next day after that. By the time they were finished, they'd practically used up Sophie's entire supply of stickers and every color of her gel pens.

Then, of course, they added to the *Mission: Kitty* film — *after* Willoughby did her makeover magic on Maggie. That gave Sophie what Fiona would call a "scathingly brilliant idea."

"I know how we can get Kitty some school clothes!" she said.

"Fiona's not here, Sophie," Darbie said. "And I don't think her dad's going to give us his credit card."

"No!" Sophie said. "Willoughby could do some outfits for Kitty using some of OUR clothes."

It took a minute for that to settle in. Then everyone talked at once.

"Aunt Emily is about to give away the things I just grew out of."

"I have stuff I NEVER wear."

"My mom will sew them so they'll fit Kitty."

Willoughby was already headed for Sophie's closet. "I'm going in!" she said.

By the next afternoon, after Darbie, Willoughby, and Maggie had brought over whatever their parents would let them part with, and Willoughby had put together outfits that they were sure would make the Corn Pops drool, the first three items on Kitty's list were checked off.

When they were gone, Sophie sat staring at the fourth request. Kitty wanted to talk to "Dr. Amy."

*I promised Fiona*, she thought. *But I promised Jesus too.*

Fiona. God. It wasn't like there was a real choice to make. But Sophie gave it one last prayer try.

*Jesus, could you just pop Fiona right down here in front of me, so I can at least explain to her?*

She even waited five minutes. Fiona did not fall from the sky. Sophie dialed the phone.

"Bunting residence, Genevieve speaking," said the smooth voice on the other end.

"Hi, this is Sophie."

"Sophie! How nice to hear your voice!"

Sophie sagged onto the step, where she sat with the phone. "How nice to hear yours too."

"I was going to call YOU tonight. I have a message for you from Fiona."

"Is she okay?" Sophie said.

"If 'okay' means she's so miserable she didn't even use any three-syllable words on the phone—sure—she's okay."

"No," Sophie said, "she's wretched."

Genevieve gave an agreeing murmur. "Any messages for her from you?"

"Tell her I miss her so much I'm going off my nut," Sophie said.

"Done. What else you got?"

Sophie squeezed the phone. She could just hang up now.

*I could also, like, die of a guilty conscience,* she thought.

"I need to talk to Dr. Bunting," she said.

Genevieve laughed softly. "Did you really think she was HERE?"

"Oh," Sophie said. "Duh."

"I could give her a message for you."

Sophie sucked in her breath. This could be the perfect solution. If she had Genevieve tell Dr. Bunting that Kitty wanted to talk to her, Fiona might not be so mad at her.

"Could you just tell her—"

Sophie got a sudden picture of Genevieve taking down her message on the official pad in the kitchen—and Dr. Bunting putting it into a pocket with all the rest of her messages—and getting to it somewhere between operations—

" 'Tell her—,' " Genevieve said.

"Could you just ask her to call me REALLY soon?" Sophie said. "It's about Kitty—and it's really, really important."

"I'll write URGENT on it," Genevieve said. "And I'll make sure she gets it as soon as she gets home." Sophie could almost see Genevieve smiling. "If she gets in at three o'clock in the morning, do you mind if I give it to her tomorrow?"

"That's fine," Sophie said. "I don't think my parents would like it if she called in the middle of the night."

"Probably not."

"Well—thanks," Sophie said.

"Sophie?" Genevieve said.

"Yeah?"

"I miss you. Maybe I'll bring Izzy and Rory over to play with Zeke if it's okay with your mom. Then you and I can talk."

"That would be great!" Sophie said.

When they hung up, Sophie didn't know whether to feel better because Genevieve might come over and make everything fall into the place where it was supposed to be, or to go nuts every time the phone rang after that because it might be Dr. Bunting calling.

She was lying across her bed with her head hanging upside down when Lacie came in.

"I don't even want to know," Lacie said.

"Fiona told me one time that if you let all the blood go to your head, you can think better," Sophie said.

"Is it working?" Lacie said.

"I don't know yet."

Lacie climbed up beside her and hung her own head over the side.

"All it's doing is giving me a headache," she said after a minute. She sat up, and Sophie rolled onto her side.

"What are you trying to think about?" Lacie said.

"Hair."

Lacie tugged at a piece of Sophie's. "You definitely have enough of it. Your hair's thicker than mine now."

"Not MY hair," Sophie said. "Kitty's."

"Is she losing hers already?"

Sophie nodded. "And I promised God—you know, Jesus—I'd get her anything she needed. And she says she needs hair—and she says a wig looks fake."

"She's right about that—unless it's a good one—and those are WAY expensive."

Sophie flopped her head down on the mattress. "If I could, I'd give her mine."

Lacie leaped off the bed and pulled open Sophie's desk drawer.

"What are you doing?" Sophie said.

"Looking for a ruler. Hang your head down again."

"Why?"

"Just do it. I'm gonna measure your hair."

Sophie flung her head over again, and Lacie got on her knees and went at it with the ruler. Then she rocked back and sat on her heels.

"I heard about this one thing, Soph," she said. "And I think you CAN give Kitty your hair."

"Are you serious?"

"Come on." Lacie grabbed Sophie's arm. "We have to get on the Net."

Daddy was alone in his study, the glare of the computer screen on his face, when the two of them skidded to a stop in the doorway.

"Uh-oh," he said. "How much is this going to cost me?"

"All we need is ten minutes on the Internet, Daddy," Lacie said.

"Now I KNOW it's going to cost me. Okay, what are we looking up?"

"I think it's called Love Locks or something like that."

Daddy leveled his blue eyes at Lacie. "LOVE Locks? You don't need to be looking at a dating service, Lacie."

"It's about HAIR, Daddy! It's Locks of Love—that's it."

He looked at both of them and then tapped his fingers on the keys. Sophie stared at the screen, her heart pounding. *She could actually give her hair to Kitty? How could that be?*

"Is this it?" Daddy said.

"Yes—that's totally it. Listen, Soph."

Lacie read from the screen about how Locks of Love took donations of hair and made them into beautiful, realistic wigs for people who were suffering from hair loss due to chemotherapy. The wigs, it said, were free to the patients.

"It says hair has to be at least ten inches long."

"How long is mine?" Sophie said.

"Ten inches from your chin to the ends. That would still leave you enough for a really cute bob or something."

Sophie looked at the pictures of the girls with their wigs that looked like their own hair. Their faces were puffy and some of them looked too old in their eyes. But they were all smiling, because they weren't bald.

"How old do you have to be to donate?" Sophie said.

"Scroll down, Daddy," Lacie said.

Daddy leaned the desk chair back and looked at Sophie.

"You really thinking about doing this, Soph?" he said.

"It's for Kitty," she said.

"Hair grows back, you know," he said.

"And mine grows really fast. It'll be long again before seventh grade's over."

"I was talking about Kitty's hair," Daddy said.

Then he turned back to the computer and scrolled down. Sophie thought his eyes looked wet.

"Okay," he said. "Looks like you made the team." He shook his head. "Now all we have to do is convince your mother."

Lacie and Sophie slept on the couch in the family room so they could catch Mama the minute she and Daddy went to the kitchen the next morning. From the way Mama was grinding the coffee beans until they were probably in a fine powder, Sophie could tell Daddy had told her about Locks of Love.

Lacie opened her mouth, a plea already outlined in her eyes as far as Sophie could tell, but Daddy shook his head at them and nodded at the snack bar stools. They climbed onto them, Sophie tucking her legs under her so she'd be high enough to beg Mama straight in the eyes if it came to that. It looked like it was going to.

Mama poured the water into the coffeepot, pushed bread into the toaster, and pulled out a frying pan. Sophie thought she would go *nuts* waiting. Still Daddy shook his head at them and calmly poured himself a glass of orange juice.

Just when Sophie could hardly stand it another minute — and Lacie had her place mat rolled into a tight scroll — Mama came over to the counter with a package of bacon and cut it open while she talked.

"I'm proud of you for thinking of this, Dream Girl," she said. "But cutting all your hair off isn't going to make Kitty better — you know that, don't you?"

"She isn't doing it to make Kitty well, Mama," Lacie said. "She's — "

Mama lifted her eyes to Lacie. "Was I talking to you?"

A chill went through Sophie. Mama never used that tone unless one of them told somebody to shut up or called someone a pig-face or something. Lacie looked at Daddy like she expected him to rescue her. He just put his finger to his lips.

Sophie wanted to pull her hair into a mustache, but she didn't. She had to be clear about this.

"I know it isn't gonna cure her leukemia," Sophie said. "But it WILL make her feel better. I don't even like thinking about her starting middle school with a bald head."

"Senora LaQuita is making her some adorable hats," Mama said.

"WHICH some idiot is going to snatch off her head first chance they get," Lacie said. And then she clapped both hands over her mouth and said between her fingers, "Sorry."

"It's true, Mama," Sophie said. "And Kitty's parents won't have to pay for it if Locks of Love makes a wig out of MY hair. And it'll be real hair and she won't feel like a freak. She just wants to feel like she's normal."

Mama stopped flopping bacon strips into the frying pan and looked up at Sophie again. She looked like she had a heinous headache.

"I think you've done enough for a twelve-year-old," she said. "I'm so proud that you have a heart so big that you want to do everything—but this is an adult decision."

Sophie swallowed hard. She knew what she had to say, but getting it to come out of her mouth was a whole other thing. Across the kitchen, behind Mama, Daddy was nodding at her.

"Actually, Mama," she said, "and I'm not being disrespectful—but it's a God decision. I promised him I would do whatever he asked me to do, no matter how hard it was. So I HAVE to do it."

"But how do you know God is asking you to do this?"

"It was on Kitty's list. She said she wanted hair. I'm doing everything else—I have to do this one thing too."

For the first time, Mama looked around at Daddy. He looked back over his juice glass.

"God didn't write that list," Mama said. "Kitty did."

Sophie felt her heart plunging right down to the pit of her stomach, where it made a hard knot. An almost-angry knot. Lacie patted Sophie's leg under the counter and then raised her hand.

"Can I just say one thing?" Lacie said.

"Go for it," Daddy said, before Mama could answer.

"There isn't anything on that list that goes against what God says in the Bible," Lacie said. "And after all, it's just hair."

"It'll grow back," Daddy said. His lips twitched. "It grows way fast."

Mama looked at Sophie, and the tears came. "Your beautiful hair," she said.

"She'll look really cute with short hair, Mama," Lacie said.

"Willoughby's aunt can cut it," Sophie said.

Mama closed her eyes and nodded.

# Eleven

Sophie could hardly breathe. "So are you telling me that I can do it, Mama?" she said.

Mama nodded again. The bacon sizzled and popped below her.

"I'm calling Willoughby!" Sophie said, sliding off the stool.

"Uh, Soph," Daddy said. "It's six o'clock in the morning. You might want to cut her a little slack."

Sophie thought she would go mental before Mama finally said it was a reasonable hour. Willoughby gave a couple of poodle shrieks and said she could already imagine how her aunt Heather would fix Sophie's hair. She called back ten minutes later and said Sophie was on for one o'clock that afternoon.

That gave Sophie plenty of time to gather Darbie and Maggie. And plenty of time to stand in front of the mirror and imagine herself without the acorn-colored hair draped across her shoulders. She pulled it all up in the back and tried to loop it so that it was just chin length.

*You have great hair*, she could hear Genevieve say.

*Your hair is super thick*, Willoughby said in her memory. *I can do all kinds of cool things with it.*

*Your hair's thicker than mine now,* Lacie seemed to whisper in her ear.

Sophie stared at her reflection, but she couldn't see a chin-length bob. The mirror was a blur.

Sophie closed her eyes and imagined Kitty walking into Great Marsh Middle School wearing a newsboy cap to match her Willoughby-designed outfit—and B.J. cruising past and plucking it off her head, with Julia and Anne-Stuart screaming, "Gross!" until the entire seventh-grade class joined them in a chant.

Sophie shook away the tears and realized she was holding a strand of hair under her nose like a mustache.

"I won't be able to do THIS anymore," she said to her mirror-self. "And that's okay—because I'm not confused."

So with her Corn Flakes on each side of the stylist's chair—except Fiona and Kitty, of course—Sophie watched Willoughby's aunt Heather cut straight through the perfect thick braid Mama had made, place it on the counter, and transform her into someone she barely recognized. When Aunt Heather was through trimming and blow-drying and curling, they all gazed with her into the mirror.

"You're as precious as you can possibly be," Aunt Heather said.

"You look so much OLDER," Mama said.

"I can't wait to try different stuff with it," Willoughby said.

"This is CLASS," Darbie said.

"I liked it better before," Maggie said.

When they all glared at Maggie, she said, "Kitty will look good in it though."

Aunt Heather placed the cut-off braid in a plastic bag and then in the padded envelope Mama had brought, just like it said on the Locks of Love website, just the way the actual person had told Mama on the phone that morning. The person

228

on the phone had also told Mama that the majority of all hair donated came from children who wanted to help other children. Mama had cried again.

But she wasn't crying now. She looked like she was so proud she could have made an announcement on the six o'clock news. She did the next best thing and took them all to Dairy Queen after she put Sophie's hair in the mail.

Sophie spent the rest of the afternoon trying not to look at herself in the mirror every ten seconds. When Daddy got home, he looked at her from all sides and said, "Looking sharp, Soph. Looking real sharp."

"She doesn't look 'sharp,'" Lacie said. "She looks fabulous."

That might have been the best compliment of all.

The phone rang right after supper, and it was Genevieve for Sophie.

"I have the evening off," she said. "I thought I'd come over and see you, if that's okay."

"It's MORE than okay," Sophie said. It was all she could do not to tell Genevieve about her haircut. She wanted to see the look on her face when she saw her.

But it wasn't Genevieve's face Sophie saw when she opened the front door. It was Fiona's. They both screamed at the same time, bringing the entire rest of the LaCroix family running.

"Fiona!" Mama said. "You're home early!"

"They couldn't stand her at camp any longer," Genevieve said behind her. "I had to go get her today."

Sophie flung her arms around Fiona's neck. Fiona put her hands on Sophie's shoulders and held her out at arm's length.

"What did you do to your hair?" she said.

Sophie twirled around. She'd figured out that it felt cool to have her hair swing and bounce around her face. "Do you like it?" she said.

Fiona gave a slow nod. "I think so. I have to get used to it."

"I have SO much to tell you," Sophie said. She turned to Mama. "Can we go up to my room?"

"Like we could stop you," Daddy said on his way back to his study.

Genevieve held up Fiona's backpack. "We brought this just in case."

"You don't even need to ask," Mama said. "I'm going to make some welcome-home—something."

In seconds they were both on Sophie's bed talking over each other.

"I can't believe you're HOME—"

"I was totally DESPONDENT—they had to let me—"

"SO much stuff has happened—"

"Like you making a honking-huge decision without ME."

Sophie stumbled over her own next sentence. "You mean my hair?" she said.

"Well, yeah. Don't we usually discuss major stuff like that?"

"But wait till you hear why I did it," Sophie said.

She told Fiona *some* of the things that were on Kitty's list and *all* about Locks of Love and how she'd had to turn inside out to convince Mama and how Daddy *and* Lacie had stood behind her. When she was done, Fiona still had her arms folded.

"I thought you'd think it was awesome," Sophie said. "It's for Kitty!"

"Kitty's hair is gonna grow back as soon as she goes into remission," Fiona said. "Which is probably going to be any day now."

"I thought it was going to take at least a year."

Fiona finally smiled. "Since when did Kitty ever follow the rules?"

Sophie waited for the Fiona pump-up that always happened when Fiona put things in their right places. But Sophie didn't feel all-of-a-sudden hopeful. She felt a little annoyed.

"I don't think she gets to decide," Sophie said. "Even SHE knows it's going to take a long time."

Fiona tossed her head. "Only because people have been telling her that," she said. "That's one of the reasons I couldn't stand being away at camp. SOMEBODY has to tell Kitty not to listen to all these heinous predictions." She got up and pulled a pen out of the cup on Sophie's desk. "I have to get caught up with you guys on letters—I'm writing her one right now and telling her not to believe all that stuff. She's not as sick as they say she is. I know it."

"Fiona," Sophie said. "I have to tell you something else that was on Kitty's list."

There was a tap on the door. "Phone for you, Soph," Lacie said. She poked her head in and stuck the phone out toward Sophie. "It's Dr. Bunting. I thought she was calling for Fiona, but she said she wanted to talk to YOU. Go figure."

Sophie could hardly take the telephone from Lacie. When she did, her fingers were as stiff as claws around it.

"Why is my mom calling YOU?" Fiona said.

Sophie watched the door close behind Lacie. If she went out in the hall, Fiona would follow her. If she asked Dr. Bunting to call another time, she might not ever catch her again. And besides, Fiona would still ask eight thousand questions. There was nowhere to go and nothing else to do except what she had to do, what she'd promised Kitty—and God—she would do.

"Hello?" Fiona said to Sophie.

But Sophie put the receiver to her ear and said, "Hi."

"Genevieve gave me your message," Dr. Bunting said. "Sorry I haven't gotten back to you sooner. What's up?"

She sounded brisk, like she was already doing three other things, and Sophie was tempted to tell her it wasn't *that* important if she was too busy. But she took a deep breath and, under Fiona's bullet gaze, said, "Actually—I have a message for you from Kitty."

"Oh?" The three other things Dr. Bunting was doing seemed to stop. "What's going on?"

Sophie closed her eyes so she didn't have to look at Fiona. "She asked me to ask you to call her. She said you're really nice to her, and you explain things the way nobody else can."

"Ah. She has some questions then. Her mother said SHE was going to call me if Kitty needed me."

Sophie squeezed her eyes shut tighter. "She said her mom wouldn't because she thought you'd be too busy."

"Never too busy for this. I'll call her. Let's see—what time is it—it's not that late. I'll call her right now. Thanks, Sophie. Is my daughter over there driving your parents up a wall?"

"She's here," Sophie said slowly. "Do you want to talk to her?"

Dr. Bunting gave a short laugh. "Tell her she's busted for breaking out of camp early. No—don't tell her that. Put her on, would you?"

Keeping her eyes down, Sophie held the phone toward Fiona. "She wants to talk to you now."

"Well, I don't want to talk to HER," Fiona said.

Sophie put the phone back to her ear. "She said—"

"I heard." Dr. Bunting sighed. "All right, tell her we'll talk tomorrow."

She hung up. Sophie took her time doing the same.

"I wanted to tell you, like, right before she called," Sophie said. She still wasn't looking at Fiona.

"Sophie, how COULD you?" Fiona put her hand out and jerked Sophie's chin up. "You PROMISED me."

"But I promised God I would do anything he asked me to do—you know, through Jesus. I didn't know he was going to ask me to do THIS."

Fiona's face was almost purple. She paced the floor at the foot of the bed, waving the gel pen. "So your promise to GOD means more than your promise to ME."

Sophie blinked. "Well, yeah," she said.

The phone rang, but Sophie didn't pick it up. They could hear Mama talking downstairs and then hurrying up the steps. Fiona and Sophie were still staring at each other when Mama burst through the door, talking like she was out of breath.

"That was Dr. Amy again. She just talked to Kitty's mom. Kitty gets to come HOME in two days!"

There was a chorus of squeals, which Lacie and Zeke joined, even though Zeke probably had no idea what was going on.

"We have to get that house in perfect shape," Mama said. "So get some sleep tonight."

The moment the door closed again, Fiona turned to Sophie. "See?" she said. "She wouldn't be coming home if she weren't getting better."

"I guess not," Sophie said. She wished for the first time all day that she had her long hair again so she could pull it under her nose. She was that confused.

"Okay, so I forgive you," Fiona said. She slung an arm around Sophie's neck. "I can see how you'd be pulled in. Stick with me, Soph."

There was so much happy excitement over the next two days that Sophie started to believe that Fiona was right after all. Now that all the Corn Flakes were back together, with Kitty on her way, they went to work at full Corn Flake speed, finishing their *Mission: Kitty* film for her private viewing, making "Welcome back, Kitty!" banners, and fixing up Kitty's room.

They were putting on the final touches when the Colonel and Mrs. Munford pulled into the Munfords' driveway with Kitty in the backseat. Mama had told them to wait until the K-sisters had a chance to do their thing, and then they would have their chance.

That didn't actually take as long as it would have at *her* house, Sophie was sure. Kandy and Kelly and Kendra and

Karen and Kayla each gave Kitty a hug and then didn't seem to know what to say.

And actually, for a moment, Sophie didn't either. Seeing Kitty took all the words away.

She looked sort of puffy in her face, and even her china nose looked swollen. But the rest of her was as thin as a stick, and although she was smiling, her eyes somehow seemed thin too.

On her head she wore one of the hats Senora LaQuita had made for her, quilted with a turned-up brim and a silk daisy on it. There was no hair sticking out. Not anywhere.

"Supper's ready for you," Mama said to Mrs. Munford. "Kayla can warm it up when you're set to eat. She has dinner duty tonight."

Mrs. Munford's eyebrows went up. "Dinner duty?" she said. "Kayla?"

"We'll leave you alone to get settled," Mama said.

"Can't they stay for a little while?" Kitty said. Even her whine seemed thinner.

"You have to rest," her mother said. "Or you're going to be right back in the hospital."

Kitty whispered something in her mom's ear, and Mrs. Munford sighed and whispered into Mama's ear. Sophie's stomach got queasy.

"Tell you what," Mama said. "I'll take the rest of the girls home and come back for you, Soph." She smiled and headed for the door. "Let's go, Corn Flakes."

They all gave Kitty and Sophie longing looks as they followed Mama, except for Fiona, who looked downright angry.

"You have to go in your room and lie down though," Kitty's mom said to her. "And no horsing around."

Kitty sprawled across her bed with a look of pure delight on her face. "I'm home," she said.

"I missed you," Sophie said. "We all did. Fiona TOLD us you would get better fast, and I have to admit, I didn't believe her—"

"Don't believe her," Kitty said. Her puffy face was serious. "I'm only home until my next treatment, and there's going to be a bunch more. That's why I have to ask you something before your mom comes back."

Sophie sat carefully on the edge of the bed. "Ask me anything," she said. "ANYTHING."

Kitty looked straight at her. "Did you know I might die?" she said.

"No!" Sophie said. "You aren't going to die!"

"I might."

Sophie could feel her eyes narrowing. "Did Dr. Amy tell you that?"

Kitty shook her head. "Sebastian told me when I asked him. And the doctors at Portsmouth said it too, and the counselor that comes to talk to me. It's the truth. I could die from leukemia."

Sophie could hardly get her mouth to move. "I didn't know that," she said. And she wished she didn't now.

"So here's my question—and this is really important." Kitty got up on her elbows. "I know you talk to God and Jesus all the time, so you could tell me, Sophie. If I die, am I going to go to heaven?"

# Twelve

❋ ⌂ ✺

Sophie could do nothing but wish Jesus would appear right there, in Kitty's room—or at least Mama. Kitty's father *did* come in and say Mama was back.

"But we didn't get to talk long enough!" Kitty wailed.

The Colonel motioned Sophie out of the room. "Tomorrow," he said. "Oh-nine-hundred or after."

Sophie had no idea what that meant. She kissed Kitty's cheek, and Kitty whispered, "Come back soon. I really need to know."

Sophie nodded and escaped.

When they got in the car, Mama said, "Talk to me, Sophie."

Sophie couldn't get the words out fast enough. Mama's hands kept getting whiter on the steering wheel, and she didn't say much until they got in the house and talked to Daddy. His face turned as white as Mama's hands were.

"I just don't think Sophie should be the one to talk to Kitty about death," Mama said, holding on tight to Sophie. "Cutting her hair is one thing—but this?"

Daddy pinched the bridge of his nose between his fingers and closed his eyes. "Okay—here's the game plan," he said. "We call Dr. Peter tomorrow, and we all sit down and discuss this."

"Is he back?" Sophie said.

"Got in a few days ago," Daddy said. "He called to see how you were doing."

Sophie's stomach knot loosened up a little. "Can we do that, Mama?"

"All right," Mama said, although she was giving Daddy a very hard look. "But the final decision is ours."

"Dr. Peter would be the first one to agree," Daddy said.

Sophie didn't say anything. There was no arguing about it this time.

Mama didn't let Sophie go over to Kitty's the next day, and then she said she would rather not have a house full of Corn Flakes because she needed some quiet time to think.

Sophie couldn't find anything to do to pass the weeklong day. She could only see Kitty in her mind, hear her saying, *I might die.*

*How could she die?* Sophie thought. *She's only twelve years old!*

And if she did, what would that be like? She'd always thought heaven would be a place where you could do whatever you wanted and not have anybody think you were weird. But now that somebody she knew, somebody she really loved, might actually leave the earth — it didn't sound so wonderful.

*Kitty wants to go to middle school*, Sophie thought. *She wants to have a boyfriend — someday — and have sleepovers with us until she graduates from high school. She can't do that if we're not with her.*

Sophie wanted to say it all out loud — say it to Jesus so he would know by her tone that she was *not* happy about this.

*But if Mama heard me*, she thought, *she'd never let me talk to Kitty — maybe ever again —*

Sophie couldn't even finish that thought. She tiptoed down the stairs and out the kitchen door and crept along the edge of the garage, like Sofia making her way through the alleys of Marseille. Only this was real. It felt like something *was* after her—and there was only one person who could help her.

She could hear Zeke on the swings in the side yard, shouting something about Spider-Man. Sophie got down on her hands and knees and crawled behind the azaleas. She could feel her throat getting thick.

*The last time I was here, I was Sofia,* she thought.

She closed her eyes—tight—but Sofia wouldn't appear, and Sophie knew why. It wasn't because Aunt Emily said it would upset Darbie or because all the adults thought the Nazis chasing the Jews was too dark for them to think about with all their other sadness.

*I'm sorry, Sofia,* Sophie breathed to her in her dream-mind. *It's just because you can't help me right now. You can run away from the Nazis, but I can't run away from Kitty's—maybe—dying. And you can save your father, but I don't know how to save Kitty from not going to heaven—*

Sophie opened her eyes and looked up, over the tops of the azalea bushes. "And you're not the one I need to be talking to anyway."

Closing her eyes one more time, she whispered, "Jesus—is it ever okay to change a promise I made to you?"

She gave a little snort.

"Okay, so that was a lame question. I said I'd do everything you asked me to do for Kitty—I just didn't know I had to do THIS."

She asked him why Kitty had to think about stuff like this when she was so young and why she had picked *her* to tell Kitty whether she was going to heaven or not and what was she supposed to say anyway?

When she ran out of questions, there was only one thing left. It was her image of Jesus, looking at her with his kind eyes.

"I guess you're not mad at me for not wanting to do this," she said. "I guess you know it's hard."

*Duh*, she said to herself. *He knows everything.*

So, then, he knew what she was supposed to say.

"So, will you TELL me?" she whispered.

She didn't expect an answer, not from his lips anyway. "I should have brought my Bible out here," she said.

That was where the answers always were. She couldn't risk going back to the house. She could still hear Zeke, shouting that he was Spider-Man, and that the enemy didn't have a chance against him.

"He thinks Spider-Man is YOU," Sophie whispered to Jesus. "I gotta straighten him out on that."

Suddenly Sophie's head came up and she banged it on the garden hose reel.

"I have to tell Kitty too!" she said, in a voice *much* louder than a whisper.

She slapped a hand over her mouth and waited for Zeke to appear, but he was too involved in swinging his way to Spider-Man victory.

Kitty had said it herself: she *knew* Sophie was going to heaven because she talked to Jesus all the time — and believed in him — and obeyed what he said.

"So that's what I have to tell her, right?" Sophie said.

She closed her eyes and saw Jesus' kind eyes. "But I still don't understand why she has to deal with this right NOW," she said. And then she started to cry.

A while later she heard Mama calling her name, and then she heard Daddy's car pull into the driveway — too early to be off work—and then another car. She could tell it was Dr. Peter by his voice calling, "Hey, Spider-Man!" to Zeke. But she stayed behind the azaleas.

"Because what if they don't LET me tell this to Kitty?" she whispered. "How's she ever gonna know?"

"She sure won't if you stay in here talking to yourself."

Sophie jumped and banged her head again. Lacie was crouched down, peering between the leaves.

"They're all waiting for you," Lacie said. "Mama's about to have kittens because she can't find you. So come on—you're never going to find out unless you go in there."

When Sophie walked into the family room, Mama looked at Dr. Peter and Daddy and said, "Now do you know why I'm against this? Look at her—she's upset."

They had obviously started without her. Sophie sank heavily onto the couch next to Dr. Peter. There wasn't even a chance to say hi to him.

Daddy was looking at her like his scientist-self. "Are you upset, Soph?"

"Rusty!" Mama gave Daddy one of her hard looks.

Dr. Peter didn't say anything, so Sophie took a deep breath.

"I'm only upset because I'm afraid you won't let me talk to Kitty. I know what to say now."

"May I?" Dr. Peter said to Mama.

She barely nodded. Sophie's heart was going like a racecar engine.

Dr. Peter said, "How would you tell her whether she would go to heaven?"

"I would tell her that she was right, that I'm going to heaven because I know Jesus and I talk to him and I obey him and I believe he'll take me up there—or wherever it is."

No one talked for a minute. Mama pulled a tissue out of the box.

"Sounds pretty good to me," Daddy said finally.

"Of course it does, and I'm proud of Sophie," Mama said. "But why does SHE have to be the one?"

"Because," Sophie said. "We have to do whatever God asks us to do—in love—no matter how much it hurts."

Dr. Peter put his hand up. "I told her that."

"And so did Genevieve—AND the Bible," Sophie said.

Daddy sat forward in his chair and put his hand on Mama's knee. "We can't argue with that, Lynda," he said.

"All right," Mama said, in a less than happy voice. She blew her nose hard. "But I want us to be there and Dr. Peter—and I guess Kitty's parents—"

*Hello?* Sophie wanted to shout. She'd pictured it as just her and Kitty. Why did half the city of Poquoson have to be there?

"I'd like to suggest this," Dr. Peter said. "Just a suggestion—but let Sophie talk to Kitty, and I can be there if you would be more comfortable—if it's okay with Kitty's parents, and if it's all right with Sophie."

Sophie nodded.

"And the two of you can talk to Kitty's parents about what Sophie's going to say beforehand."

"What if they won't let me do it?" Sophie said.

"Then we have to respect that," Mama said.

"Respect that they don't want her to know Jesus?" Sophie said.

"Let's take it one step at a time, huh, Soph?" Daddy said.

It was hard for Sophie not to pray for all the steps to happen at the same time.

The Munfords agreed to meet Sophie, her family, and Dr. Peter at Anna's Pizza for the talk—because that was where the Munfords wanted to go so Kitty could get out a little.

Dr. Peter and Kitty and Sophie picked out songs on the juke-box while Sophie's parents talked with Kitty's parents. After a few minutes, Sophie heard Colonel Munford say, "It's fine with me. That's a whole lot better than what I could come up with."

"At least we got past Step One," Dr. Peter whispered to Sophie. "Now you can let the grown-ups deal with the Munfords, okay?"

Sophie was *more* than happy to do that. The waitress sailed over with a pizza held above her head and set it down on the separate table Dr. Peter had set up for the three of them.

"I don't know if I can eat pizza yet," Kitty said over the extra-cheese pizza she usually wolfed down. "I still get kinda sick."

"I'll eat your piece," Dr. Peter said. He took a bite and nod-ded at Sophie.

Kitty pulled her hat down tighter on her head. People were stealing stares at her from other tables. Sophie could tell that Kitty could tell. She wished the wig was made already.

"Do you get to answer my question now?" Kitty said.

"Yes," Sophie said. There was no frozen mouth. No hand squeezing a fork or the edge of the table. The words flowed out of her, better than they had with Mama and Daddy and Dr. Peter. Better than she'd imagined saying it, over and over and over. It was almost like Jesus himself was doing the talking.

When she was through, Kitty looked from Dr. Peter to Sophie.

"I already believe in Jesus," she said. "Because Sophie does, and she's the best person I ever knew. So what do I do now?"

"Oh, Kitty," Dr. Peter said. His eyes were sparkling. "Sophie and I have so much to share with you."

But it obviously wasn't going to be right then. The door opened, and the fading outside light ushered in Julia and Anne-Stuart and a tall, reddish-haired woman who looked around Anna's as if she were Anna herself.

"Don't look," Sophie whispered to Kitty.

But Kitty did, and she put her hand on top of her head and pushed down on the hat some more. But when she pulled her hand away, it caught on the brim and flipped it off. Kitty's whole head, with its few lonely patches of thin hair, was exposed to the world.

Sophie and Kitty both fumbled for the hat, but it was too late. Julia and Anne-Stuart came straight to their table like picnic ants.

"Okay," Anne-Stuart said.

"Nice do," Julia said.

"She's having chemotherapy," Sophie said. She could barely keep her voice from rising to a scream, or from adding, *morons!*

"Oh," Anne-Stuart said. "Sorry." Her sneer faded, but she still stared at Kitty as if she were a freak of nature.

"Yeah, sorry," Julia said. Something unfamiliar flickered through her eyes. "What's wrong with you?"

Kitty looked at the extra-cheese pizza. "I have leukemia."

"It isn't contagious, is it?" Julia took a step backward.

"No," Kitty said. "You can't catch it."

Julia and Anne-Stuart still gaped at her. Sophie had never known them to be without a word to say.

"So," Julia said finally. "Are y'all coming to middle school orientation tomorrow?"

Sophie looked back at her in surprise. Was it tomorrow? She hadn't gotten a stomach knot over middle school since Kitty had gotten sick. She didn't have one now.

"We'll be there," Sophie said.

"See you, then," Anne-Stuart said, sniffling. The two of them hurried back to the tall woman, buzzing at each other like bees.

Dr. Peter, who had been silent the whole time, said, "Corn Pops, I take it."

"See how heinous they are?" Sophie said.

"I thought they looked a little scared."

*Oh*, Sophie thought. *THAT was what it was in Julia's eyes.*

"I can't go!" Kitty said.

Sophie looked at Kitty. The fear in *her* eyes was bigger than Julia's.

"I'll be the only one there wearing a hat!"

"We'll all be there with you," Sophie said. "All the Corn Flakes. Hey—we could ALL wear hats—you have enough of them."

Kitty shook her head. "What if they won't let me keep it on—they have rules about hats. Or what if it comes off? Or what if somebody pulls it off? You know some Fruit Loop is gonna do that!"

Sophie didn't know what to say. She couldn't make it better.

But all the way home, all she could hear in her head was Kitty saying, *I'll be the only one wearing a hat.*

*I've been the "only one" a lot of times*, Sophie thought. *The only one who was weird. I know what that feels like.*

But no matter how hard she squeezed her eyes shut, Sophie couldn't imagine how it would feel to walk into that huge middle school tomorrow, already stressing about all the new stuff they would have to do, already worried about whether they would be in the same classes. And to have a hairless head on top of all that.

*I don't know how it feels, Jesus!* she cried out to him in her mind. *How can I help Kitty if I don't know how it feels?*

The answer came, quicker than it ever had before. When she got home, she went into Daddy's medicine cabinet and pulled something out and went to the kitchen, where he and Mama were getting ready to have their nightly decaf.

Mama saw what was in her hands, and she slammed her cup on the counter.

"NO, Sophie! Absolutely NOT! This is where I draw the line."

"What?" Daddy said. "What do you have, Soph?"

Sophie set the clippers on the counter. Daddy immediately shook his head.

"I have to agree with your mother on this one," he said. "You can't shave your hair off. You'll regret it the minute you do it, and there's no way we can put your hair back on."

"Kitty can't put hers back on either," Sophie said.

"You are not Kitty!" Mama said. "You can't suffer everything she has to suffer! You're twelve years old!"

"I don't know," said a voice from the doorway. Lacie dropped her purse on a chair and came to stand beside Sophie. "I was telling them at youth group tonight that it's like Sophie's not just twelve — she's more like sixteen or seventeen in her soul. Maybe older."

She put her hand next to Sophie's, and Sophie grabbed onto it.

"Lacie, don't start," Mama said.

But Daddy put his hand up. Sophie thought he might drop over any second from the scary look Mama was giving him.

"Let's just hear Lacie out," he said.

Lacie squeezed Sophie's hand tighter. "How long have we been worrying about Sophie because we didn't think she'd ever grow out of the dreamer phase? Now she's showing all this maturity, and you want to hold her back?"

"You think it's maturity?" Daddy said.

"No!" Mama said. "I think it's a beautiful thought, but I don't think it's going to seem that beautiful when she looks in the mirror with a bald head. It's bad enough seeing our Kitty that way."

Mama's face crumpled and she sagged against Daddy's big chest.

"But I'm not sick like her, Mama," Sophie said. "And I can't make her better—but I CAN make her feel like she's not all alone. No matter how much it hurts ME."

"And it's gonna stink," Lacie said. "You're gonna catch so much flak from those snob-girls."

"I know," Sophie said. "It'll be worse than ever."

Lacie looked at Mama and Daddy. "See?" Lacie said. "She knows what she's up against. She's not pretending everything is going to turn out just fine the way Fiona is. That girl is in total denial."

"Maybe if the Corn Pops and the Fruit Loops have ME to bully," Sophie said. "It'll keep them from dumping it all on Kitty."

Daddy started to nod. Mama pounded her fist weakly on his chest, and then she looked up at Sophie.

"Are you sure, Soph—are you really SURE?"

Sophie just picked up the clippers and climbed up onto a stool.

Daddy took them from her, and Mama wrapped a towel around her shoulders.

"At least you have a decent-shaped head," Lacie said. "You might not look that bad. It'll make your eyes look bigger."

Lacie kept on talking while Sophie watched her reflection in the oven door; watched as her shiny scalp appeared.

She imagined Jesus watching too.

With his kind, approving eyes.

# Glossary

**ad lib** (add-lib) when you act in a movie or play without a script, and make lines up on the spot

**agenda** (a-jen-duh) a series of plans or ideas that can control someone's actions

**ALL** (acute lymphoblastic leukemia) (a-cute limp-fo-blast-ick loo-KEY-me-uh) a type of cancer that attacks the white blood cells that normally fight infections. ALL creates white blood cells that can't fight off infections and makes the person very sick. It's the most common cancer in children.

**au pair** (oh-PARE) a fancy French word for a nanny; specifically a young person who lives with a family and takes care of the kids and the housework

**blackguards** (BLAK-gards) very rude and nasty people

**bogey** (BO-ghee) an Irish slang word that actually means snot (gross!), but basically tells people you feel really stupid

**chemotherapy** (key-moe-THAIR-a-pee) really strong chemicals that are used as a treatment for cancer

**class** (klas) not a group of students, but a nifty word that means something's really cool

**CVC** an abbreviation of cardiovascular ventricular catheter (car-dee-oh-VAS-cu-lar ven-TRI-cue-lar CATH-et-er), or a fancy tube through which medicine is put into the body

**despondent** (de-SPOHN-dent) feeling completely depressed, to the point that you become almost zombie-like

**desperate** (DEHS-pret) without hope, sometimes doing extreme things to avoid a certain situation or thought

**devastating** (DEV-as-tate-ing) when an event is so awful and unimaginable that it makes you feel helpless

**disconcerting** (dis-cohn-CERT-ing) a word that describes something that just doesn't seem right, and makes you feel awkward and confused

**ecstatic** (ek-sta-tik) so incredibly happy it makes you almost crazy with joy

**extraterrestrial** (ex-trah-ter-RES-tree-all) something from outer space, or something so strange it seems like it came from outside this world

**flitters** (FLIT-turs) a feeling of being really excited and a little jumpy, and your body gets a little shaky while you wait for something to happen

**heinous** (HEY-nus) unbelievably mean and cruel

**holiday** (HA-leh-day) a British word for vacation

**inquisitive** (in-KWI-zeh-tiv) being really curious and asking a lot of questions

**liberty** (li-burr-tee) freedom; "not at liberty" means you're not allowed to say or do something

**meltdown** (MELT-doun) something that happens when things become too much to handle; losing control of yourself because of the stress

**oh-nine-hundred** (oh-nyne-hun-dread) 9:00 am in military speak

**reef** (rEEf) an Irish word that means to attack someone with your words

**remission** (re-MEH-shon) the time when cancer symptoms aren't active and the person starts to get better

**scathingly** (SKATH-ing-lee) according to Darbie, wonderfully brilliant

**two-thirds** (too-therds) approximately 66 percent

**scenario** (see-NAIR-e-oh) a series of events that could occur; worst case scenarios are they worst possible things that could happen

# Sophie Flakes Out

*Nancy Rue*

Meet Sophie LaCroix, a creative soul with a desire to become a great film director someday, and she definitely has a flair for drama! Her overactive imagination frequently lands her in trouble, but her faith and friends always save the day. From best-selling author, Nancy Rue, comes two-in-one bindups of the popular Sophie series.

Sophie Flakes Out: Sophie wants more privacy like her friend Willoughby, who has plenty, until Willoughby's father finds out about her fast, new friends. His harsh punishment makes Sophie wonder what rules they need to follow.

Sophie Loves Jimmy: Sophie doesn't get why a rumor should stop her from being Jimmy's friend – until the Corn Flakes start believing the whispers. Now Sophie wonders how she and the Flakes can ever be friends again!

*Available in stores and online!*

# Sophie Steps Up

*Nancy Rue*

Sophie LaCroix is a creative soul with a desire to become a great film director someday, and she definitely has a flair for drama! Her overactive imagination frequently lands her in trouble, but her faith and friends always save the day. This bindup includes two-books-in-one, Sophie Under Pressure and Sophie Steps Up.

*Available in stores and online!*

# Sophie's Drama

*Nancy Rue*

Sophie LaCroix is a creative soul with a desire to become a great film director someday, and she definitely has a flair for drama! Her overactive imagination frequently lands her in trouble, but her faith and friends always save the day. This bindup includes two-books-in-one, Sophie's Drama and Sophie Gets Real.

*Available in stores and online!*

# Sophie's Friendship Fiasco

*Nancy Rue*

Meet Sophie LaCroix, a creative soul with a desire to become a great film director someday, and she definitely has a flair for drama! Her overactive imagination frequently lands her in trouble, but her faith and friends always save the day. From best-selling author, Nancy Rue, comes two-in-one bindups of the popular Sophie series.

Sophie's Friendship Fiasco: Sophie tries living up to other's expectations, but lately she's letting everyone down. When she misrepresents the Flakes – with good intentions – she loses their friendship. Will they ever forgive her?

Sophie and the New Girl: Sophie likes the new girl who joins the film club. She's witty and unique, even if she is a bit bizarre. When the camera goes missing, the other Flakes are quick to accuse. Will Sophie be able to identify the real thief?

*Available in stores and online!*

# NIV Faithgirlz! Backpack Bible, Revised Edition

Small enough to fit into a backpack or bag, this Bible can go anywhere a girl does.

Features include:

- Fun Italian Duo-Tone™ design
- Twelve full-color pages of Faithgirlz fun that helps girls learn the "Beauty of Believing!"
- Words of Christ in red
- Ribbon marker
- Complete text of the bestselling NIV translation

*Available in stores and online!*

ZONDERVAN®
.com

# NIV Faithgirlz! Bible, Revised Edition

*Nancy Rue*

Every girl wants to know she's totally unique and special. This Bible says that with Faithgirlz! sparkle. Through the many in-text features found only in the Faithgirlz! Bible, girls will grow closer to God as they discover the journey of a lifetime.

Features include:

- Book introductions—Read about the who, when, where, and what of each book.
- Dream Girl—Use your imagination to put yourself in the story.
- Bring It On!—Take quizzes to really get to know yourself.
- Is There a Little (Eve, Ruth, Isaiah) in You?—See for yourself what you have in common.
- Words to Live By—Check out these Bible verses that are great for memorizing.

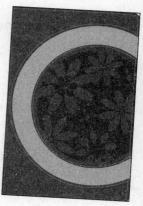

- What Happens Next?—Create a list of events to tell a Bible story in your own words.
- Oh, I Get It!—Find answers to Bible questions you've wondered about.
- The complete NIV translation
- Features written by bestselling author Nancy Rue

*Available in stores and online!*

**ZONDERVAN®**
.com

# Talk It Up!

*Want free books?*
*First looks at the best new fiction?*
*Awesome exclusive merchandise?*

We want to hear from you!

Give us your opinions on titles, covers, and stories.
Join the Z Street Team.

Email us at zstreetteam@zondervan.com
to sign up today!

Also—Friend us on Facebook!

www.facebook.com/goodteenreads

- Video Trailers
- Connect with your favorite authors
- Sneak peeks at new releases
- Giveaways
- Fun discussions
- And much more!